"To the list of splendidly crusty New Englanders created by the likes of John Gardner and John Cheever, add the name of Howard Elman, the protagonist of Ernest Hebert's impressive first novel."
— *Philadelphia Inquirer*

"What makes *The Dogs of March* a brilliant book is Mr. Hebert's ability to portray ordinary people, the kind of people novelists usually ignore or sentimentalize. He catches them so exactly that one feels a rush of love and recognition, of common humanity."
— Anatole Broyard
New York Times

"*The Dogs of March* is just the book to give to your nice auntie if she thinks New England was invented by Grandma Moses. The first few pages, which evoke a wonderland of junk automobiles, will change her mind in a hurry . . . A fine first novel."
— *Minneapolis Tribune*

"Novels such as this one make me wonder how many other books the author has written because when a 'first novel' is this poised, this sure of its balance and depth, chances are it's not a first book at all—only the first published . . . This story seems simple enough but, of course, in the hands of a skillful writer, simplicity speaks with eloquence . . . The book is rich in detail. The prose goes light and dark with imagery in this contemporary story which seems, often, ancient. A seasoned, thoughtful book."
— *Boston Globe*

"What makes *The Dogs of March* so interesting is Ernest Hebert's ability to see the lives of a New Hampshire working-class family in a way that is clear and whole and to make them into the material for a novel that is both compassionate and amusing."
— *Chicago Tribune*

"A neatly constructed and deeply-felt first novel . . . a book that you ought to read."
— Alan Cheuse
Los Angeles Times

THE DOGS OF MARCH

ERNEST HEBERT

THE DOGS OF MARCH

UNIVERSITY PRESS OF NEW ENGLAND
Hanover and London

UNIVERSITY PRESS OF NEW ENGLAND
publishes books under its own imprint and is the
publisher for Brandeis University Press, Brown University Press, Dartmouth College, Middlebury College Press, University of New Hampshire, University
of Rhode Island, Tufts University, University of
Vermont, Wesleyan University Press, and Salzburg
Seminar.

Published by University Press of New England,
Hanover, NH 03755
© 1979 by Ernest Hebert

University Press of New England paperback edition
published in 1995.
The Dogs of March was first published in 1979 by The
Viking Press and simultaneously in Canada by Penguin
Books Canada Limited.

Printed in the United States of America 5 4 3 2 1

Acknowledgment is made to Alfred A. Knopf, Inc., for
permission to reprint lines from "The Man with the
Blue Guitar" from *The Collected Poems of Wallace Stevens*
by Wallace Stevens. Copyright 1936 by Wallace Stevens
and renewed 1964 by Holly Stevens.

Library of Congress Cataloging-in-Publication Data
Hebert, Ernest.
    The dogs of March / Ernest Hebert.
       p.   cm. — (Hardscrabble books)
      ISBN 0–87451–719–2
      I. Title. II. Series.
  PS3558.E277D64   1995
  813' .54—dc20   94–44580
  ∞

To the memory of my uncle,
Monsignor Joseph Ernest Vaccarest

CONTENTS

Things as they are have been destroyed.
Am I? Am I a man that is dead

At a table on which the food is cold?
Is my thought a memory, not alive?

Is the spot on the floor, there, wine or blood
And whichever it may be, is it mine?

WALLACE STEVENS
"The Man with the Blue Guitar"

THE DOGS OF MARCH

1: WORK-FOR-PAY

Teeth, straight teeth. The thought surfaced, but he pushed it back
into the depths, for this was early morning, when the mind
could do such things. It was the time of day to take small, familiar pleasures, like a fisherman taking undersized trout, enjoying
their frisky tugs, then throwing them back into the water, to rise
to his hook another day. He dressed, and his forest-green work
clothes were full of the good, greasy smell of mechanical things.
The dinner pail clanked musically in his thick hands and sent a
subtle trembling through his fingers for a moment, and, unaccountably, an image appeared in his mind of the dromedary on
his pack of Camels; of North Africa; of Pasha, a tank named for
a whore; of Pasha herself, who was dark and moist in a land of
yellow light and parched earth. He stepped outside, and Novem-
ber's chill slapped his face.

Howard Elman was coming awake.

He paused by an overturned wheelbarrow to survey his land.
Birches, a score of junk cars, a swing on a limb of a giant maple,
a bathtub in the garden, a gray barn, a house sided with fading
purple asphalt shingles, a washing machine riddled with bullet

holes—to Howard, these things were all equal in beauty. He saw no ugliness on his property. As nature felled weak trees and scattered fallen leaves, so Howard Elman dispensed with machines that would not work. To his eye, his yard and field beyond were one, as to the eye of a mariner the ocean often merges with the sky.

He began to walk, moving with bearlike grace, bearlike awkwardness. At the driveway—ruts packed-down gravel, center grassed—he paused again, to ponder what car to drive to work this morning. The De Soto? The GMC pickup? The Ford wagon? To Howard, the De Soto was the epitome of luxury. True, the seats had been slashed long before he bought the car; true, the original maroon paint had faded to the dreary brown of dried blood, and rust spots pitted the body like impetigo. It didn't matter to Howard. The De Soto had power—power brakes, power steering, power windows, a powerful V-8 engine. Power was the bringer of well-being, Howard believed. In driving the De Soto, all one had to do was "settle in and aim it, and watch the world go by," he would say.

The GMC pickup was a kidney rattler, a back straightener, a feet freezer—and a trickster. Its gas gauge worked most of the time, so that he would forget when it didn't work. The carburetor stalled the engine at stoplights, especially in the rain, and anytime—it seemed—he was in a hurry. The defroster did not defrost. The front end was always out of line. Yet he loved the pickup. It was an old, untrustworthy, but unendingly interesting friend. It had tricks but no secrets, and he would not part with it any more than he would willingly part with an arm or a leg.

The most faithful of Howard's cars was the Ford wagon. It was reliable and economical. It never failed to start and burned little oil. It was the best car he had ever owned, and he hated it. He hated it because he could not improve it, only screw it up. It was too perfect, too self-regulating. Somehow, he felt diminished when he drove it.

He chose the De Soto.

It started and died. He pumped the accelerator (he called it the "exhilarator") four times, cursed—"You filthy, rotten son-of-a-cock-knocker"—and turned the key again. The De Soto whined like a kicked dog and then started. He lit a Camel, enjoyed a deep drag, and, with a deliberate effort, relaxed his eyes and shoulders to preserve the euphoria of half awakeness.

He pulled onto the road, jammed his foot on the gas pedal, and he could feel the tires kick stones. The car rose up the hill toward Swett's huge house, which looked down on Howard's fifty acres and beyond to the Vermont hills across the Connecticut River. Everett Swett had been a man to beat all flesh and blood dear to him, thought Howard—wife, children, dogs, cats, cows, and pigs. He once smacked Howard's son, Freddy, on the ass when the boy was young, and Howard had marched into Swett's barn, picked him up on his feet, and shaken the buttons right off his overalls. The two men were good neighbors after that, and even went bird hunting together in the upland behind Swett's house. Swett died the prettiest of deaths, full of morphine after his tractor threw him and crushed his chest. Howard did not see a wet eye at his funeral. Ann Rae Swett cleared out of the house within a week, moving in with her eldest in Nashua. The house was empty now, up for sale. Somebody had better buy it soon, before some kids put a torch to it, Howard thought.

The De Soto pulled onto the highway, the change jarring him slightly, so that he did his trick with eyes and shoulders. Full awakeness would be on him soon enough: the slamming of shuttles, the odd smell of the shop, as if something had died in the walls, lint in his nostrils, faces—faces of Charley Kruger, Cooty Patterson, Mr. Lodge, and William, goddamn William. He let the De Soto carry him as if he were a passenger and not the driver. He fished what he could from his half awakeness.

Begin half awake in the village of Darby. Drive ten miles to full awakeness in Keene. Drink to get to half awakeness at night. Engine yawning at fifty-five. Stay half awake and live twice as long. Live fully awake and burn up. Eight miles to full awakeness. Lose the miles. Trees like ironwork holding up the sky. Somewhere, in heaven, in an orchard, a big buck. A big buck, Freddy. Shh, Freddy. Thank the gun-cold day. Think, feel, push, pull, shove, climb, lift, stroke, punch, shoot, and fuck for warmth. One mile to full awakeness. KEENE. Shrub trimmers. Grass cutters. People who swallowed their own spit. Stoplight. Tap, tap, tap on the steering wheel. Coming into full awakeness. Stoplight. Tap, tap, tap. On the verge of full awakeness. Monday morning. Seven A.M. Lodge Narrow Fabric Co., Inc. Punch in. Full awakeness.

For a fraction of a second the colors were too bright, the noises too loud; the push of the floor against the balls of his feet was too hard. Then the morning's meanness came, like a bitter medicine.

"Goddamn you, William, go wash your hands."

"Jeez, Howard."

"How do your hands get so dirty?"

"Working on my car. Jeez, Howard." William wiped his hands on his blue jeans.

"Go wash your hands."

"It ain't your web."

"Ain't you smart. It's my ass if the web's dirty, and if it's my ass it's your ass." Howard moved closer, like a body puncher in a boxing match.

"Fan belt was squealing."

"Ain't you smart."

"Squealing so loud it hurt your ears."

"Ain't you smart."

"Jeez, Howard."

"Go . . . wash . . . your . . . hands."

"Jeez."

William stuffed his hands in his pockets, turned, giving Howard a hidden finger, and marched to the men's room. He was a little angry with himself. He knew better than to get in

Howard's way first thing in the morning. Nevertheless, the incident, along with others like it, served to bolster an already-well-developed confidence. After all, it was doubtful the Marine Corps had a drill instructor who would yell as loud and as often as Howard, and Howard didn't bother him a bit. This was good training; someday, years hence, he'd probably thank Howard. He shifted his thoughts to sex, entered the men's room, took a leak, and forgot to wash his hands.

Howard stood amidst the clatter of the looms, waiting for the meanness in himself to dissipate, tapping his foot like a man keeping time, in spite of himself, to music he hated. *Work-for-pay, work-for-pay,* went the clatter of the looms. William, stupid William, incredibly stupid William, twenty-twenty-vision-and-blind-stupid William. But the rage inside him was not against William Potts; it was against Charley Kruger. Charley Kruger: who could weave tirelessly for eight hours and not sweat; who wore a clean white shirt every day and shined his shoes; who spoke in a soft voice, as if he knew everything; who, nonetheless, had nothing in his head, no longings, no lust, no foolishness, no criminality, no privacies, the light of his presence like the light in a supermarket—bright, efficient, cool, and yet punishing, making you blink and believe there was something wrong with the way you saw things. Charley Kruger needed somebody to dirty him up. *Work-for-pay, work-for-pay,* sang the looms.

Some of the morning's meanness began to escape from Howard like a nauseous gas, so that he imagined he smelled something bad from himself. He moved to the next aisle. He was sorry he had raised his voice. He yelled too much, especially at Freddy. That would lose him the boy one day, surer than he was going to hell. And yet he continued to yell, yelled when he was making a joke, yelled because he could not understand how people could be so stupid, and, conversely, yelled out of shame when his deepwater ignorance was roiled. Just once he wanted to bring together all those he had offended so he could say, "Howard yells, but he don't mean nothing."

There was even more to his yelling than Howard was aware of. He would not admit to himself he was getting hard of hearing, and as a result he yelled all the time, even when he thought he was speaking softly. Furthermore, he set strangers against him by another habit growing out of his poor hearing. He stared fixedly at others' lips as they spoke. He had a coarse, pitted face, and his practice of shaving at night, instead of in the morning, gave him a perpetually unkempt look. When he stared, his mouth twisted into a grimace, and his gray bullet eyes seemed to shoot into others' most private thoughts, when in fact he was using his eyes to help him hear.

"Hello, Howie." It was Fralla. She whacked him on the fanny, tossed him a lewd look, and chugged down the aisle to her inspection table, her big ass bouncing like a barometer on Judgment Day. The meanness in him hissed out. Everything was all right; he was not going to kill anyone. He savored the after-image of Fralla's ass for a moment, faced the loom, and kicked the metal housing—but not too hard.

Howard made sure William was winding web, and then he got himself a cup of coffee. He did not check his weavers. There was no sense in making sure a man on piecework was busy. Of course he was busy. The coffee in Howard's cup jiggled as if the cup were held by a badly frightened man, but Howard's hand did not shake, never shook. The floor beneath him vibrated from the machines in the shop.

Howard considered one of those machines now as he sipped his coffee. Anticipation of the morning's work brought him pleasure. He'd make it run, could make anything run. The thing would start and it would work the way it was supposed to, and as a gift for his labors, he would experience a moment of low ecstasy, private and sweet, something to be secretive and superstitious about, as if revealing it to someone else, or hunting down its source within himself, would diminish its power. It was a wide-web loom, one of the oldest in the shop, perhaps as old as the founder himself, Ira Lodge, who (it was said) was currently full of tubes in a rest home. The machine was silent now, the shuttle stopped in the shed of the loom. Howard stooped, peered into the black gears, sneezed, and called for Cooty Patterson.

"Clean the crap from under that thing," Howard said with the same gruff affection he reserved for his daughter Heather.

Cooty, as usual, stank. Howard thought of him as old, although he was only sixty. He was a small gray-haired man with a perpetually worried look on his face. He was one of Howard's only two friends. The other was Ollie Jordan, who was one of the shack people of the town of Darby.

"They're in the shop again," said Cooty, quivering like a bird on a wire in a cold rain.

This was familiar territory: Mr. Lodge and Mr. Gordon were prowling the aisles again. Everyone in the shop was trying to guess just what was going on. Howard didn't know Mr. Lodge's first name, although he was president of the company and the founder's son. Mr. Gordon talked with a Southern accent; he was obviously an expert in something. Recently, the two of them had been seen moving about the shop, asking questions and making lists.

"What difference does it make?" asked Howard.

"There's something wrong; I can tell," said Cooty.

"Cooty, they ain't laid nobody off," said Howard, getting to the root of the old man's fears. Without work to keep him busy, Cooty would drown in his own nervous sweat.

"Ought to stay up in the office where they belong," he said. Lint puffs stuck to his brow.

"Listen up," said Howard. "You are going to die in this shop right here under wide-web looms, lay your head down one afternoon, right after coffee break, and not wake up."

The prophecy cheered the old man. He got down on his knees and worked his slight body behind the loom. With the little broom he carried—the one tool of his trade—he began to sweep up the lint puffs that were stuck to the grease on the machine and that covered the floor.

It is cozy here, he thought. The sounds of the shop seemed far away, like a distant train. He began to think about turtles, those wonderful creatures that could look at a wet rock for hours and see a hundred things.

"Take the goddamn cover off when you get done so I can get in there."

Howard's voice, far away.

Howard left to refill his coffee cup. Such liberty was one of the advantages of being a foreman. He didn't have to wait until nine-thirty for a coffee, and he didn't have to tiptoe to the bathroom to sneak a smoke. He straddled a bench that ran along the hall. Behind the bench were stores of warps, bins of spare parts, and boxes of web packed for shipment. Often Howard would wander back there. It was quiet and musty, making him feel something unexpected was going to happen, as in a forest when there is no wind. Occasionally, he'd flush a couple of kids goofing off from the shipping department, and they would slink away.

Mr. Lodge and Mr. Gordon walked slowly down the stairs from the office with Filbin, the dyes foreman. Howard watched intently. Mr. Gordon kept a step ahead of the other two. Sleek as a fisher, with sly eyes, he always looked as if he were making plans. Filbin was silent, grim, and a little afraid, as if he suspected the stairs might collapse. Mr. Lodge, dressed for church, preached to Filbin. Mr. Lodge wore a smile that puzzled and annoyed Howard. It revealed some displeasure in the smiler. But then, why smile? He could not understand why some people smiled when they weren't pleased, or how they'd learned such a smile, or what it was for. Howard figured that Mr. Lodge smiled at Mrs. Lodge like that and at manure piles and when somebody died.

Mr. Gordon spoke to Filbin, who turned white, as though he had been caught in a lie. Mr. Gordon was young and smart. Howard wondered what the hell he was doing here. Probably, he'd been hired to shape the place up. Howard remembered Mr.

Gordon interrogating him. ("What does Patterson do?" "Been here thirty years." "But what does he do?" "Loom fixer." "What's the broom for?" "Sweeping.") In Howard's department, only William needed a foreman. One fifty-year-old foreman for one eighteen-year-old boy. Howard waited for the day they would demote him to loom fixer and get rid of Cooty, who couldn't weave because of his arthritis and couldn't fix machines because he didn't have the head for it. Eventually, they'd lay off clumsy boys like William and hire girls with clean hands to wind web for the minimum wage. Howard knew all sorts of ways to save the company money, but he was keeping his ideas to himself because he could not see how they would benefit those of his kind; and, too, because he believed such ideas were somehow wrong. Despite the seeming stupidity of those in charge, what they changed and what they left alone was right because they were in charge.

Mr. Lodge nodded good-bye to Filbin and then, spotting Howard, waved to him—half greeting, half command—to come over. Howard ignored the gesture, looking through an imaginary hole in Mr. Lodge's belly, beyond the stairs, beyond the walls, beyond the city, into an imaginary orchard with imaginary deer breathing white-frosted breath. Mr. Lodge smiled and moved in, stepping lively, a military officer's walk. He whipped his hand off his hip like a gunman.

"Come up and have your coffee with me." He tugged Howard's hand as Howard struggled to keep it limp.

Howard hated handshakes, considered them bad omens. People who wanted your money shook hands, along with funeral mourners, wedding celebrants, strangers, drunks, and worthless bums you hadn't seen in twenty-five years.

Mr. Lodge's office cowed Howard as Mr. Lodge could not. The great gleaming desk, the wall-to-wall carpet, the aerial photograph of the shop, the picture of a Chinaman who seemed to be wearing a bathrobe, Mr. Lodge's golf trophies—these immobilized Howard. He was afraid that if he moved he would break something and that if he spoke he would say a dirty word.

Mr. Lodge led him to a plush chair next to his desk. He poured coffee into fancy mugs. Only Mr. Gordon remained standing, half camouflaged by a jungle plant in the far corner, instinctively choosing the site that any predator would.

"Cream? Sugar?"

"Black!" Howard shouted. (He hated black coffee.) He took the mug and searched for a place to put it down. Carpet too bumpy. Chair arm too dangerous. Desk unthinkable. He ended by holding the awful black liquid between his knees.

From the pocket of his checkered jacket Mr. Lodge removed a gold pen shaped like a golf putter. He used it as a prop for his chin during meditative poses, as a pointer, as a gavel, as a pacifier. It reminded him that life was like the game of golf, each day a different course with its unique terrain, each project a hole with its particular grade of difficulty, each encounter a shot requiring a tool, a mood, and some luck to execute it properly. Howard Elman was a long putt: you had to stroke firmly, and you couldn't expect to hole that narrow cavity of a brain in one shot. Mr. Lodge tapped his upper front teeth with the putter face of the pen.

"How's that boy of yours?" asked Mr. Lodge.

"Good." Howard could feel the looms vibrating beneath him, and somehow he derived some comfort in knowing they were not far away.

"Sophomore now at Plymouth, isn't he, Howard?"

"UNH."

"Yes, ah, UNH." The putter-pen, snapped by a forefinger, was sent spinning onto a blank sheet of white paper. "What's he majoring in?"

"Don't know." Howard had only a faint idea what "majoring" meant. He struggled in his deepwater ignorance. "I think maybe he wants to be a dentist," he blurted.

Mr. Lodge, pleased with this outburst, pressed on. "An education can take a man far in this world," he said.

"Yuh, that's right." Howard turned his head ninety degrees from Mr. Lodge and caught the eye of the Chinaman in the picture, who appeared to be thinking, probably about something to eat, Howard figured, for he was thin and unhealthy-looking. The pause in the conversation, a bit awkward for Mr. Lodge, rested Howard a little.

"I always felt . . ." The putter-pen was tracing the Greek letter sigma in the air.

"What?" Howard's eyes shifted quickly from the Chinaman to the scurrying lips of Mr. Lodge.

"I always felt—and strongly, too—that education is a potent force in shaping a man's life." Mr. Lodge waited for this to sink in, putter-pen on his chin.

Howard wondered what the hell he was driving at.

Mr. Lodge changed pace. "You've been here over twenty years."

"Since the war ended."

"I started here for my father about the same time, after the same war." (Except that Mr. Lodge had been an officer, a headquarters officer at that, and so perhaps not the same war, thought Howard.) "Simple times, when you think about it."

"You mean the war?" Howard's tone was incredulous.

"Cancel that," said Mr. Lodge with an accompanying hand signal. "I meant everything then was so much easier to understand. We knew the enemy then, didn't we?"

"You mean the Germans?"

"No, no," said Mr. Lodge. "Not exactly. I meant that the world itself has become more complicated, more . . . more . . ." He held the putter-pen out like a microphone.

Howard, who was expected to nod with some acknowledgment, continued to stare straight at Mr. Lodge's lips. Land, house, family, car, tools, guns, garden, beer, work—the quest for the squaretail trout—neither more complicated nor less complicated, but the same.

"More . . . more complicated. Never mind. Let me get to the

point." Mr. Lodge rose, took a golfer's stance, and stroked smoothly in at Howard with his putter-pen, saying, "I'm running for Congress next year."

Everything made sense now to Howard. Mr. Lodge had been cut out from the start to be a politician. He was well dressed, well spoken, gray haired, and full of shit.

"Why, I'll vote for you," said Howard.

Mr. Lodge gave a single-syllable laugh, dropping his putter-pen. "I appreciate the gesture. What you should understand, why we've called in the supers and the foremen, is to announce that the company has been sold."

It's stuffy in here, Howard thought, and his mind strayed. An odd smell. Rabbit pens.

"Who the fuck to?" Howard grimaced at his unmanageable tongue.

"To the Pensacola Cane Exports Company, PCEC. It's a conglomerate."

Howard nodded wisely. He had no idea what a conglomerate was. He groped in the waters. Conglomerate—Congo, Africa; cane—candy cane, sugarcane, cripple's cane; exports—ex-wife, egg-zits, Ex-Lax; glomerate—many canes, many wives; Pensacola—it was in Florida, goddammit. He sipped his coffee violently, hating it as he hated his ignorance. Words and patterns of words were the problem. It shamed him that he could barely read a newspaper, that any reading was tiring, humiliating work. The talk of the educated, the talk in books, confused him, as if on purpose, as if education itself were a conspiracy to make certain that the knowledge of the world was unavailable to him. And yet he believed in his own intelligence, took pride in the way his thoughts came together like the cocking of a revolver. But the words were never there to express the thoughts, and so his private stock of knowledge was forever his secret, sealed inside by his ignorance.

"Tomorrow," said Mr. Lodge, "we'll pass out a Xerox explaining it all. The transition should be smooth, eh, Ben?" Mr. Gordon slunk forward, smiled, but said nothing. "I'm going to stay on as a consultant, Howard, though I won't be in the office every day. Mr. Gordon is going to be the plant manager."

"They laying anybody off?"

The question startled Mr. Lodge, embarrassed him. He smiled, glancing at Mr. Gordon. He realized he had three-putted the conversation.

"No changes for now," Mr. Gordon said sweetly.

Howard lay on his back under the damaged machine. Cooty had done his usual meticulous job of sweeping, and yet a few lint puffs had found their way back to tickle Howard's nose and stick to his sweat. The lint puffs looked like the fuzz on a Christmas-tree angel, thought Howard. White, weightless, and always in motion, tumbling one by one down an aisle, flying in formation over the looms, falling like snow, rising like ashes from a fire; there was something sinister about the way they seemed to carry on business, perform duties, create strategies, repeat habits, as though mocking the duties, strategies, and habits of the shop. Something was always going on in the shop—ants trooping between the floorboards, spiders hypnotized to stillness by their webs, flies in search of sex and garbage, rats singing *chi-ki-ki chi-ki-ki* in the walls, birds fearfully trying to find their way out of the attic, birds trying to find their way in. This was all well and good and natural. But the lint puffs were not natural. You could shoot a lint puff point-blank and it would continue to be a lint puff. Of such substances were the dangerous things made.

"Flashlight!" called Howard.

Cooty's sneakered feet, all that Howard could see of him, shuffled away, returned, and then a small, gnarled hand appeared between the sneakers.

The belt from the electric motor to the main drive shaft of the loom had fallen off. A ten-minute job.

Howard decided to loosen the shaft, move it back, and jump the belt onto its groove.

"Three-quarters open-end wrench," he commanded. Sneakers

moving off, bare floors, knees in pants too big, old hand, wrench.

"Howie, one of these teeth is gone."

"What?"

Knees, face, stink of sweat and breath. "One of the teeth on that nylon gear you put in is chipped."

"I know that," Howard shouted. "It's been like that for three months."

"Oh." Sneakers only.

The machine would run with a chipped tooth, Howard thought. Teeth, after all, didn't have to be perfect. *Teeth, straight teeth.* The thought thrashed about on the surface of his mind. Freddy had said to him, "Heather has got buck teeth; she needs braces to make them straight," and Howard had replied, "Ain't you smart."

The boy had read to him, drawn a book from his pocket.

"You can tell the real poor from the fake poor by the condition of their teeth. The real poor have poor teeth while the fake poor have rich teeth. The real poor are poor forever, irrespective of any money they make, because they are penned by illiteracy and cultural deprivation, and you can see their agony in their mouths, in their yellowed teeth, in their blackened teeth, in their crooked teeth, in their toothless cries. The fake poor are poor by choice, and you can see their richness—their college degrees, their good manners, their health—in the finely constructed jewelry boxes of their mouths, and, at last, you can see them cast off their poverty with a well-placed smile. . . ."

Howard had interrupted him, shouting, "Ain't nothing wrong with Heather's teeth. She can bite as good as you and me. Your mother has got teeth like that and your sister Charlene and your sister Pegeen, and there ain't nothing poor about them, except maybe for Pegeen and that ain't her teeth's fault. There's only you and your sister Sherry Ann that got pretty teeth, and she's a whore and you're a snob since you been to college."

"You don't understand my point," Freddy had said, shaking

the book at him, and Howard had knocked it from his hands.

The boy had backed away from him, not frightened really, just disgusted with him. Didn't the boy understand that it wasn't the teeth business that had set him off, that it was the reading, the slap in the face at his ignorance? And didn't he understand that his father's words never found their way to his lips in the same shape in which they had left his mind? College had taught the boy a technique for thinking, a plan for putting things in their place, a pleasure of mind, a code only the educated could understand, and now—Howard knew—the boy, in his own way, was trying to teach him that technique. But didn't he understand that it was too late? Howard had tried to signal to his son in his own impossible code—shouting, violence—that he was too old, that the limits of his thinking were confined in the hard, jagged walls of his illiteracy, and that the depth of his ignorance plummeted for miles. Why didn't the boy understand? Elenore understood; even Heather, at age eleven, understood. The boy had his own special brand of ignorance, Howard thought. Like father, like son—two cheeks of the same ass.

Howard half fitted the belt onto the groove of the shaft.

"Cooty, we're going to jump this whore on."

"Loose belt, eh?" said Cooty.

"Belt's loose."

Sneakers pattering.

"Not yet!"

"Not until you say, Howie."

"Tease her on, and holler up so I can get my hand out of here."

"Read-dyy, now!" shouted Cooty, turning the machine on for a split second, then shutting it off.

"Didn't make it. Leave it on a little longer."

"Read-dyy, now!" Cooty shouted.

"Almost, almost. This time it goes on."

Belts, pulleys, shafts, gears, male ends and female ends—mysteries to Cooty Patterson. He had spent nearly all his life in factories and had never learned how machines worked. To him they were odd arrangements of metal, grease, rubber, wood, and plastic, which, through the genius of men greater than himself, magically created rubber ducks, inkwells, matches, and other interesting objects. There was nothing in his head that knew how to make or fix things.

"What's holding you up?" Howard shouted.

"Ready?"

"Of course I'm ready. You think I'm down here playing with myself?"

"Now, Howie." But Howard did not hear.

Cooty turned the machine on. The belt caught on the shaft, and the shuttle banged out of the shed. Cooty shut the machine down, except that something was still running—*uhhhh*, he could barely hear it through the clatter of the looms in the shop; *uhhhh*, as if the belt were loose and still running and spinning on the shaft. At the same time, a tiny object jumped across Cooty's feet. He thought it was a lint puff, and he bent to pick it up. It was the little finger of Howard Elman's left hand.

2 : THE .308

Howard Elman driving, drinking a beer, thinking, forgetting what he thinks.

Toward Darby. Into the shroud of a late-November afternoon. The finger carried off by a wind, to return perhaps some night years hence as he lay floating, as old men do, in a shallow sleep of bright, tossed colors. Swett's place empty as a yawn. Below, his own fields spotted with his belongings. Television antenna, up a tree, in danger of falling over.

Howard Elman and the De Soto were home.

"What are you doing here so early?" asked Elenore. She was a soft, small-boned woman, narrow and rounded in the shoulders and broadening at the hips, and listing slightly, like a pear. She had tired eyes and plump white cheeks that cried for a pinch of red, and even with her mouth shut, part of one of her long upper teeth protruded over her thin lower lip.

She eyed Howard suspiciously. She didn't like events to steal up on her. Then she noticed his bandaged hand and came to him and lifted the hand into her own.

"Lost my little finger at the shop," he said.

17

"Does it hurt?" she asked. She was relieved, he could see, as though she had imagined something far worse.

"It don't hurt," he said. "They stitched it, and numbed it up. Don't even feel like I got a hand."

He sat at the kitchen table and she brought him a beer, knowing without having to ask that he would want one. Given her feelings about alcohol, the act was remarkable, and he was grateful.

"I was working on wide-web looms," he said to her, trying to clarify the accident in his mind. "I felt this snipping in my finger, and then nothing. Must have blacked out. Next thing I knew I was standing in the aisle, and Mr. Gordon says, 'Get his finger out of his mouth,' and William Potts says, 'I ain't getting near him,' and Cooty Patterson is on his knees like he wants to sweep up, because he don't know what else to do. So I took my finger out of my mouth, and I'll be damned if there weren't no finger there."

Elenore began to become suspicious again. "When's it going to be better?" she said.

"It ain't going to be better—it's gone," Howard said. He knew what she was getting at. She was afraid he'd be out of work; she was thinking they were going to starve. Elenore thought the worst or she thought nothing at all. "It don't matter, because the company's paying," he added, although really he wasn't quite so sure. He was vaguely aware of workmen's compensation, but he suspected that as a matter of course, the workmen were never actually compensated. He did not reveal the suspicion, because he knew that whatever his fears, Elenore's would be greater.

She quieted for a moment. He guessed that she sensed he was concealing something from her. Helpless anger surged through him, and he twisted in his chair.

"So you'll be here for a while," she said.

"A while."

"Freddy's coming home tomorrow for Thanksgiving," she said. "Why don't you go get him."

The suggestion drew off his anger, and he found himself pleased. But as usual he masked his pleasure.

"He ain't crippled; he can bum a ride," he said.

"Course he can," Elenore said, and let the phrase hang there.

"Um," he said. He wanted her to talk him into picking up the boy.

"If you go get him, you can bring home his laundry," she said.

"I suppose."

"I daresay the ride will do you good," she said.

"I daresay . . ." he said, and they both knew the matter was settled. Tomorrow Howard would drive the one hundred miles to the university and fetch the Elmans' only son. Howard imagined Freddy sitting on a pair of sheets puffed with laundry, his nose in a book. For the moment he was happy.

Howard sat at the kitchen table for about a minute. Then he went to the barn, staring blankly at a Dodge slant-six engine that had been hanging from a chain for four months. He retrieved a shovel and grub hoe that had been in the garden since spring and returned them to the shed. He marched briskly down the cellar, like a man with a mission, except that he had no mission. He opened the fuse box and shut it, whisked the dust off a few of Elenore's preserves, checked the damp spot on the earthen floor with a push of his foot (it was still soft), all the while lugging his numbed hand, shaking it, squeezing it, trying to lend to it some substance. Eventually he returned to the kitchen. He didn't know what to do with himself in this free hour before supper. *Work-for-pay, work-for-pay,* ticked his clock, but he wasn't working, and no command came to eat, drink, fix, drive, screw, hunt, fish, sleep, paint, dig, behold.

"Where's Heather?"

"Down the road."

He helped himself to another beer. Elenore gave him a hard look, but she said nothing. She hated drink, feared it. Her father, mother, brothers, sisters—all were alcoholics. She tolerated

Howard's chronic but moderate beer drinking, but she could turn crazy when he was drunk. Once, after he had come home crocked, she had hit him over the head with a quart jar of tomato preserves. The resulting scene had sent their daughter Sherry Ann into a ten-minute screaming fit.

He watched Elenore knead a meat loaf. There were spots on the backs of her hands, and the joints were starting to knot from arthritis. Still, they were slender hands, stiff and glistening like a cluster of twigs after an ice storm.

She had changed since her latest operation, a year ago. She seemed older, weaker, and full of new thoughts. It seemed as though she were always sick, always having operations. He could not understand how she could be religious, devoted to a God who made her suffer so. In the early years of their marriage, she had worked a full-time job (as an aid in various nursing homes), cared for a house, and raised a family. But she hadn't worked since the last operation, and he doubted whether she could ever work full-time again.

He remembered the first time he ever saw her, thirty-three years ago, when she was a girl of fifteen. The state had taken her from her alcoholic family and put her in Uncle Jack's foster home. Howard was only a boy himself at the time, but on his own, doing the only thing he knew, working as a farmhand for board, room, and a few dollars a week. He remembered she had a boxed lip from the back of Uncle Jack's hand, and scared eyes, hunted eyes, and something else, something magical. What was it? He could not remember.

"I daresay," Howard said, pacing, holding his bandaged hand in the palm of his good hand. "I daresay . . ." He wanted to say something about their early love. "I daresay," he began for the third time.

"Stop daresaying and start saying," Elenore said, impatient.

"Uncle Jack was the closest thing I ever seen to a father," Howard said, "but—no doubt—he was the meanest man ever to walk the face of the earth, meaner even than Swett."

"He wasn't so bad before Marlene got sick," said Elenore.

"She was already in bed with sores when I got there," Howard replied, still searching in a part of his mind for a way to say something about their early love. "I admired how she kept her hair all done up, even though she couldn't even go to the toilet alone."

"That wasn't her hair. That was a wig."

"Nooh?"

"After all these years you never figured that out?"

"I never doubted bacon come from a pig either," said Howard.

"Oh, she was bald all right. Had a few hairs here and abouts, but most generally you'd say she was bald. Poor thing. I turned sixteen the day she passed away."

Elenore's right hand left the meat loaf, which had nearly taken on its final shape, and she made the sign of the cross, leaving a greasy spot on her forehead.

Howard continued to pace, thinking. He was seventeen when he went to work for Uncle Jack, or so he suspected. The truth was, he didn't know how old he was. His age, along with other facts about his origins, had been lost as he was shuttled from foster home to foster home. Home, hell, he thought. The state would send him to a "home," which was always a farm, and the farmer would be paid by the state to feed him and care for him, and the farmer would work him ten hours a day for no wages. Eventually he would get into trouble, and the state would send him on to the next "home." All the while, it settled in his mind that he loved land and hated working land. So when it came his turn (thanks to World War Two money), he bought this little farm, fixed the house, put in oil heat and insulation, pruned the apple trees (once every ten years), laid out a garden, and made a solemn promise to himself and to a hundred boulders that sat like judges in his fields that crops, cows, chickens, and horses (the stupidest of creatures, in Howard's view) would be raised on other farms by other fools. "Up yours, Uncle Jack," he said silently, "and good riddance to horseshit." Well, not quite. He had kept a pony for his daughter Charlene.

Charlene had been conceived in Uncle Jack's hayloft, and Howard and Elenore had to get married. Not that they were burdened or shamed by the situation. In the circles they grew up in, pregnancy was regarded as part of the courtship.

He tried again to say something about their early love.

"I daresay . . ." He paused, began again, "I daresay," paused again, and asked, "When's supper going to be ready?"

"When it's always ready," Elenore answered.

"Where's Heather?" he nagged.

Elenore glared at him. He finished his beer and immediately opened another. He checked the weather seals on the kitchen windows, and then peeked at the top of the refrigerator for no good reason.

"Why don't you go to the dump?" Elenore finally said in exasperation.

It was just the right suggestion, and Howard was grateful for it. He patted her on the rump.

One-handed, he loaded four battered galvanized trash cans onto the pickup. As he was backing the truck out of the drive-way, he saw the lights go out in the kitchen. Elenore would be walking slowly into her sewing room, which she had converted into a shrine for Mother Mary. She would be kneeling on the bare floor, praying, hunched over like some creature in a circus. He could see her in his mind's eye kissing the tiny crucifix of her rosary. He didn't mind her religiousness, but he hated the kneel-ing. If he ever decided to talk to God, he resolved to stand up to Him. He drove off, nursing his beer and occasionally shaking his numbed hand, trying to get some feeling into it.

Elenore belonged to no parish, confessed to no priest. She was a TV Catholic, her romance with the Church having begun in the 1950s as a flirtation with Bishop Fulton J. Sheen and his televised sermons. Later she followed Sunday Mass on Channel 22. She had learned the rudiments of Catholicism from a set of catechisms she bought at a rummage sale. It was hybrid religion, but Elenore was devout and faithful to it.

Something at the dump burned with a low hiss, and Howard strained for a moment to listen to it. It was a pleasant sound, like Elenore's praying. Years ago, when she first got her catechism, she would read to him as they lay in bed, he with his arm thrown over his eyes to shield them from the light, listening as if to crickets.

Who made us? God made us.

Why did God make us? God made us to know Him, to love Him and serve Him in this world and be with Him in the next.

Wonderful entertainment, Howard thought. Good questions and good answers, like parts in a machine.

The Elmans ate supper as usual at five-thirty.

In Freddy's chair sat Music, Heather's cat, like the girl plain but athletic, with little interest in keeping clean. Music pawed food out of his dish onto the chair, sniffing in a suspicious crouch, half closed his eyes, purred, and began to feed. Heather, too, purred, imitating the cat, but improvising, so that one heard in the purring the melody of a popular song. Heather scrambled potatoes and peas into a greenish mortar and constructed a fortress of the food, imprisoning her meat loaf within. She called her father's attention to the creation; he grunted in approval. She then ate a doorway into the fortress and released the meat loaf, attempting to cut it into the shape of a star. This effort met with failure. She plucked a piece of meat with thumb and forefinger and ate it. Another piece went under the nose of the cat, which took the chunk between its two front paws, sniffed it, dropped it, and smacked it off the chair. Music then did a 360-degree turn in midair and resumed feeding. Girl and cat purred for the duration of the meal.

Half of Elenore's plate was demurely sprinkled with meat loaf and peas. Two blocks of store-bought cake occupied the other half. Cakes, pies, puddings, ice cream, came often to her table and to her dreams. Indeed, sweets had shaped her body like a drop of honey. She ate with her back straight and her head up, a slightly uncomfortable, formal pose of reservation and gravity.

For Howard, eating was a sort of meditation exercise. He remained silent during the meal and unaware of those around him, the act of eating a ritual of fork, hand, and mouth; his head approaching the plate until it was just a few inches away; the bite; and then the procedure reversed—the tide comes in, the tide goes out. Later, in the living room, Heather sang to her homework; the cat dozed in electronic warmth on top of the television, which played to no one yet dominated the room; Elenore sprawled in her chair like a hastily dropped overcoat.

Howard shook his hand. The numbness had left, and was replaced by a vibrating sensation, as if something were laughing at the stub of his finger.

"Hurt?" asked Elenore, head thrown back, jaw slack.

"What?"

She pointed to her hand.

"Starting to hurt," said Howard, "and it's buzzing." He banged the hand against his hip, preferring the pain to the buzzing.

"They give you any pills?" Elenore asked.

"I ain't taking no pills."

"When you hurt enough, you'll take 'em."

"Ain't you smart," Howard retorted with his best sarcasm.

Elenore snapped her mouth shut in resigned scorn. She knew more about pain than he did. You could begin with ideas about how to behave, how to live, how to die, and the ideas would take you through the first few stages—the fear, the rage at the unfairness, the disgust—but eventually there would be only the pain, a pure, white-hot sun in the belly, and all previous notions of order would be revealed as false gods of the prideful mind. In the end, you would surrender. They would turn you onto your belly and whisper to one another, and you would not care; they would jab you with a needle, and you would not care.

The pain vaguely frightened Howard. It was the odd, tingling sensation, as if a stranger with unknown powers and intent had got inside him. And, too, he saw his own foolishness at his small fear, knowing that most pain was self-inflicted. A deer could walk for hours with a bullet in its gut, could choke on its own blood, could lie breathing its last on a bed of decaying apples, and still suffer less than a man curled up safely in a trench, fearing guns, fearing not guns but the noise of guns, fearing not noise but that there would be a flash and no noise, fearing in the end a continuum of soundless flashes in which he would not know if he were dead and blown to hell or alive and insane (it was so; he had seen it), whereas the deer would die perfectly, without thought, without confusion, in the end without pain, slipping away with the softness of falling snow.

"I'm going up the hill and see Ollie, goddammit," Howard announced, startling Elenore with his sudden good humor.

"Going to get drunk," Elenore said.

"No I ain't," Howard said, spacing his words, self-satisfied at an idea that had just popped into his head.

"Going to get drunk," repeated Elenore.

Howard smiled at her slyly. "Going to trade for a new deer rifle for Freddy," he said. "Christmas is coming early this year."

"You say it, and you believe it," said Elenore, "but I know you're going to get drunk."

"Oh, I may have a couple," he said, shaking his tingling hand. He marveled at her ability to magnify a tiny truth into a general principle.

The shack people were the invisible people of the town of Darby, indeed of all the towns in Cheshire County. The shack people lived in the town and yet were apart from it. They did not vote at town meeting; they did not join the Darby Volunteer Fire Department; they were not seen at quilting bees, sugar-on-snow parties, or square dances, although occasionally they showed up for the annual Fourth of July picnic on the town green. Their homes, which seemed calculatedly ugly—shacks, trailers, run-down houses—were scattered among beautiful trees, beautiful fields, beautiful stone walls. So much beauty surrounded them that it was easy for the other people of the town, the nice people, as they liked to think of themselves—the farmers, the commuters to Keene, the new people (all of whom seemed to have college degrees and big bank accounts)—to see only the beauty, as though no one could be truly poor in the midst of beauty. When the nice people thought about poverty, they thought about city ghettos full of black people. However, there was one family of shack people in Darby that was well known—the Jordans. Every town in the county had its family of "Jordans"—illiterate, uncouth, congenitally defective. It was as if the nice people singled out and focused upon a family so ridiculous and so beyond all help that the other shack people became that much less visible, and thus the nice people's guilt about local poverty was blunted.

The Jordans lived in the shadow of a great sign, forty feet high and two hundred feet long, that sat on a windy crest and faced the interstate highway, three miles away on the Vermont side of the Connecticut River. BASKETVILLE—EXIT 8, said the sign. Behind it was a series of shacks and sheds, the outbuildings of an old chicken farm whose main house and barn had burned years ago. In the sheds resided dogs, cats, goats, pigs, rodents, cows, and chickens, ranked according to the rules of a rough feudalism in which a pig named Grunts was lord. In the shacks resided Jordans, similarly ranked, whose lord was Ollie Jordan.

Howard's pickup rolled into the yard. Something crunched under a wheel. Dogs were out of the sheds yapping at his ankles the moment he stepped out of the cab. He cradled two six-packs of beer under his arm. Even in the cold air, with the hill wind crying through the frame of the great sign, he could detect the smells of the place: pigshit, garbage, piss, and something else, intense and sweet like a dead animal—the Jordans themselves. Willow Jordan yelled to him, from somewhere in the dark, "Come to fix the lights?"

Howard opened the door to the shack without knocking. A tiny girl with a snotty nose lunged at his leg. He picked her up, kissed her roughly on the cheek, and set her down. Her hair had captured the smells of the house. He followed the sound of the television into the next room—an adjoining shack, really. Here most of the Jordans were gathered. Helen Jordan, Ollie's common-law wife, gave Howard a cold look, wiped her mouth, and looked away. She had long, saggy breasts that fell like tongues to her waist and flopped about in a loose-fitting cotton dress. Edith Jordan, who was Heather's age but two years behind her in school, sucked on her thumb. Floyd and Fletch Jordan, twin boys age fourteen, wrestled in a doorway, which led to yet another shack, where their father, Dale Jordan, lay snoring-drunk on a bed. Back in the television shack, Noreen Jordan, only sixteen and unmarried, lay asleep on a couch, her child at her breast. On the floor sat Ollie's deaf-and-dumb hunchback son, Turtle, pursing his lips and squinching his eyes. It was a moment before Howard realized that Turtle was mimicking his facial expressions.

Turtle and Willow—the latter was outside—were Ollie's eldest sons. They were both mimics; they were both defective; they were both favored by Ollie. Neither had been to public school, although Willow had been sent by the state to Laconia for a year when he was young. They did not look like brothers. Willow was heavy and dark, Turtle slight and blond. Howard suspected they'd had different mothers.

At a card table sat Ollie Jordan, cleaning a shotgun. His body was hard and angular, like chicken feet. His face was dominated by a potatolike nose, coursed with purple veins and smashed red capillaries. Every thirty seconds or so, his hand jumped to the nose to scratch it.

"Ollie, you need a bigger place," said Howard.

Ollie Jordan glanced at Howard's bandaged hand, but said nothing. Under his rules of etiquette, it would be up to Howard to raise the subject of the lost finger.

"The bigger the house, the more people fill it," Ollie replied, pronouncing one of his many laws.

They broke into the beer Howard had brought. Ollie gave a

can to Turtle, telling him something in Jordan sign language.

"I heard Willow outside," said Howard.

"He climbs up the sign and hollers his goddamn head off. God damn him, yes!" The nose brightened, as though signifying the torment caused by Willow.

"Can't you shut him up?" asked Howard, knowing perfectly well there was no way short of murder to shut up Willow Jordan.

"Dog barks and you kick his ass twice and he still barks, it means he's going to continue to bark." Ollie lit his corncob pipe and scratched his nose.

"I ain't had a dog since the little girl's collie—or whatever kind of breed that goddamn animal was—was run over," said Howard.

"You want a dog?"

"Don't want a dog. Want a deer rifle for my boy."

"Nobody wants a good dog anymore. All they want's a house dog. You bring a good dog in the house and you kill his nose."

"I never could understand that collie," said Howard. "She'd wait by the road for hours to chase cars."

"Every critter, animal or man, has got a stupid streak," Ollie said.

"Ain't that the truth. Goddamn."

"Goddamn."

"Goddamn."

"That boy can shoot a rifle, all right," said Ollie.

"Freddy's the best natural shooter I ever saw," Howard bragged.

"Natural law," said Ollie.

To Ollie Jordan, laws were the presents nature bestowed upon the thoughtful man, as the town dump bestowed useful materials upon the wise scavenger, to be gathered and put together after one's own fashion, private creations for private uses rather than principles standing alone. "Trout feed after a rain" was law if you caught trout after a rain; people saying "How are youuu?" and dogs sniffing one another's hind ends were laws for some people and some dogs; and Ollie could understand and respect such laws and see how they meant the same thing and how they served the respective species without ever having a desire to adopt the laws as his own.

"Got a nice little three-oh-eight. Ain't been fired maybe two or three times."

Howard nodded, and Ollie left to get the weapon, which he kept in a box under lock and key.

Howard's head felt light, but not from the beer. He was feverish. A crazy image appeared in his mind: a tray of spare parts for wide-web looms that included nuts, bolts, cogs, pins, and his own little finger.

Ollie returned with the rifle and gave it to Howard, and then he spoke in sign language to Turtle, his fingers twirling like those of an old woman knitting. Turtle went into the kitchen and came back with a single bullet.

"Used to have a scope on it," said Howard, inspecting the weapon.

"Owned by a Massachusetts hunter."

"You fire it?"

"No. But you can." Ollie took the bullet from the hunchback, gave it to Howard, and put an empty beer can on top of the television set.

Jordans gathered around Howard, expecting entertainment. Edith, thumb still in her mouth, fled to the kitchen. Noreen remained asleep with her baby. Howard sighted the rifle at the can, wincing at the pressure of the gun on his bandaged hand.

"I'm going to hit the goddamn screen," he said.

"Goddamn, it's only across the room."

Goddamn you, Ollie, Howard thought. Howard's hand was as tender and pulpy as a rotted melon—as any fool could see. But Ollie Jordan, who was not a fool, could not see. Every man a fool in his own way. He could refuse to fire the weapon inside, but that would insult Ollie. And he would rather shoot the television or Ollie himself than insult him. He decided to fire the damn thing one-handed.

The resulting explosion temporarily deafened Howard and scrambled his perceptions. He felt as though he had been thrown back in time, into a den of cavemen. Turtle Jordan lay on his back, arms spread, a faraway look in his eyes, as though something very beautiful had happened. Noreen, child screaming soundlessly at her breast, sat bolt upright, a terrified look on her face, as though she believed she had awakened in hell. Floyd and Fletch writhed on the floor belly-laughing, reminding Howard of a silent movie. On the television screen, a man with a suit and tie chased another man with a suit and tie. Disgraceful—well-dressed men behaving like that, Howard thought.

The voice Howard heard next might have been Willow's whispering through the bullet hole in the wall, a meaningless message that Howard's brain, desperate for order, would invest with words. But in fact the voice was Ollie's, emerging from the silence as he inspected the beer can critically.

"You hit it a little high, Howie," he said, "but I don't believe it shoots high. I believe you pulled it."

Then Howard heard the child crying and the teenage boys laughing, and Noreen shouting, either at him or at Ollie, he couldn't be certain, "You bastid, you bastid, you bastid."

Howard agreed to give Ollie a chain saw for the rifle. The gun was worth more, but Ollie owed Howard the difference in compensation for repair work that Howard had performed on his vehicles over the years. Nor would Howard deliver the chain saw. It would stay in his barn, and he would continue to use it, bound by the unwritten, unspoken agreement to maintain it or have on hand its equivalent in case it wore out. This winter, next winter, the winter after, perhaps never, Ollie would come by with Turtle to fetch his saw. Their method of barter had evolved over the years, and neither would have been able to explain how it worked. Listening to them talk, a stranger could not guess that a bargain had been struck.

The finger that he did not have began to itch, and as he lay in his bed, soft pear of Elenore beside him asleep or perhaps faking sleep, he wished he had got drunk so that sleep would come like a door's shutting. *Come to fix the lights?* If she had been faking sleep, she would by now be asleep, for she would know by his breathing that he was not drunk, and so her ancient fear would be laid to rest for another night. *Come to fix the lights?* He had missed a few minutes of his life today. They had floated off with the lint puffs in the shop. He tried to scratch the finger, and discovered that something that wasn't there couldn't be scratched, though it could itch. *Teeth, straight teeth.* It was going to be a *collld* winter. Ask Willow. Ask Willow nothing, for he was an animal. Observe and behold. You could observe the behavior of humans ad infinitum and never know how cold the winter would be, but the animals could tell you. He scratched the finger that was not there until pain overrode the itch, and a tiny trickle of blood wet the sheet. As the pain subsided, the itching returned. How was it that something that no longer existed could make you feel?

3 : THE GIFT

Half awakeness. North Africa. A vast and harsh blue sky. The land yellow and gleaming like the back of a gold watch. If you closed your eyes and listened to the music of the tank, you would think of bears.

Howard was on the road, traveling east to Durham to fetch his son for Thanksgiving. Beside him was his Thermos of coffee—treasure. The morning was gray and unpleasant, the sky falling into the hills like soot. A rock wall angled without purpose through a field. A great mound of highway salt, covered with black plastic, held him in awe for a moment, then faded from his thoughts forever.

The image of a fourteen-year-old boy appeared in his mind, himself years ago. He had run away from a farmer who overworked him in the summer heat, and had wandered in the woods for days before they found him. He had eaten insects, preferring the ones that went *crunch* between his teeth to the soft-bellied ones. Eventually hunger brought spiritual power, as if requirements for food, sleep, warmth, had vanished; brought yellow dust to the sunlight; brought ecstasy.

In the sound of the tires' whirring, he began to hear the music of the tank, and he lapsed into a reverie of bears.

Then, in momentary panic, he snapped his head around. The gun! Had he forgotten it? The .308, tucked into its brown vinyl case, lay on the back seat like a sleeping child.

He could not remember driving the last ten miles. The Ford had hypnotized him, guiding itself. What had he been thinking about? Something pleasant, something large, something that might instruct by virtue of its being rather than by example. The image of a boulder glittering with mica crystals took shape in his mind. No, that wasn't it. The thought was gone, fallen into the memory like a coin dropped through the layers of cold in a deep lake. He lit a cigarette, as he always did when he was annoyed. Thoughts were like anything else you owned, he believed. You could tinker with them, put them away, leave them around, even destroy them, if you were willing to put up with trouble. But if you lost them, you were violating certain self-evident rules of conservation, and you were a damn fool.

He sipped his coffee, watching the trees along the road as another man might watch a sporting event on television. A troop of poplars was overtaking a swamp that was drying up; an ancient, recently fallen maple now lay waiting for a decent burial in the snow.

He relaxed his shoulders. "Christmas is coming early this year," he said aloud. They would hunt Sunday with Cooty and Ollie and maybe Willow, and Freddy would handle the new rifle with the grace and ease of a good roofer nailing black felt. With some effort, Howard called for last year's deer hunt from his mind.

The hunters had stopped to rest, Willow skinning a stick for the fun of it, Ollie scratching his nose with high seriousness, Freddy breaking out a book from under his jacket, an act that both irritated his father and filled him with pride.

"Nice here," said Cooty, eyes weepy from the cold. He sat on a stump and emptied snow from his galoshes, which for reasons of his own he refused to buckle. He wore earmuffs, a huge brown tweed overcoat, and a felt hat. Beside him was a cardboard suitcase filled with a pint of liquor, a Thermos of coffee, cups, and sandwiches. He looked like an aging Fuller Brush man. He opened the suitcase, and Ollie reached into it.

"Cooty, why don't you get yourself a rifle?" Ollie Jordan bit into a lettuce sandwich, making a tiny crashing sound in the stillness of the forest.

"*Chickachickachicka.*" Willow mocked a red squirrel up a tree.

"I wouldn't know what to do with a gun," said Cooty.

"*Chickachickachicka.*" Willow waved his knife at the squirrel.

"Trade you for a nice little ninety-four," said Ollie. "Owned by my cousin Pearly. Always took care of his things."

Cooty shook his head violently.

"He's scared of guns," said Howard. He took a snort of liquor, enjoyed the electric shiver down his spine, and sipped his coffee.

"My sister Jean was scared of birds, afraid they'd get in her hair," said Ollie. His nose glowed; it hurt him in the cold.

Freddy's old Marlin lay in the snow at his feet. The boy handled the weapon as if it were something unpleasant, and yet he could shoot through a keyhole and unlock the door.

They were ready to move on now, but they waited patiently for Cooty to go to the bathroom and gather his things. The presence of Cooty on the hunt was very important. He was the spectator who must be entertained and instructed. He raised the level of the hunt to a public event, so that they hunted with more care, more self-consciousness, more responsibility to their own standards.

Ollie and Howard worked the uphill side of the ridge, and occasionally they could see Swett's place looking pretty in the snow-covered fields. Freddy and Willow took a stand along a deer trail. Freddy was happy because he had time to read. Willow didn't care where he hunted. Cooty tagged along with Howard and Ollie.

Ollie had already killed a deer this fall. But that was not hunting; that was winter food gathering. In the old days Howard and Ollie jacked deer with a lamp. But Howard had got steady work, and with prosperity came responsibility and fear of the law. He hadn't shot a deer illegally in fifteen years. He ate beef. He believed he had made progress.

They saw no deer or signs of deer. They were joined by Freddy and Willow, whose luck was equally bad.

"Ain't no deer here like there used to be," said Ollie.

"I believe they're on the other side of the ridge," said Howard.

"I expect the dogs run 'em up there in the winter, but I don't see why they don't come down at this time of year. Plenty of feed here," said Ollie.

It was difficult to cross the ridge because of a series of ledges, and the going was hard on that side of the hill, wild and full of tangles, with no trails.

"*Chickachickachicka.*"

"Willow, there ain't no squirrel here," said Howard.

"*Chickachickachicka.*"

"It's a wonder he don't shoot one of us or his own toe," said Howard.

"Oh, he will someday," said Ollie.

Freddy and then Cooty began to dance to warm their cold feet. It was three o'clock. The hunters decided to go home.

The climax of the day came unexpectedly. They had reached the road not five hundred feet from the Elman house. Howard saw a movement in some young birches, but before he could react, Freddy had snapped his rifle to his shoulder and fired. There was the sound of an animal crashing through brush. Freddy appeared stunned, as if the rifle had gone off by itself.

Boom! Boom! Boom! Willow sprayed the trees with buckshot and took off on the run. Freddy resumed his foot-warming dance. "Willow, you goddamn fool!" Howard shouted. Ollie was delighted. He loved to see Howard angry.

The deer ran three hundred yards and dropped. It lay panting, tongue out, eyes open. When the men arrived, Willow was already at work slicing its belly. The deer appeared aware of what was happening, but blissful, as if it were drugged.

Ollie knelt beside his son, guiding him gently, subtly, so that Willow gutted the deer properly and yet was not denied the ecstasy of knife work.

Howard's heart beat furiously with joy. He put his arm around Freddy. "Nice buck. Beauty, beauty, beauty," he repeated.

Freddy watched gravely as Cooty struggled, suitcase in hand, to reach the hunters. Freddy's face was calm, but Howard could feel him shaking all over, as if he were hiccupping violently.

A few leftovers of the hunt memory remained, and Howard cooked them into a pleasing mental stew—Ollie trying unsuccessfully to explain to Cooty the difference between a white birch and a gray birch; a place where folds of ice hugged a ledge; an unresolved, spirited argument with Ollie about the nature of the bad breath of bears (like a fart—Howard; like a dead horse—Ollie).

Howard's attention turned toward the gloomy day, one of those days that portend winter. "Goddamn, winter's coming," he said aloud in the confines of the Ford wagon.

He loved winter more than the other seasons, loved a tender snowfall, loved the savage north wind and the blinding light off a frozen lake, loved most a blizzard, which he faced head-on like a bison. He would not admit these things, however, because in his superstition he believed that by revealing desires about sacred subjects, such as weather and seasons, you would likely receive the opposite of what you wanted. Therefore, at this time of year, Howard could be heard complaining about cold, moaning over oil bills, claiming that if he had the money, he would take his family to Florida and never come back.

Ever since he was a boy, Howard had taken secret pleasure in disasters. Blizzards, floods, and hurricanes thrilled him as if the excesses of nature were his own. Disasters were his allies, his brothers; he himself was a disaster waiting to happen, he thought with pride. All his life he had misunderstood the phrase "bull in a china shop" to be a compliment.

Fires were an exception to his love for disasters. The hot wind of a forest fire fatigued him, weakened muscles as well as determination, made his stomach queasy. When Elenore talked of the pains of hell through eternal burning, he asked her almost politely to keep quiet, as if telling her loudly to shut up might ignite something in the room.

For an hour Howard slumbered in a driver's mood. He saw everything, he saw nothing; he was bored, he was amused; he passed a few cars, a few passed him; he remembered, he forgot; he was in North Africa, he was in Durham, New Hampshire.

Howard parked the Ford in a lot behind the dormitory. He carried the rifle by the handle of its case with pride and assurance. To Howard, there was nothing odd about a man with a rifle on a public street. Yet when he saw a girl with an armful of books, he thought it peculiar, even shameful. Books to him were objects that were meant to be stationary, and to transport them in plain sight was somehow inappropriate, like displaying a naked dummy in a department-store window.

Nor did it strike Howard that giving his son a Christmas present on the day before Thanksgiving in a dormitory room might be inappropriate. Giving and receiving presents on traditional occasions—Christmas, birthdays, weddings, anniversaries—held little meaning for him. Sometimes he bought his wife a gift for their wedding anniversary, and sometimes he did not. (One year he gave her a twenty-dollar bill.) Santa Claus baffled him. Even as a child, he regarded Santa as just another fat old man with signs of alcoholism around his eyes and nose, a creature whose exploits were not even plausible. Who could believe in a man who presumed to drive a machine powered by deer across the sky, who employed dwarfs in a toy shop at the North Pole, who entered a house through a chimney? Early in their lives, Howard's children were told there was no Santa Claus. Their mother bought the gifts; their father paid for them.

If Howard did not practice the amenities of giving, he was not against giving altogether. In fact, he was generous to a fault. He was a master at giving his wife presents she did not want or wanted under different circumstances. Over the years, he had surprised her with perfume she dared not wear, dresses she could not wear, hats that could wear her, candles for which she had no use, expensive appliances she would rather have chosen herself, and knickknacks whose function she was at a loss to understand and whose beauty she was at a loss to appreciate. And so, slipping the rifle out of its case, Howard—with the egotistical elation of one who considers himself the giver rather than the receiver—entered Freddy's room.

Father and son looked at each other as if each had come across a crime. Both spoke at the same moment. Freddy said, " 'Lo," and Howard said, "Where'd you get that goddamn beard?"

"I didn't get it; I grew it," said Freddy.

"Ain't you smart," yelled Howard. This phrase he could utter in a hundred ways, to convey degrees of sarcasm, exasperation, frustration, criticism, irony, cosmic outrage, even affection; a phrase that filled in when he had no other words; a staple—like rice or potatoes or refried beans—that could be fed into the maw of a starved vocabulary.

"You're always yelling at me," yelled Freddy.

Dark hair enveloped his face from the bottom of the eyes to the throat. A pink slash showed where his mouth was. His ears were partially hidden.

"You look like a goddamn A-rab," yelled Howard.

"The word is Arab," yelled Freddy.

"Ain't you smart," yelled Howard.

"Arab, Arab, Arab," yelled Freddy.

"Ain't you smart," yelled Howard.

"Oh, I ain't smart," yelled Freddy, with emphasis on the "ain't."

"I'll smarten you up," yelled Howard, taking menacing steps forward, rifle at order arms, its butt skipping along the floor.

Freddy stood his ground, teeth clattering, clenched fists quivering at his sides.

The two stood breathing fire on each other for a few seconds.

Then Howard backed up. He realized he had been wrong. For a man who had never learned to apologize, he did his best. He brought the rifle to present arms, and said, "Merry fucking Christmas."

"No, not to me," said Freddy.

"Trade it for a shotgun, then," said Howard.

Freddy shook his head no no no no and retreated.

Howard remained in the middle of the room, holding the gun in offering.

"Ain't nothing wrong with this rifle," he said.

"I'm not interested in killing animals," said Freddy with a shrug of hopelessness.

Dread rolled over Howard. College had pulled his son apart, scattered beliefs, habits, and loves like so many bits of a machine, and was now rebuilding him into a customized version of Freddy Elman.

Howard slipped the rifle into its case, zipping it to the top and folding the zipper back so it wouldn't show. He toted the rifle to the car and laid it gently in the back seat with the caution and reverence of a man placing flowers at the bier of a loved one, or a bomb under a church seat. Freddy followed with his laundry bundles.

The Ford sped away from Durham faster than it had come in.

Howard was like a mariner, first drifting in sunshine, then lost in the fog—think, feel, think, feel, think. . . .

No doubt college had changed the boy, Howard thought, much as war or marriage or third-degree burns changed one. The beard, the long hair, the strange-colored patches on his trousers—these were harmless enough. Why was it, then, that he, Howard Elman, was so appalled? Surely it must be because Freddy Elman, as Howard knew him, soon would vanish. This had to be so, he figured, because the human brain could hold only a few ideas at one time. Education was not so much addition as it was replacement. For every idea gained, one was lost. He glanced at his son with love and mistrust.

An uneasy peace prevailed while Howard told the story of how he had lost his finger at the shop. The war resumed when Howard changed the subject.

"What the hell they teaching you there?" asked Howard abruptly, but without malice.

The question caught Freddy by surprise; he was tussling with his own thoughts.

"You learn about Machiavelli. And like that," he replied.

An Italian? An artist? A shoemaker? A pope? A gangster? A goddamn fascist? Admit it, Howard said to himself, you don't know. College had put things in Freddy's head that were not in Howard's head and likely never would be.

"How far away is the moon?" pestered Howard.

"Two hundred and forty thousand miles," said Freddy.

"They teach you much geography over there?" Howard was probing, like a doctor feeling for a cancer.

Freddy shook his head no.

"They teach communism?"

Freddy shrugged, showing he thought the question was meaningless.

"Teach disrespect for your family?"

Freddy made a face.

"Teach about the war?"

Freddy shook his head no.

"I can't watch you nod your goddamn head and drive this goddamn car," Howard yelled.

"Quit asking me stupid questions," said Freddy.

The boy was right, Howard realized. He was asking stupid questions, and he was minding someone else's business, a worse offense than common stupidity.

Howard tried to relax his shoulders, but his mind would not drop into its driver's doze. It roamed like a lost ship in search of land. He brooded.

Freddy, too, brooded. What had once been familiar, even comfortable, now seemed alien and harsh: his father's green work clothes, smelling of grease; the crushed cigarette packs on the seat; the rusted oil filter that rolled around in the back; the empty foam cups and beer cans shoved under the front seat; Freddy made a silent vow of neatness.

Pictures of his family flashed through his mind: his mother, sitting in her chair, thumbing her rosary beads and hissing her prayers, her eyes lost, as though someone had hypnotized her; Charlene, lecturing Heather on the subtleties of go-go boots. Charlene had got pregnant in high school, and so at seventeen had married Parker Harris. Freddy had to agree with his father's description of Parker: He was a good provider and a dumb shit. Thanksgiving Day meal this year was at Charlene's. Freddy dreaded it. He had contemplated begging off, but he wanted to see his sister Heather. Indeed, he wanted to do something for her, get her away from the family, save her from getting pregnant in high school and marrying some garage mechanic. He wanted his little sister to grow up to be beautiful and sensitive and cultured, and share the company of the thoughtful. Such persons, he noted, did not have buck teeth. It wasn't that he disliked his family. Not really. It was just that as a sophomore in college he believed he had outgrown them. He was determined to save his sister from ignorance.

"Maybe . . . maybe you can explain it to me, about the gun, I mean," said his father.

"I just want to stop the cycle of killing," Freddy said. "It isn't necessary. It isn't even necessary that people eat meat. And it certainly isn't necessary that people make war on people. I'm doing my small part to change the species."

"Umm," said Howard.

Freddy could see that his father did not understand his pacifism, and he began to feel frustrated and strangely lonely.

Meanwhile Howard was thinking. He wanted to tell his son that people went to war because they enjoyed it. But he said nothing. He drove on, slipping into a driver's doze.

The sky is black and the sound makes you shiver, and God, it's only midday. Howard had seen them in Africa, a sky full of grasshoppers that blotted out the sun and ate all vegetation, the kind of enemy that took everything you owned and left you intact. This was real horror, worse than getting shot or blown up in a war.

"I remember when we was in Africa ..." Howard began.

Oh, Jesus, thought Freddy, he's going to start telling war stories.

4 : THE CREATURE

Later that night, the finger that wasn't there throbbed in an uneven rhythm, like a leaky faucet, and Howard could not sleep. Thoughts floated to the surface of his mind: the smell of decay, softness, like a dead log; the sweet heavy air of August. He put his arm around Elenore. She curled into a protective knot. Howard opened his eyes. Cool, electric-white moonlight filled the room.

"Harvest moon," he said.

"Wha—?" questioned Elenore, but she was not awake.

He dressed in the half darkness and stood by the window. The stars were like the debris found far out at sea, tossed and isolated.

He decided to look in on the children. Heather lay on her back, feet sticking out of the blankets, the cat nestled on her stomach. He watched and listened. He had to be reassured that there was life in the room. He came closer, and he could hear the cat purring. He covered Heather's feet, and the cat leaped to the dresser. He squeezed the child's foot through the covers, and bent and kissed her lightly on the neck, and left.

Freddy lay on his side, arm thrown over his head, bottom

sticking out, in the manner of his mother. Howard stood in the doorway. He would come no closer. There were boundaries here. He thought about the coils of barbed wire the infantry used to lay during the war. The arm came down heavily, and he heard a pig sound from the bed. There was life in the room.

Downstairs the moonlight pressed in on him through the windows, as if it could be felt, like a wind. He wanted to go outside and look at the sky, but decorum held him back. Man must have his reasons. Man does not abandon habit even for beauty. He put a crescent wrench in his hip pocket, believing somehow that reason and tool were one, and went outside. The moon looked like a buffed, slightly dented hubcap. The moon, they said, traveled around the earth, which traveled around the sun, which ... Well, it too must travel around something. He wondered if college taught Freddy where all these objects in the sky were going, and how they had got started. It was obvious the universe was a mechanical contrivance—like a washing machine, with perhaps two or three rules governing its operation— as opposed to a living creature. Everything in the sky moved in circles around everything else, without touching. He thought about the ocean again.

There was something odd about the horizon, and it took him a moment to figure out what it was. There were lights on at Swett's place. A car, rather splendid in the moonlight, was parked in the driveway. He was going to have neighbors. Howard was jealous. He had come to think of Swett's acres as his own since the place had been abandoned. Now he felt diminished. He paced off eighty yards to the marker between the two properties, a snaky, falling-down stone wall. There he stopped.

From the wall he had a fine view of the Swett house, about three hundred yards away upslope. The two properties shared a field strewn with gray boulders, which cast long, creaturelike shadows in the moonlight. On one side of the field was a row of sugar maples beside the town road that emptied into the state highway about a mile away. On the other side was a dense forest of mixed hardwoods and pines. Here the land became very rugged and steep. Farther up, near the ridge of the hill, were hemlocks growing out of jagged boulders. There had been quarries on the Donaldson Township side of the ridge, it was said, but Howard didn't know for sure. The deer in the area used the ridge for their winter yards.

He heard a sound from the Swett house—perhaps a door opening and shutting. Then he saw a figure, moon shadowed, loping away from the house into the forest. A dog, he guessed. But, no. It didn't run like a dog, or like any dog Howard had ever seen. It was about the size of a small doe, with a curved, erect tail. He watched it come back into the field, only to have it vanish before his eyes as clouds moved across the face of the moon. When his eyes picked up its movement again, it was running right at him at full speed. For a moment he lost it again in the darkness, and then the moonlight was strong. The features of the thing were sharp and clear. Howard moved his arm across his eyes, as if to protect them, and the thing veered away at the wall and disappeared into the woods. Tiny electric shivers danced along his spinal column. He had seen a silver-haired creature with the moon-dazzled face of a woman. Just a damn dog, he told himself. But he was shaken.

The Elmans gathered for Thanksgiving dinner at 42 Elliot Street in Keene, the home of Parker and Charlene Harris and their three small children. Pegeen, Howard and Elenore's second daughter, stayed home in Lowell, Massachusetts, this year. She was ill. Sherry Ann, the third daughter, had run away with a sailor three years ago and was heard from only intermittently.

Reginald Harris, age six, spilled a glass of milk on his turkey platter. His father, Parker, laughed and laughed, "Houp, houp, houp, houp," showing a mouth full of jagged black teeth.

Parker had no opinions, no conflicts. He neither took nor gave, desired nor submitted; he marshaled no forces, yet was invulnerable. He grinned most of the time and laughed the rest of the time. He laughed at a fig and a broken nose and a rainy day and a goat and a Volkswagen and a pile of butchered chickens as if they were all the same thing. In Parker Harris, a perfect blend of stupidity, ignorance, luck, and emotional stability had come together to form a contented man.

"Houp, houp, houp, houp." Presently Parker laughed at Freddy's beard.

Freddy suffered the laugh in silent anger, but his father tried halfheartedly to come to his defense.

"Parker, will you pipe down so the rest of us can eat," he shouted.

Charlene gave Howard a vicious look.

"Charlene!" bellowed Howard.

"It's his house. He can say what he pleases," said Charlene.

"He don't say nothing. He just goes haw, haw, haw," said Howard in a poor imitation of Parker's whooping-cough laugh.

"Don't pick on him," said Charlene.

"You both pick," said Elenore, almost as an aside.

"Houp, houp, houp, houp." The tears came, and Parker almost fell off his chair, and he laughed all the more at himself.

Freddy stormed off to the living room and opened a paperback book.

Heather ran to the bathroom.

Charlene's youngest began to bawl, and the next one joined in. Reginald, the oldest, said, "Ca-ca, ca-ca, ca-ca, ca-ca . . ." until his mother slapped his hand, whereupon the child began to laugh.

Elenore and Charlene glared at Howard. They blamed him for the commotion.

Howard became sullen. He remembered Thanksgiving meals at his house. Things were different then. They were pleasant.

Freddy sighted over his book—*The Stranger,* by Camus—as if it were a surveyor's transit. He was measuring his father and his brother-in-law as they sat at the kitchen table. With their cotton work clothes, they reminded him of soldiers, soldiers of factories, soldiers of highway departments, soldiers of gas stations, soldiers of dumps, their uniforms worn on all occasions save for weddings and funerals. Parker's dirty blue shirt hung over his broad hips. The sleeves were haphazardly rolled up, and there was a button missing at the waist, so that you could see his navel. By contrast, his father was impeccably dressed. He could be counted on to wear forest-green work suit, white t-shirt, red and white suspenders, scuffed shoes or work boots, and white cotton socks, and always the buttons buttoned on his breast pockets, although this meant buttoning and rebuttoning the cigarette pocket twenty times a day. Difficult to tell whether the habit was an expression of personal pride or a Pavlovian trick played on him by the army.

Freddy began now to read his book. He felt more kinship toward Camus' characters than toward his family.

After the meal the family gathered in the living room, where a color television played. It was simultaneously watched and ignored, like a much-loved but never-listened-to president—say, Dwight Eisenhower. The Harris children were dispatched to the playroom, a bombed-out area of drool, dried vomit, urine, smashed toys, crayon drawings on the walls, bitten furniture, and its own television set, the only object in the room that was undamaged and working the way it was supposed to. The door was kept closed and the children were left to themselves, unless their screams became especially loud.

The playroom was the exception to an otherwise well-kept house. Although she worked thirty hours a week at Grant's department store, Charlene found time to be a fastidious housekeeper. Indeed, the living room was clean and orderly to a fault. It served as a kind of museum for Charlene's horse objects, which included more than a hundred paintings, statues, carvings, and books. The walls were decorated with frilly blue paper on which frolicked creatures with the bodies of horses and the facial expressions of angels. Shaggy, iridescent blue carpeting covered the floor, and heavy drapes of a deeper shade of blue obscured a newly installed picture window that faced the street. The room was furnished with a matching living-room set in the Mediterranean style and resembled the inside of a new mobile home. The children were prevented from entering the room by a gate fashioned to look like that of a Western corral. Parker was not allowed in the room unless he was wearing clean pants. Anyway, he preferred watching the tiny Japanese television on the kitchen table.

Howard did not like the living room, because it reminded him of a funeral parlor, though he admired his daughter's creative touch. He felt that every room in a house ought to have things to put your feet on and some bare floor where you could spread out the parts of a rifle or motor.

The living room made Elenore slightly suspicious because there were no pictures of Jesus or Mother Mary, not even a crucifix on the wall. She suspected that Parker was too unsuffering a soul to believe in God, and she feared he was leading her daughter and grandchildren down the road to good-humored atheism, but she had promised herself never to meddle in her children's lives once they were married, and besides, criticism was tiring. She liked this house, though; it was smaller than her own and easier to take care of, and the temperature was even throughout, and there was no whistling of the wind in cracks and no creaking of floorboards and no moaning from the attic; in fact, as far as she knew, there was no attic, and this struck her as civilized.

Charlene had resented Parker when he got her pregnant her senior year in high school, not because she didn't want to marry him but she had to give up her horse, Gentle Harriet. Soon afterward, however, she started her "museum," as she called it, and it had sufficed. Every evening after the children were asleep, she sat in her easy chair in the living room and sipped hot water flavored with lemon and sugar, and leafed through one of her many picture books on horses. She was a sensible woman, and she knew the real thing had never been as good as this.

Elenore and Charlene sat on the couch talking about how

Pegeen had become stooped after her last pregnancy. Freddy sat in the easy chair reading his book. At his feet on the thick carpet, Heather leafed through Charlene's books on horses. Howard and Parker played knock gin at a card table brought in for the purpose. Howard almost always won the games, but got little satisfaction, because Parker gave the impression he was not really trying, just humoring his father-in-law. On the television, the Detroit Lions were getting beaten by the New York Giants.

Howard brought the cards very close to his eyes, like a jeweler about to inspect a strange gem. Four kings, eight and ten of hearts, six of clubs, two aces, and the three of diamonds. He peered over his cards at Parker, who was watching him. Houp, houp. Howard drew the nine of hearts. He discarded the six and knocked with five points, burning Parker for twenty-two points. Houp, houp, houp, houp.

"Stooped," whispered Charlene.

"Stooped," whispered Elenore.

Freddy looked at his book, but for the moment he had ceased to read. *"Remembrance of sleep lies as softly as fur."* He had not meant to give up hunting. It had just happened. It was as if while he slept one night, someone had whispered in his ear that he should not hunt. He liked the woods and the iron-cold air, and he liked snapping the rifle to his shoulder as the game came into view. But he did not like the killing, the thing lying there, bewildered, eyes open. No, he did not like the eyes. He imagined that the stranger in Camus' book had eyes like that. He looked around the room and saw the bewildered eyes of his family.

The picture in his mind vanished now, and he was not thinking or reading but watching television. Someone had scored, and the crowd was cheering.

The De Soto, that magic carpet of an automobile, flew from Keene, its turkey-stuffed pilot, Howard Elman, comfortable now that he was out of his son-in-law's house and able to concentrate on important matters—gathering snow tires for winter.

"The breeze through the window," sang Heather, as Freddy

The Creature : 49

accompanied her on his harmonica, "tips the old woman's rocker, first forward, then back, and blows through her thin gray hair."

Elenore fell into a light sleep. Every few moments, her body twitched, her eyes opened, her jaw dropped—startled—and her eyes closed again.

The Pickup: You put five hundred pounds of rocks in the bed and it would grip snowy roads like a tractor, no matter what tires were on it. Still, there was something foolish, even disgraceful, about a man who did not put snow tires on his vehicles. Thus, compromise. A couple of recaps would do.

"It brings to her ear girlhood dreams of Queen Isabella," sang Heather.

"Noooo," moaned Elenore weakly. Howard shook her gently so the unpleasant dream would sift to the bottom of her mind.

The Ford wagon: He had bought a new Sears tire last spring on an impulse; it was a beautiful tire, a technological wonder, a black jewel with a wonderful smell, worthy to be placed at the altar of a demanding God. He would sacrifice it to the Ford.

The De Soto: Two snow tires, with just enough tread to last one winter, were in the barn at this moment beside a mangle, a coal shovel, and an exquisite toy metal dump truck. The image brought him the slightly desperate pleasure that the thought of stew brings to a hungry man. Perhaps someday he and Freddy would hold an intelligent discussion on tires: the dangers and merits of the recap, the dearth of real whitewall tires these days, the sham known as the radial tire being perpetrated upon the public, the importance of keeping air pressure at twenty-nine pounds per square inch.

Elenore awakened. She slumped in her seat and wept softly. Howard lifted her tightly clasped hand, opened it—it was empty—and placed it on her lap. It was the best he could do by way of tenderness. Elenore's weeping was solemn and quiet, her body shaking just a little, like the shimmer of a leaf. She wanted even in sleep neither to disturb nor be disturbed. The children sang on.

Howard flirted with an old idea of building a camper on the back of the pickup, plywood sides painted blue, with a tiny gabled roof and a window and a screen door. It would look like a bob-house on wheels. He would take Elenore across America and show her Montana, the Mississippi River, Detroit, and the Great Salt Lake. He had the idea—erroneous, he knew—that she was unaware of these places and that the sight of them would somehow bring the girlishness back to her cheeks. But of course he would never build the camper. He was not a spore blowing in the wind. He was as rooted as a tree. He breathed deeply, and emptied his mind.

Parked in the Elman driveway was an expensive, nearly new foreign car. It was a beautiful thing, pretty but strong as a well-made toolbox, thought Howard. He guessed it was the car that had been at Swett's place last night. He parked away from it, perhaps fearing a comparison might put the De Soto in a bad light. "Wait here," he said firmly, a reflex action rather than expectation of danger.

A tall, square-jawed, too-well-dressed man stood by the Mercedes. He signaled—"Eh, Zoe"—toward the barn, faced Howard, and smiled hugely, like a figure in a poster advertising cigarettes.

Howard did not acknowledge the smile. He folded his arms and waited for the stranger to come to him.

A woman about forty, with golden but wrinkled skin, emerged from the barn. The tall man fell in step with her. She wiped something from her fingers.

"We've been looking for you," said the woman with authority, as if Howard had been wrong in not being home. "Thought you were here. Saw the cars." She pointed toward the low sky. "So many cars. . . . I am Zoe Cutter, and this is my brother, Ronald Thorpe. I've bought Mr. Swett's properties."

Howard did not so much avoid her hand as she extended it as move away. Freddy jumped from the De Soto, his own hand outstretched in an obvious effort to preserve the sanctity of the amenity. Zoe Cutter understood and swung her still-extended arm toward Freddy. They shook hands like old friends, a bond already created between them.

"My name is Frederick Elman, and that's my father, Howard, and my mother and sister." Elenore and Heather shyly got out of the car.

Ronald Thorpe shook Freddy's hand and stepped smartly backward. Freddy and Mrs. Cutter chatted amiably, individual words clear to Howard, but the conversation garbled, like radio talk sometimes. He didn't quite know what to do next, and then Ronald Thorpe offered him a cigarette. He accepted.

"Nice car," Howard shouted, with a toss of the head at the Mercedes.

"I suppose it is," said Ronald Thorpe in the kind of rich baritone that can be heard for miles.

"Her car," said Howard, guessing.

Ronald Thorpe nodded. "I don't drive." He was bragging.

"How do you get where you want to go?" asked Howard.

"In the city, a car's a nuisance—unless you have a lot of money, which of course, ha, is never a nuisance." He threw a glance over his shoulder at Zoe, then gave Howard a knowing look, raising his eyebrow a full inch.

Howard was puzzled but pleased by this large, harmless man. "You, ah, thumb when you want to go somewhere?" asked Howard.

"And get mugged? Run over? Arrested? I think not. You take taxis, the subway when you have to. It's not so bad, unless you're working in Albany or some equally awful place, which of course I haven't done in years."

Howard knew now that when Ronald Thorpe said "city," he meant not Keene, nor a thousand places like it, but New York.

Howard was prepared to like Ronald Thorpe—a nice man, not malicious or cunning. A show-off, maybe even a fool, though not a damn fool.

"Invite 'em in the house!" shouted Elenore.

Heather stood apart, her head moving back and forth from beautiful Mrs. Cutter to handsome Mr. Thorpe as if she were watching a tennis match.

They sat at the kitchen table, Howard and Ronald Thorpe drinking beers like two strangers in a friendly bar, Ronald Thorpe talking about the perils of Albany and Perth Amboy and the Atlantic City of recent years, Howard nodding his head and grunting politely but not listening, watching the woman talking in hushed tones with Freddy across the table.

What she had wiped from her fingers was grease, glistening on the bone of her wrist, skin loose and freckled and golden, hands aging faster than the rest of the body. Somewhere in the lines of her face was the figure of an animal, but he could not identify it. Fisher, fox, hunter-bird, otter—no, none of those, not an animal from a place like Darby. Her eyes were blue and steady, almost motionless, two patient spiders in the corners of a small room. It took him a moment to solve the mystery of the gold skin and of the other lines that weren't part of her facial structure, oddly patterned lines like a series of mistakes repeated by a loom. The sun. The woman spent too much time in the sun.

Elenore sipped tea, raptly intent on her husband. She could not tell whether she was jealous of Mrs. Cutter. Some emotions came strangely these days, startling and strong as ever, yet only faintly recognizable.

Music, the cat, hid under the stove. He could not distinguish one human from another, but he knew the count of everything in the house and the count was wrong, and therefore danger was near.

"Darby. Lovely." Mrs. Cutter pronounced the name of the town "*Dar*-bee" instead of "*Dah*-bee," the way the locals said it. To Freddy the word had been said correctly for the first time.

"Are you the man on the television?" Heather broke in, and in a moment the Elmans realized that yes, they had seen Ronald Thorpe before, on television.

"A fan, ha," said Ronald Thorpe, and he drew Elenore and Heather to him with his voice. Afternoon soaps for the last fifteen years. Before that, Broadway, when the theater was theater. Murdered occasionally on prime time. (Grips stomach, rolls eyes, expires with a shudder, much to the delight of the Elmans.) Made three movies. Not liked by Bogart and other short leading men. Most recently, commercials. (Does his gaseous Goodyear-blimp voice. Elenore giggles; she has fallen in love with him. He is a giant rabbit. Heather rollicks with mirth like a shaken piggy bank.)

A good audience. Much better than Albany. For the first time, Ronald Thorpe was happy to be in New Hampshire.

Zoe Cutter continued to chat with Freddy. She told him of her plans to open a country boutique in the barn. But she also listened. After all, there was the business of finding out what these people were like.

Freddy talked about the intellectual famine of his early years, his thirst for knowledge and experience, his lack of any specific goal.

Howard gradually became detached from all this, not quite understanding, a little dazed, ethereally happy. He could not remember seeing his family so animated, so entertained.

It was dark before Zoe Cutter rose and Ronald Thorpe wiped his mouth with thumb and forefinger and moved the second empty beer can to the center of the table for good luck.

"Walk 'em to the car," shouted Elenore, searching for a rule of etiquette. Somewhere out there was a mountain of manners and proper living.

"I intended to," shouted Howard, louder still.

"Oh, it's not necessary," said Ronald Thorpe. The Elmans ignored him. Struggling to be gracious, they followed the new neighbors to the Mercedes, which shone faintly under the electric-white moonlight just coming into the valley.

"You'll come to visit, Frederick," said Zoe.

Freddy nodded vigorously.

"Nice car," said Howard. "What did you pay for it?"

Freddy stiffened with embarrassment.

"I'm not sure. It was a gift from my husband before he died.... You, ah, do have an interest in automobiles, don't you?" Mrs. Cutter said, in slightly threatening tones.

"Spectacular night," said Ronald Thorpe, trying to head Zoe off before she got into that line of discussion.

A cloud slipped under the moon, and it was very dark. Ronald Thorpe, quickening his step, reached the car well ahead of the others. He opened the door on the passenger side of the Mercedes. Then Howard saw it, the dog with the woman's face, coming out of the moonlight, leaping in slow motion, it seemed, from the car, and snarling viciously.

"Kinky, Kinky—what has got into you?" Zoe's sharp command stopped the Afghan hound just short of Howard. It bared its teeth, spitting saliva.

"Kinky! Stop it this minute," Zoe said.

Howard took a step forward. "You ain't going to bluff me down, you son of a bitch. Not in front of my own house, you ain't."

"Back, Kinky, back—I've never seen him like this," said Zoe.

Howard took another step forward. "If he was my dog, I'd shoot him," he said.

The dog feigned an attack at Howard's leg, but Howard refused to move and the dog backed up. Man was clearly beginning to emerge the winner over his animal adversary.

Zoe took the Afghan by his collar, slapped his face, and marched the not-too-reluctant animal to the car. "In, Kinky, in, in, in!" and she shut the door.

"Keep your dog to home before he gets shot," Howard snarled at the woman. He turned his back on her before she had a chance to speak, and headed for his house.

Freddy started to apologize to Zoe. She ignored him. She stared at Howard and then at his junk cars glinting in the moonlight. She was calm.

"It's just a dog, Howie," said Elenore, following her husband.

"You shut up. You shut up," he said.

5: THE EMPLOYMENT OFFICE

What of it? A lot of people were out of work, happy and rich with welfare and unemployment checks.

It was hot in the house, and Howard told Elenore so.

"It ain't never hot in this house," she said.

Goddamn cold-blooded woman. He fetched the .308 and put on his checkered coat and the matching cap with the hard visor. It was a cold, bright morning, with frost on the field just ready to burn off. He sat on a wooden plank in a shadowed spot under the eaves of his house. He picked a target, the side mirror of a 1947 Chevy coupe about forty yards away. He had bought the mirror at Sears five years ago and mounted it himself. That long ago? My Christ! Once it had been a good car. It might be running today, he reflected, were it not for his stupid rage. The carburetor had iced up at a stoplight in the square in Keene and stalled him. He was so mad that when he got the car going again, he drove it into the field that night and abandoned it with the key in the ignition. The key was still there, and the car had not been moved since. He fired—*k-pow, k-pow, k-pow, k-pow*—the shots steady and regular as a strong heartbeat, the mirror broken and smashed.

Mind blank, he waited, as if for a train. Time passed. The sunlight warmed the frost to dew. It shone brightly on the 1947 Chevy, and because of a trick of the light, flame seemed to spurt from the bullet holes where the mirror had been. A movement up the hill by Swett's house snapped Howard to attention. Instinctively he brought the rifle to his shoulder. In the sight was the woman's hound, tail curved but erect, head up, confident as a cocky prince. The animal disappeared into the woods and came back into the field lower on the hill. Howard followed it in the sights to the stone wall, where it cut sharply and raced to the road. He turned the rifle to the old Chevy and shot up the windshield until the magazine was empty. He smelled the deathly incense of the burning gunpowder, and the cold made him uncomfortable. He trained the weapon on the woman's house. A wind had begun to blow and swirled some dried leaves like lint puffs about the house. Beyond, the sky was empty. He waited until the air around him was clean and he was shivering. Then he went inside, poured himself a cup of coffee, and backed his ass against the radiator.

Assets: full tank of heating oil, food in the freezer for a month, three cars that ran and others in the yard for parts, eight hundred dollars in the bank, nine-room house and fifty acres of field and woods, one dug well (can't flush toilet regularly during dry summers, or pump sucks air), one brook, and hundreds of granite boulders, which were not so much assets as spiritual markers that reminded him that he, Howard Elman, man, was at once great, because he could know rock and rock could not know him, and insignificant, because he was as temporary as a dewdrop on a blade of grass, whereas the rock had reflected a thousand nuances of the sun at midday for a thousand years and would continue for another thousand.

"It's Tuesday," Elenore announced. Her shins were white and lumpy, and he could just make out the beginning of the scars on her knees where the doctors had taken out veins.

"I know it's Tuesday."

"And you ain't getting no job staying home."

He flamed her with a look. Elenore went into the next room and stood by the window, keeping her back to her husband. She thought about warm sunlight in June, lest she begin to shake. She could not tolerate the thought of poverty, for the thought of it led to the thought of abuse. With no job, he would begin to drink, she feared, and she would grow sickly, and the county would come and take Heather away and put her in a place like Uncle Jack's and someone would abuse her, and Elenore could not stand the thought of that. Bad food, hard work, dirty talk, things that crawled in the bed—these could be tolerated. But not abuse. She was sobbing.

"Goddammit," said Howard. He led her like an invalid to her chair and brought her a cup of tea. "I'm going down to that unemployment office now," he told her.

As Howard left, he was filled with the same inexplicable elation that had surged in him the day Mr. Gordon announced that the shop was moving to Baptist Creek, South Carolina.

While Howard watched the Cutter house over the sights of a rifle, Zoe Cutter watched the Elman house through her new sliding glass doors.

Elman was firing his gun. She couldn't see him, but the shots rang out clear and horrible, like the sound frogs make when you run over them on an August night. She imagined him crouched in the snow for his gunnery practice, the hulks of appliances and automobiles in his yard for targets, grim and angular under their caps of snow. Elman, she decided, was one of those male animals that ought to be castrated for its own good and for the good of other creatures. Cats that dragged themselves home half dead after meaningless territorial encounters; pigs that ate the young they had sired; men who murdered animals in drooling ecstasy—all manifestations of the male ego, that small-dictator part of the brain that was wired directly to the genitals.

Deliver us from evil. Deliver us, indeed, she thought, and a picture discovered thirty years ago in a *National Geographic* magazine formed in her mind: forested hills, fields that rode the lower slopes, a tidy stone wall bordering a country lane, white birches in the foreground like two angels, white church steeple just showing behind maples in the background. She remembered that day. The apartment was crammed with stuffed furniture and incongruous knickknacks, though it had all been bought new, except for Aunt Sally's exquisite china closet, a crack in the glass, empty, ashamed—inherited. "Puh-*leasse,* the radio," her mother said, raising her hands to her temples like Sarah Bernhardt dying delicately but elaborately. Outside, broken light reflecting from the tenement windows littered the street, the sky a dull yellow, which Zoe associated with her mother's suffering (used to oppress her children the way other mothers used love). Tornado weather.

Zoe (then Gladys) had never been a religious girl, but she looked at that picture of the New Hampshire village as if it were a page from the Bible. Deliver us. Deliver us from Kansas City. Deliver us from our mother, who will not keep her hair clean and who makes a disgusting noise when she eats apples. Zoe had carried a picture of the village in her mind all these years, though she had given up the dream of actually finding the place. Still, the picture in the mind could not be given up, and it was the picture in the mind, beautiful and perfect, that fired her anger now as she surveyed the real fields and woods through her binoculars.

There was so much to be done with this land. The stone wall, looking like the crooked furrow of a mole, must be straightened and the stones properly stacked; the crowded woods must be weeded, so the strong trees would grow tall and thick while the weak and stunted were mercifully killed; the trunks of apple trees, glutted with rot, must be cleaned and the branches pruned. These things could be done, but the land still would not be right, because of the eyesores at the Elman property. Chaos reigns over order. Ugliness dominates beauty. Intensity beats wisdom every time. *Poof!* She imagined the field on a warm summer day without Elman's house and clutter but with the barn, a solemn tortoise on a green sea. She reconsidered. Perhaps the barn should be removed also. *Poof!* Leave no reminders—a good motto for maintaining mental health. Now she flew above her passions and prejudices in that wonderful airplane of her judgment: Elman and his house must go; the barn could stay.

She made an entry in her date book, "Call Bert Reason on E.," and another, "Sue Reason." If Reason couldn't work out a deal with Elman, she would sue Reason for selling her this property under false pretenses, or whatever the lawyers could come up with. It was nothing personal. She liked Reason and his mile-a-minute talk, the occasional flickers of good sense. Over the years Zoe Cutter had won more lawsuits than she'd lost, but financially she had about broken even after legal fees were paid. No matter. Inside she was richer for the suits. They were good therapy. They helped release aggression, kept the mind busy, contributed to the gross national product, and provided an education in American law and human psychology. An ideal hobby.

The dog scratched at the door. She let him in, pulling burrs from the hairs on his belly and scattering them outside. The dog went to his rug by the fireplace and immediately fell into the ecstasy of half sleep. In New Hampshire he was Kinky, but in New York he was a blue-brindle Afghan hound Ch. Sandia Starstreak, and very valuable. She wondered if local thieves knew enough to steal him. She would have to talk to Miss Flagg about that.

She started an egg and spread *The New York Times* on the dining-room table with the care of a sea captain laying out charts. The key to good nutrition, Zoe believed, was to put one of everything in a relaxed stomach. For breakfast, one glass of orange juice, one poached egg, one strip of bacon, one pear, one cup of black coffee, and one slice of faintly buttered whole-wheat bread, toasted. She scanned the room for something out of order. She imagined the recent issue of *Country Life* was set crookedly in the rack, and she straightened it. She combed her hair and checked herself to make sure she was properly groomed. Then she sat with some severity, looked at the paper, and sipped the juice. She followed this regimen every morning, even when Ronald came to visit. She was not one to break her own rules. *The New York Times* was delivered every morning by Arlene Flagg, the storekeeper's maiden sister. Zoe was the only person in town to receive this unusual service, and she knew the word would spread that she was a woman of some means, a little eccentric. She realized she must not appear too aggressive. Rich, slightly aloof, yet helpful, quirky but not ostentatious—these were the qualities they admired here. In the afternoon she walked the mile to the store, sometimes staying in the road, sometimes following the fresh skimobile trail that wound through the woods, beginning on the other side of the road from Elman's property. Here were trees, a black and silver brook, the crunch of her footfalls, the cry of a winter bird. Peace after four hours on the phone. At the store she picked up her mail and chatted with Arlene and Harold. She walked home with the mail and the *Wall Street Journal* under her arm.

Zoe ate with a slow, clocklike rhythm, so that meal and paper were devoured at the same rate. On the front page of today's *Times* was an Associated Press photograph of a lunatic getting shot by a policeman. The man was brown with large lips, a pencil mustache, and the eyes of a cow. His right hand, holding a gun, was raised in a kind of comic desperation. She winced. Killing such people was a bad example, and photographing them was in bad taste. Something like a stun gun ought to be invented to disable lunatics temporarily—and (she was pleased to think) photographers. It would be the safe thing, the kindly thing, and the just thing. Why not? "Call Bernard C.," she wrote. She took a tiny bite of egg. Bernard Church was president of the Sand Hill Arms Company in Newark, and Zoe was chairman of the board.

She made a note to demolish a wall between the dining room and a useless pantry that smelled of old milk. New Englanders packed too many rooms into one house, the way their forests grew too many trees in a small space. It was going to cost thirty thousand dollars to make this house into what she wanted. She wondered whether it was worth the trouble. It might be best to raze the place and put up one of those huge-windowed houses with interesting roof lines. She filed the idea in her mind.

She looked at her date book. It was going to be an average day, thirteen phone calls. There were two phones in the house, one in the living room and one in the bedroom upstairs. Each had a long extension cord so she could wander from room to room, even walk out to the porch on warm days. It gave her pride to think she was one of those people who could think on their feet.

One could administer the world by telephone, Edward had told her. He liked that word, "administer." It was resilient, diplomatic. After his stroke he ran his business affairs at home. He didn't want his associates (his word) to see his face half paralyzed, not out of any self-consciousness but because he was a polite man, and he thought of his half smile, half grimace as a breach of etiquette. A dozen times a day she put drops in the eye that could not blink. Opened, the eye wandered until it grew tired, and he would flick it shut with his little finger. Closed, the eye rested, though seepage worked its way up from deep within and gathered around the lid and hardened once exposed to the air. After five years, she knew his business as well as he did. With the second stroke she took it over completely. Amazing, the complexities of the human mind. Toward the end he would not eat from a plate directly in front of him. He would see the food, know what it was, even hold a conversation about it, but he would not eat from it any more than one would eat the page from a menu. Move the plate a foot to the right, and he would feed. His sphere of perception had been reduced to a tiny atoll of knowledge. Old age caught up to him all at once, she thought. Grief had come and gone with the cruelty of an ugly season, and she remembered it almost nostalgically as a time when she had exceeded her normal range of emotions. Occasionally, to prove she still had those emotions, she would open the captain's chest in the library where Edward's ashes were kept. She would hold the jar up high like a priestess and think the word "love" and shudder. "Call Bit," she wrote. (Steven Bittenbender was director of the Edward Hayes Cutter Apoplexy Research Foundation.)

After breakfast she washed the dishes and tidied up. Then she went into the library, or the room that would be a library once the house was renovated, and undressed. Kinky wandered in and made the mistake of staring at her bare, freckled body. "Mongrel!" she said harshly, and banished him to the shed. Kinky put his face between his paws and whimpered in dumb misery, a sinner ignorant of his sin. Zoe refused, as a matter of policy, to be looked at naked in full light by man or beast. She could have a face-lift and more, but waging battles in a war that was destined to be lost was poor use of resources, she thought. Once a woman reached forty, Zoe believed, she should dress well, dress her age, and not spend too much time in front of mirrors. She oiled her body, lay on the slick cot, and clicked on the sunlamp. The gentle warmth was better than sex, better than hot soup.

She thought about Frederick, wondering whether under the black pirate's beard his face was as brutish as his father's. The idea tantalized her. The boy's note had said:

Dear Zoe,

Can you put me up for the holidays? I want to see my mother and kid sister at Christmas, but . . . well, you know. I just don't care to argue with him anymore. Very depressing.

If you'd like, I'll strip the paint from the paneling downstairs as payment for board and room.

—Frederick

Brazen, insistent, yet offering a fair bargain. She admired that. She'd phone him today. Fourteen calls. The sexual thought returned. She toyed with it awhile, and then it melted away.

Howard decided to pick up Cooty on his way to the employment office. He had not seen the old man since the shop closed, two weeks ago. They would form a team at the employment office, Howard supplying the leadership and force of character, Cooty the technical know-how to fill out the forms.

The hallway of the rooming house was musty, as if no one lived in the building, and full of distorting echoes. A hundred-watt bulb cast a harsh yellow light along the dirty corridors. Howard didn't bother to wipe his feet. He walked up three flights of stairs, and as usual barged into Cooty's room.

His first perception was that Cooty's smell was faint. Then he saw a large black woman with a terrified face looking at him from Cooty's cot.

"You ain't no policeman," said the woman.

"No, I ain't."

"You get out of here." The woman's skin was chalky and unhealthy-looking, and she was wearing Cooty's galoshes.

"Where's Cooty?" Howard stepped forward like a soldier. Cooty's smell was gone completely now, replaced by the smell of cigarettes, wine, and something else he couldn't quite identify, strong like burdock.

"Don't know no Cooty."

"He lives here," Howard shouted with authority.

"The old man?" asked the woman.

"Cooty Patterson. Lived here for years and years," said Howard with exasperation, which lifted some of the terror from the woman.

"He don't live here no more," said the woman, her voice getting higher and higher. "He wasn't taking care of himself, and they see him in the street, sweeping, and they call the cops and they come and take him up there to Concord."

The word "Concord" sent a tremor through him. He felt like an intruder now, and the woman sensed it and rose from the sagging cot and brought her smell closer to him like a weapon. Here were Cooty's things, but Cooty was far away. Only his faint smell lingered, and soon that would vanish. An image came to Howard of the troopship dead in the water, and of darkness officially pronounced and the need to master an urge to whistle. Howard backed out of the room.

He remembered a black boy in Headquarters Company who was bald. His name was . . . Willie. What had happened to Willie? Howard couldn't read black faces any more than he could read the Gideon Bible. He couldn't tell whether the look in the woman's eyes was fear or some ravenous appetite, a lust known only to black people. There was something about blacks, as there was something about books, that was evil, and that something was what he could not know about them. Long ago it had become implanted in his mind that blacks brought sickness to whites. He thought about the woman's smell. What sort of sickness? He strained his memory. Willie was a supply clerk, a private, and he helped St. Pierre with the mail. The sickness theory was foolish and unfounded, he knew, and yet it held him. The sickness was insanity. Spores of insanity were shooting off from the woman's skin like fireworks on the Fourth of July. He held his breath. Willie? Willie had been transferred to Italy and later got shot nicely in the kneecap and earned an early discharge.

Was Cooty Patterson crazy? The old man had spells of peculiarity and moments when he appeared lost in himself. Right now, Howard figured, he would be mopping an endless corridor in the nuthouse, because he had asked to be kept busy. He would be working too fast, slopping water on the walls, and an attendant with thick hands on his hips would be telling him to smarten up. At night in a room full of crazy men he would frame himself in a corner and curl up into his own sweat and stink, his mind a yard sale of images—pincushions, moon craters, what turtles think, fiddle-faddle. None of this was craziness, as far as Howard was concerned. But the authorities said Cooty was crazy, and the authorities could create truth by edict. They started and ended wars, proclaimed holidays and commandments with equal ease, and set the price of liquor. What the authorities did was not right or wrong but "correct," in the sense in which the military used that word, to mean "natural," "inevitable," "orders coming from on high." Thus, a bee's stinging was "correct." A man's protecting his property was "correct." A bear's shitting in the woods was "correct." Cooty was crazy all right, no question.

The New Hampshire Department of Employment Security building had a brick front and imitation Greek pillars on each side of the main door. Nonfunctional, white imitation wood shutters framed the windows. Along the sides of the building, the attempt to make the structure conform to something like Colonial New England architecture had been abandoned, and the walls were concrete building blocks painted beige. It was here that Howard paused. The blocks had been laid badly, and a long crack was working its way diagonally up the building. Howard was filled with a tremendous rage at the mason who had laid the wall, a rage so great he wanted to kill the man, strangle him until his eyes popped.

Howard entered the building, and the finger he didn't have began to itch.

A girl with pink, bitten fingernails asked if he had been there before, and Howard shouted, with some pride, "No, I ain't."

The bitten fingernails came quickly at him. He reached for the form, but the girl put it on the counter between them, and he suspected she didn't want their hands to touch.

Howard sat at a stout table with metal legs. Somewhere on the form, full of lines, boxes, complicated and blurry lettering, he must write his name. He held the paper at arm's length, tucked in his chin, and dropped the corners of his mouth like some grande dame sniffing her shoes for dog droppings. He found the word "name." Should he print or write? He'd come back to that problem later. "Height," "inches," "feet," in nice neat boxes. He wrote, carefully, "5" and "11." Victory. "Weight." He didn't know exactly—230, 240, something like that. He wrote "2" but couldn't bring himself to guess the last two numbers, and finally he erased the "2." The word "handicapped," which he did not recognize, faced him, its pronunciation and meaning a mystery. "Neuropsychiatric." What kind of word was that to spring on a working man? What purpose? Humiliate him, reduce him to an ash? He returned to the word "name." Print or write? This is a government form, very serious, a grave and official thing, he thought. Fill it out wrong and they'll put you in jail. He turned the form over and immediately found the word "name." He began to perspire heavily. Which side was the front and which was the back? It seemed important to begin at the beginning. Sound idea. He deliberated for a moment, put the form on his lap, and folded his hands over it. Defeat.

6 : THE HUNCHBACK'S PANTOMIME

The moment the door shut, Arlene Flagg turned to Zoe Cutter and said, "He's not from here," thus absolving the town of Darby from any responsibility for Howard Elman.

Arlene was forty-five but looked like an old woman. No, Zoe reconsidered; not like an old woman but like a good amateur actress posing as an old woman.

"He was a foster," continued Arlene from her straight-back chair in front of the cash register of Flagg's store (groceries, sundries, beer). "Both of 'em were fosters. He got her in trouble in the foster and had to marry her. One of his girls got into the same trouble. Another went to California"—here Arlene paused—"and stayed!" Her meaning was clear. You could go to California with some virtue, but if you did not return soon, you were cheap.

"How did he come to buy that house?" asked Zoe.

Arlene bent to scratch her ankle. She wore black nun shoes and baggy support stockings, which camouflaged attractive legs. "War money," she said. "He bought it from Henry Piken when he came home from the war. Otherwise he'd be in a shack or trailer like the rest of 'em."

"Town's tax base is the worst in the county because of shacks and trailers," said Harold Flagg, as—ponderously but stately—he began to make his way from the meat counter after his hushed conversation with Howard Elman. "Elman tells me that Willow Jordan is on the loose again."

"Well, I'm not surprised—are you?" she said to her brother, but did not wait for an answer and immediately turned to Zoe. "Henry Piken quit the farm to go to Boston and become a millionaire. . . ."

"Which he never became," answered her brother, white, lumpy, and fat, though curiously weightless, like a transparent bag of marshmallows.

"Not that Howard Elman ever farmed," said Arlene. "Bought a farm but wouldn't farm it. Went to work in a shop. Bragged about not farming right to Harold's face. A terrible-mannered man. Once . . . tell her about the horse, Harold."

Harold had arrived from his walk up the aisle. He was puffing. "Can't blame him too much for that, Arlene. I consider the matter of the steps more important."

"I consider the matter of the horse equally important."

"Perhaps so, but the horse did require discipline," said Harold.

"It was the way he carried it out. It reveals character."

"I guess you might be right, Arlene."

"Tell her about the horse."

"Please do," said Zoe, trying not to sound impatient.

"I will, but the steps were more important, because they affect the tax base."

"Tell her," said Arlene.

"It's well documented, though I didn't see it myself," said the storekeeper. "Howard Elman owned a horse for his eldest daughter. One day he got into a discussion with the horse, and the horse disagreed with him, and—"

"Oh, don't put it like that—a discussion. You don't discuss with a horse."

"I was trying to lend some humor to the story," said Harold.

"It's not a funny story."

"I thought it was funny."

"Some might consider the steps incident funny," said Arlene.

"Anything to do with tax dollars is not funny," said Harold, assuming the officious tone he took as chairman of the three-man board of selectmen.

"The horse incident was less funny."

"Tell me if you think this is funny, Mrs. Cutter. We taxed Howard Elman ten years ago for putting in some new concrete front steps. The assessor went out to assess his place the next year and found the steps gone. Elman had broken them up with a sledgehammer and scattered the bits in his driveway. He spoke some choice language to the assessor about the matter. Of course, we couldn't tax him for those steps the next year."

"Or since," Arlene interrupted.

"Or since."

"Now tell her about the horse."

"I meant to all along. I wanted to make the point about tax dollars."

"It was a pretty horse," said Arlene, "and that little girl cared for it well when you consider the kind of family she came from. Course, eventually she got in trouble. Lives in Keene now."

"Anyway, one day he was holding a discussion with the horse, and the horse disagreed with him and stepped on his foot. . . ."

"Howard Elman's youngest is quite the singer, you know," Arlene interrupted.

Zoe nodded to Arlene but kept her eyes on Harold. Buried in the layers of sweaty fat about his face were pretty, almost girlish features. He had a scratchy, penetrating voice.

"After the horse stepped on his foot—"

"I thought you'd finished," said Arlene.

"You weren't listening."

"It's no wonder. You never come to the point."

Such exchanges between the Flagg siblings went on all day, with neither showing a trace of humor or annoyance but talking like two veteran radio actors reading from a script. What perhaps had once been good-natured kidding between them was now mere habit, the original purpose lost.

"After the horse put its foot on Elman's foot," said Harold, doubling his plump, hairless fists, "he punched the horse between the eyes, so that it fell to its knees and wasn't right for a whole day."

"Terrible, terrible manners," said Arlene gravely.

"Frankly," said Harold, in an intimate aside to Zoe, designed to be overheard by Arlene, "it's the only thing the man has ever done that I've admired."

"Were there many horses then?" asked Zoe.

"I can remember horses tied up to that pole out there," Harold replied. He didn't bother to point it out, assuming Zoe must be familiar with it (she had never noticed it).

"There were more fields then, more agriculture," said Arlene, as if she were speaking of two hundred years ago instead of twenty. She seemed on the verge of an impassioned plea of some kind, but changed her mind, and her voice fell away.

"Father had two hundred cows," she whispered.

"Grandfather had three hundred cows," said Harold, as though trying to one-up his sister.

"And Mr. Elman keeps automobiles in his fields instead of livestock," said Zoe, bringing the conversation around to where she wanted it.

Arlene sighed, the quavering sigh of an old woman. "Fosters," she said.

Zoe marveled at the oddity of the woman. Her complexion was flawless, yet she covered her cheeks with dull powder. She walked hunched over, squinted through glasses, and, it seemed, bound her bust with towels so that her chest protruded like a bird's instead of a woman's.

Harold shook his head at Zoe's remark about Howard Elman's junk cars.

"Why don't you pass an ordinance barring them?" Zoe

pressed on, and surprised the Flaggs by snapping her fingers and smiling as if anything could be done very simply if only enough will were brought to bear.

"Everyone wants the selectmen to bar something, especially in regards to his neighbor," said Harold. He was talking over her as if to someone upstairs.

"Zoning. Do you have zoning?" Zoe said.

"Of course."

"A planning board?"

"Course we do. Law requires it."

"Could you ban junk cars if you wanted to?"

"Probably could. Not sure, though, whether it's legal. We'd have to talk to the lawyer." He was enjoying this, Zoe thought, almost as if he were flirting with her.

"Oh dear," said Arlene, glancing at the thermometer that hung outside the window, "it's getting colder."

"A front," said Harold.

"Affront?" said Zoe. She couldn't tell by his tone what he meant—it was mysterious, hurt. And then she realized, oh, yes, he meant weather. New Englanders spent a lot of time discussing the severity and unpredictability of their weather. They took it personally. Weather was family, to be argued over, put down, scorned—unless you were an outsider, and then you didn't have the right.

Zoe felt a pleasing, malicious urge to "improve" the Flaggs, chloroform them and spirit them off to a clinic in Denmark to be cleansed, trimmed, dressed, manicured, pedicured, mentally honed to fulfill what she perceived to be their potential— Harold, a slim, arrogant, poison dagger of a man, a critic; Arlene, a remote, untouchable, envy-provoking beauty, a cold, first-class bitch.

At this point the bell hanging over the door rang, and Howard Elman entered the store for the second time in fifteen minutes. The look on his face stunned them to silence.

* * *

Earlier that day Elenore Elman had watched her husband sitting on the floor among the parts of a rifle, like a giant child with his toys.

It had been pleasant having him home during the day, from the moment he received his first unemployment check a week ago. He had held it up like a prize. "Seventy-eight bucks. Feels good; feels like stealing, like a kid stealing an apple," he said. Since then he had acted like a man on vacation, working on engines in the barn by a potbellied stove, weather-stripping the storm windows, doing dozens of odd jobs interspersed with numerous coffee breaks and catnaps. Wednesday, after the first snow of winter, instead of calling Pete Andrews to plow them out, he shoveled an overly ordered path from the road up the driveway, past the house and up to the barn; and for reasons known only to himself—which by now he had probably forgotten—he cleared a narrow walkway to a derelict Chevrolet in the field. The shoveling had taken him most of the day and seemed to please him immensely, as if he had discovered that snow removal could be a fascinating hobby as well as a necessity.

Two feet of snow had fallen, and Christmas hadn't arrived yet. That was all right. Elenore believed that early snow meant early spring. In the evening, after Heather went to bed, they would sit on the couch in front of the television and talk; that is, she realized, she would talk and he listen. It wasn't as though he cared what she said, or even heard; he listened for enjoyment, the way one listens to music or a sermon. Such moments made her feel womanly. Her health seemed better now, and she flirted with the idea of going back to work in the nursing home. She missed the sense of reverence she felt when she washed the backs of the old. Like children, they were close to God, and if you were quiet and emptied your mind, you could touch Him as you touched their loose and fragile skin. She did not want to work at Heaterman's Laundry. The women there laughed evilly and used the Lord's name in vain. She looked at Howard now, scrubbing a piece of metal with a toothbrush. He wasn't a bad man, not fully grown up, true, and he had a mean streak that came and went like a thunderstorm, and at times he could be smart and stupid at once on the same subject, so that he would not listen to reason; but he was a good provider, at least until recently; he didn't turn vicious with drink, and he was often entertaining.

This was an interim period for them, she realized, between the days when Howard was a foreman at the shop and whatever was to come. The period would be brief enough. It was a gift, and she crossed herself and thanked Him.

In the name of the Father and of the Son and of the Holy Ghost, amen. She bowed her head and then raised it—and was startled to see someone watching her from the window outside. It was Ollie Jordan.

Ollie never knocked. He let himself in, or kicked the door, or shook the handle. Now he merely stood by the window, studying her, motionless except for the hand that jumped to the crimson, tormented nose. She let him in, the hunchback, Turtle Jordan, limping behind. She tried to snub Ollie, punish him for watching as she prayed, but he brushed by her as if she were invisible.

"What's wrong with the gun?" Ollie asked Howard. It was a professional's question.

"Ain't nothing wrong with it. Cleaning it." Howard stood.

"Mighty elaborate takedown for cleaning," said Ollie.

"Helps me clear my mind."

Ollie nodded. "Willow has run away."

"Hmmm," said Howard. He scratched a two-day beard as Elenore watched. There was a promise of adventure here, and she could see that he was stirred. He had a forceful face, like an iron fry pan. He could lift the heaviest appliance or snatch a fly from the air with equal ease. Even now, after all these years, she was impressed by his strength, and yet she had no confidence in his ability to take care of himself during these "adventures." He was too fearless, too inquisitive, his very strength a defect. She stepped between them, as though her presence might serve, in a way she could not have explained, as a warning. But the men talked through her, oblivious of her.

"You know where he went?" Howard asked.

Ollie shook his head slowly and pointed at Turtle, sitting in a corner. "He knows, but he won't say." He cupped his hand and brought it up to his mouth as if to drink, a gesture that spoke to Turtle.

The hunchback got on his knees, put the index finger of each hand over his ears, and curled his lower lip slightly over his upper.

"Cow?" asked Howard.

"Cow," said Ollie.

Turtle imitated the slow, lurching walk of a cow backing out of a stall. Elenore suppressed a giggle of fright. Turtle crawled, ambled into the kitchen, still a cow. He paused and made as if to feed from the linoleum. Then he snapped his head up, and extended his neck straight out as far as it would go. His eyes bulged, and he stuck out his tongue. The muscles in his cheeks twitched. He held this pose for about a minute before tumbling backward as if halved. Lying on his side, he gradually relaxed his face, at last removing the fingers from the side of his head and bringing his hands together for a moment, as if in prayer. Then he leaned his cheek against his hands and pretended to fall asleep.

"Is he fooling with us?" Howard asked.

"Don't know what he's doing," Ollie replied.

"He's fooling," said Howard.

"I wouldn't put it past him," said Ollie.

There is something wrong with this, Elenore wanted to say. This is violence, fists swinging, broken bottles, the open mouths of fish breathing out of water. But she was powerless, like the deaf-and-dumb hunchback. The men's talking, as if in ceremony, stupefied her.

Ollie Jordan put his arm out like a traffic cop, and the hunchback ceased his mime, returned to his corner, and laid his head on his shoulder as if for a nap, though his eyes were open.

The two men sat at the kitchen table, muttering like two old checker players. Elenore heated water for instant coffee. Then she went into the living room and sat opposite the hunchback.

Ollie had sent Willow and Turtle to cut firewood in Franklin Dexter's forest. Howard chuckled every time he heard Ollie use Dexter's name. Ollie had reached a casual agreement with Dexter to thin trees on his property in return for half the wood. That was twenty years ago, and Dexter (who was fond of calling himself a Connecticut Yankee) had been dead for nineteen of those years. Dexter's heirs sold the land to a Keene real-estate agent, and since then it had gone through several hands. Howard didn't know who owned it now. Meanwhile, Ollie continued to harvest trees—red maple, black birch, white birch, some oak—leaving half, well, maybe a quarter, of what he had cut stacked in Dexter's forest.

The hunchback raised his arms to Elenore, as though he wanted to be hugged, she figured, then thought better of it and looked away from her. Sitting, hands crossed on her lap, self-consciously stiff and holy, she watched him run his fingers over his eyebrows, like a cat cleaning itself. His face was soft, white, and beardless; his head was covered with golden hair in a snug, curly cap. His eyes reminded Elenore of blue hepatica. God had invested in the hunchback's face all the beauty that was due the Jordans. This thought seemed very precious, very unusual, to Elenore, and she let it settle in her mind. She brought the hunchback a cup of coffee, and he took it from her hand.

She went into the kitchen and sat with the men. "Howard," she whispered, but he did not hear. "Howard!" she shouted, much too loud.

"What's the matter with you?" he asked.

"Nothing," she said.

An important thought had come to her: A brief and pleasant time between them had passed almost as it was perceived, and perhaps the perceiving of it had hastened its departure. But after she had shouted "Howard," she discovered she had no words for the thought, and he was too preoccupied to read it in her face. So she said "Nothing," waited until they finished their coffee, and put the cups in the sink with great care. In a few minutes the men went off and Elenore was alone, itchy with knowledge.

Ollie, two hands on the wheel of his Plymouth Fury (Ollie called it his "go-to-church car," though he never went to church), drove with jerky concentration.

Ollie's love for Willow, Howard believed, was his single major flaw. Willow showed signs of insanity early in life. He had obsessions: tying knots in snakes, climbing trees and refusing to come down for days. Ollie persisted in calling Willow's insanity his "sense of humor," pointing to numerous mischievous stunts Willow pulled as evidence. It was clear even to Ollie that Willow acted according to the whims of an inner logic, which only by coincidence met the demands of the world; so Ollie took it upon himself to "educate" Willow. He tried beating him (Willow thrashed one of his sisters, as if following a good example); he tried bribing him with pies (Willow got fat); he tried talking sensibly to him (Willow memorized his phrases and repeated them for amusement); he tried shunning him (Willow wept). The "education" was good for Ollie, teaching him patience, but Willow learned nothing. Eventually Ollie gave up trying to change Willow and resigned himself to carrying him for the rest of his life like a gimpy knee.

Teeth, straight teeth. The thought of Freddy surfaced in Howard's mind, rising out of the thought of Willow and Ollie. If only one could be wise about such things as son love. He had a crazy idea to propose to Ollie: that they swap sons for a year to bring to their respective problems a fresh, detached viewpoint. Howard decided he would give Willow to the Russians, as one might donate to the Department of Agriculture a two-headed chicken. He laughed out loud at the bitter joke.

The Hunchback's Pantomime : 77

"What the hell you laughing at?" asked Ollie.

Howard told him his plan.

"Makes it easier to go around the law than to obey it," said Ollie without humor. He seemed about to explain why breaking natural laws was not good in the long run, but he couldn't think of a reason.

Both men laughed out of an inexplicable embarrassment.

As soon as they were out of the car, the wind cuffed Ollie's nose, swelling the veins from red to blue, and he began to weep, and wept all the while they were in the woods where Willow had last been seen. It was a cold, bright day with broken bits of the sun on a thin crust of snow. Willow had cut down half a dozen red maples, one on top of the other. The smell of raw wood hung in tiny hollows. Howard and Ollie found the gas can and ax in a mess of Willow's tracks two hundred feet from the work area. The tracks meandered, as if they had been made by a curious animal stopping to sniff certain rocks and trees, and then they merged and became confused, as if there a man had paced in great anxiety. Finally, the tracks showed Willow had come to a decision, for they led straight with long steps to the road, where they could not be read. Following Willow's tracks were the hunchback's—direct, economical.

At the road Ollie grasped Turtle by the shoulders, so that the two of them looked like two twisted trees whose branches had become permanently entwined. He sat the boy down forcibly in the snow, stood over him, and (it seemed to Howard) chewed him out in Jordan sign language. The hunchback looked up at him from the snow, not in fear but in reverence, as if Ollie's hands swore with great skill; but the hunchback made no return gestures, merely "listened" until Ollie exhausted himself and sat on a stump, propping his chin in his hand, as if in deep thought, though Howard knew he was resting and his mind was probably blank.

A minute passed. Ollie rested, Howard smoked, and the hunchback lay motionless on the snow. Gray birches, broken and dead, littered the shadow of a wolf pine, which had killed them by growing above them and stealing their sunlight. Birches came up first in abandoned fields and basked dreamily in the sun like so many bathers. Then the pines came, and the maples and the oaks. The gray birch is doomed to die in the shade, Howard had told Freddy. *Teeth, straight teeth.*

"Not now," Howard whispered, but Ollie heard him and was startled. He drew his hand to his nose and searched the woods with his eyes.

"That was me. Thinking out loud," said Howard, and as he spoke, he saw the soles of the hunchback's boots and knew at once where Willow had gone.

"Turtle, don't you move," he said. He flicked his cigarette away, grasped the hunchback's ankle, and with his pocketknife removed a cake wedged between the heel and sole of Turtle's boot. He showed the cake to Ollie.

"Cowshit," said Ollie.

"Cowshit," said Howard, triumphant.

"Storekeeper's barn," said Ollie, and Howard smiled. The brain is a beautiful machine, he thought.

The men knew that Harold Flagg owned the nearest barn in which cattle were still kept. He raised a few meat steers for his store, along with some laying chickens and a pompous little cock that thought he was the king of Siam, from the sound of his crowing in the morning.

Ollie held the cake under Turtle's nose and spoke to him in sign language with his free hand.

The hunchback bowed and brought his fingers to his head to imitate a cow's horns. He knelt and stared placidly at a point directly in front of Howard. In a moment his expression changed; the tongue protruded, the eyes bulged, and the cheeks drew taut. A drill sergeant making a point, a gardener staring at the sun, a man laughing uncontrollably at himself in a mirror—whatever the expression meant, Howard could not read it. Finally, Turtle collapsed in the snow, exhausted. They carried him to the Plymouth. By the time they put him in the back seat, he was asleep, and by the time they reached Flagg's store, he was having bad dreams.

Howard went into the store to get Flagg's permission to search his barn while the Jordans waited outside, because Ollie owed Flagg money. Howard had no special liking for Flagg—mainly because although he was a storekeeper, he came from farmer stock and was associated with farmers, and Howard hated farmers. They had crazy ideas about land (they couldn't leave it alone) and crazy ideas about work (they broke their bodies and the bodies of those around them with it and thought they were doing right). And he knew how Flagg could use his office of selectman to injure people he didn't like. Harold Flagg was a dangerous man. Still, Howard always took pleasure in walking into the store. Years ago Howard had a crush on Flagg's wife, a married man's pure-hearted crush. Celia Flagg died in childbirth twelve years ago, but even these days Howard could feel her presence in the store—a shawl and a light step. He let the thought steep in his mind before entering.

"Harold," he said, "you hear any chain-saw work going on this morning?"

"Road agent's been cutting up that tree that fell in the storm," said Harold. "I haven't paid any attention."

"Willow Jordan has gotten away," said Howard. "He was sawing wood and he took off."

Flagg was cutting meat, and now he began to cut more slowly. For a long moment he said nothing. He was measuring the situation. Howard decided to wait him out. Finally, Flagg said, "That so."

"We got reason to believe that he's in these whereabouts," Howard said, speaking as he imagined Flagg would have spoken.

Another pause. Flagg cut slower and slower. It was he who was doing the waiting out, Howard realized.

"We'd like permission to search your barn in case he's hiding there," said Howard.

Flagg stopped his work altogether, put his knife down, and wiped his glasses on his apron. He was in full command.

" 'We' being you and Ollie Jordan," Flagg said.

"And Turtle," said Howard.

"And why'd he send you in?" It was not a question so much as an accusation, and Howard said nothing. "You know, Howie, I got a good mind to call the sheriff. That son of Ollie's is a menace to this town. Ain't that so?"

"Um," said Howard. He knew Flagg wouldn't call the sheriff. It went against his principles to look for help from the outside.

Another pause, and Flagg nodded toward the door. Howard took the gesture as permission to search, a permission tinged with a threat.

On his way out, Howard saw Arlene Flagg, the town gossip, and Mrs. Cutter talking at the cash register. They reminded him of two old witches, brewing up something evil. He remembered now that Mrs. Cutter's car wasn't parked in front of the store. Strange. How had she got there? It seemed important to find out why the woman's car was not out front, as though it were some overwhelming question—the missing link between man and ape, the roots of war and of love, the nature of the soul, the nature of the universe, the nature of time—that he felt suddenly called upon to answer for his own survival. It did not occur to him that Zoe might have walked more than a mile from her house to the store because she wanted to. Only the mad, like Willow Jordan, did such things, in Howard Elman's view.

Outside, Howard scanned the common for Mrs. Cutter's Mercedes. It was as if there were a plot against him. With great clarity now he could see it was possible that Hitler was still alive (say, in New Jersey) and that Mrs. Cutter was really what's-her-name, Eva Bomb. Howard the soldier, dead in the snow, machine-gunned from a German car, son marching with the enemy, wife alone and numbed by prayer, youngest daughter altered in a laboratory, other daughters dim-witted in front of their television sets, land taken by the state and fenced, harem of vehicles sold down the river. The idea was comforting in a way because it was logical, perhaps even just. After all, who was he to deserve family and property?—he who had been meant by birth and inclination to hunt, fish, trap, roam from time to time like a goddamn moose, and on Saturday night get drunk and laid. What was not logical was that he had worked all these years for family and property; what was not just was that they should simply vanish and that he be left untouched, without battle, without knowledge, without even regrets. No Mercedes in sight. Troubling.

Ollie danced in the driveway to keep his feet warm; the hunchback was still but shivered violently and stared into space at some soundless, perfect world.

At the end of the driveway, they followed a path in the snow made by Harold Flagg's heavy footsteps. The storekeeper's house, like himself, was enormous, with too many additions on a delicate, now lost core, full of closed-off rooms meant for children never born. Behind the house was the barn, weathered black as a judge in robes.

They waited in the barn for a moment until their eyes got used to the darkness. The sunlight came jeweled through a thousand cracks between the boards; the air was heavy, rich, musty.

They could hear the whisper of a steer munching hay.

Another steer moved its stupendous bottom from side to side like a fat old woman preparing to sit. The hunchback warmed himself by its flank.

Ollie climbed the loft, kicking and punching the hay, and announced, in a tone of exaggerated importance, "He ain't here."

In a few minutes there was no place left to look.

Finally, as they were about to leave, the hunchback, pride or gift-giving in his eyes, led them to the rear of the barn. He tried to open a large sliding door, but it was stuck. Ollie grasped the handle and with a heave slid the door open.

As Howard remembered the event later, it was as if the moment Ollie opened the door, they were spacemen on an alien, hostile planet. The sunlight, he decided, caused the feeling, illuminating the snow-covered fields like a vast sheet of rippling, white-hot steel, the hills beyond dark and grim. In fact, as Howard remembered, he had watched Turtle begin his pantomime before he had seen the cow, though it lay in frozen gore nearly at his feet. He had been fascinated with the hunchback—on his knees, tongue out, eyes bulging, cheeks taut—and he believed that at that second he had guessed the truth before he had actually seen it, though of course you couldn't be sure about such things. It was Ollie's awed voice saying "My Jesus" that had taken his eyes from the hunchback to the steer, cut in half with a chain saw. What he last remembered, the image that stayed deep in his mind, to rise up in dreams and odd waking moments, was the hunchback's completing his imitation, his face beside the severed steer, their expressions identical, and his thought at the time, how marvelous the human mind, and Ollie's words, "My Jesus . . . my Jesus . . . my sweet Jesus, what a sense of humor that boy has got."

7: THE OFFER

The sky was still dark, dawn just easing up. Howard walked along the path he had shoveled to the derelict 1947 Chevy in his field. There he placed a half-dozen empty beer cans on the hood of the car. The snow-covered ground was littered with beer cans torn by bullets from the .308. He was preparing for the morning's target practice, the only time in the day when he had any real peace, the only time he could really think.

He went into the house and returned with a mug of coffee. And then he sat bundled in a quilt in the rocking chair on the back porch, sipping his coffee, the rifle on his lap. The cold relaxed him. He waited for dawn to spread across the sky, from black to gray, and lighter gray, and almost to white, and then the colors from the east would fly up in slow motion, broaden, and slowly fade until the sky was deep blue. He began to think.

Up the hill, they would be stirring—the woman, the actor, his own son. He could no longer think of the place as Swett's. The woman had taken absolute possession. Everett Swett in his dirty overalls spitting tobacco juice into a Maxwell House coffee can, blue as the sky—the memory was sharp and vivid, yet somehow unreal, as though Swett had not been a man he knew but a character out of a story someone had told him. *Once there was a farmer who lived on a hill in a pretty spot overlooking the Connecticut River and who carried a stick to beat his animals with.* Earlier, from his dark kitchen, Howard had watched Mrs. Cutter's Christmas tree in her living-room window, electric bulbs twinkling in imitation of stars. Pretty. Now dawn lay on the window like a bright mask. Icicles glittered from the eaves of her house, and he had an urge to pick them, as though they were bright fruit. But he remained in the shadows of his porch, sipping his coffee and smoking a cigarette.

Soon they would let the hound out for its morning constitutional. Perhaps he ought to kill it, rid himself of the sight of it. How often had he killed with a rifle? Two hundred times? He had killed rabbits, raccoons, squirrels, hedgehogs, rats, birds more splendidly arrayed than ladies at a ball, deer more graceful than dancers, a bear that troubled him with a look, once—incredibly—a fish, three times men from the machine-gun mount of the tank, Pasha, which they had ridden through the war, as though Europe and North Africa were a vast brothel for killing. The pleasure in killing was a small, passing thing, like the pang he felt at the sight of the first scarlet leaves of fall. A man fifty years old ought to have sufficient wisdom to override such a pleasure, he thought.

Chickadee-dee-dee! Same bird as yesterday, somewhere near the barn. Unaccountably, he wondered whether bears watched men from the edges of forests. An exciting idea. *Chickadee-dee-dee!* Some birds chirped for their own pleasure, or called other birds. Not this bird, he figured. This bird called out of some mournful, brainless duty, like a woman praying at the deathbed of her drunken-bum husband.

He had felt a change come over him the day he and Ollie tracked down Willow. He had realized that his elation, his vacation mood, at being out of work had been false, a trick of his mind. He was a desperate man in a desperate world.

Howard had whispered to Flagg the news that a steer had been killed, and Flagg had put on his rubber boots and his coat and waddled with him to the barn, where Ollie and Turtle waited by the severed steer. "Can't you keep that son of yours under control?" Harold began, almost calmly. "Some people can make a town look bad, make us the dumping ground for all the riffraff in the county." Then his face had reddened as he took hold of his idea. "Somebody ought to have that idiot committed before he hurts someone." Spittle formed at the corners of his mouth, and he pointed to the carcass of the steer. "Exhibit A, stupid, senseless, and utterly prideless." Howard had broken in, "Jesus, Harold, it's just a goddamn cow." And Harold had gone on about the problems of farmers and taxes and a slew of other things that Howard didn't understand; nor did he see what they had to do with the issue at hand. Despite his anger Harold had seemed somehow relieved, like a man loosening his bowels after days of constipation. Finally, exhausted, panting, at peace with himself, it seemed, he warned Ollie that Ollie hadn't heard the end of this.

They found the chain saw on the other side of the field. Ollie started it, and it worked fine, although the chain was clogged with bits of flesh and the handle was sticky with beef blood. They found Willow shivering in the woods nearby. Ollie beat him on the spot with fanatic despair before taking him home, where he undressed him and put some dry clothes on him and Helen Jordan fed him some soup.

And all the time at the Jordan shack gloom was enveloping Howard. Parts of him were dropping away—his finger, the affections of his son. Soon there would be nothing left.

The sky over his fields was beginning to whiten. He had a vision of the shop, of quiet looms and an empty parking lot.

Face it, he said to himself, you're not going to find a job. He was too old, too ignorant, too ugly. Still, he would continue to search with something like diligence, making looking for a job into a job. Weekdays he drove to Keene at nine A.M. and returned at five P.M. He established routines, took coffee breaks, and gave himself an hour for lunch, which he ate in the park, no matter how cold the weather. Then, first without realizing it and later realizing it, almost with pleasure, he violated all the rules he had created. He missed appointments with Mr. O'Brian at the employment office; he extended his coffee breaks; he concocted excuses not to follow up job ads; he drank an extra beer at Miranda's Bar in the afternoon.

Mr. O'Brian had a boy's beard and an old man's eyes. Once he told Howard that twenty law schools had turned down his applications for admittance. Every Monday he wore a tie with dolphins on it. Howard liked him. Mr. O'Brian suggested that Howard register for a night course, paid for by the U.S. government, at Keene High School. The course was called Development for Adults Recovering Economically (DARE), which meant, as near as Howard could figure out, reading. He refused to take the course. Illiteracy, he tried to explain in his way, arms one with a certain narrow, gloomy, yet unique perspective on the world. As he spoke, an image passed through his mind of a caravan of black Cadillacs on their way to a cemetery. A silence. A baffled look on Mr. O'Brian's sad face. Whatever Howard had said had made no sense. It struck him that if he went to school and learned to say what he wanted to say, he would probably no longer want to say it. Mr. O'Brian told him, gently, that he was stubborn. Howard was touched.

Despite his fears of education, Howard occasionally found himself daydreaming about sitting at a desk, writing on white paper with the sure, elegant strokes of Mr. Lodge drafting a check. At such moments he would look at Mr. Lodge's letter of recommendation and admire the quality of the penmanship, lovely as a cluster of deer prints in the snow. By contrast, his own handwriting was as large and sprawling as the wreckage of a fallen tree.

Written on paper of the company that no longer existed, lettering full of swagger, Mr. Lodge's note read, "I am happy to recommend Howard Elman. He worked for my father and me for many years, and we have found him to be reliable and enthusiastic. F. JOHN LODGE." Mr. Lodge had written the same note for all his former employees. The phrase "worked for my father and me for many years" was included in William Potts' recommendation, though William had worked at the shop only six months before it closed. Howard was unbothered. Mr. Lodge's handwriting had transcended everything. Indeed, Howard was ashamed that once he had thought badly of Mr. Lodge. He vowed to vote for Mr. Lodge for ... what was it? Governor? Whatever, he'd get Howard Elman's vote. In fact, Howard hadn't voted since Ike left office.

He had seen William Potts last week at Miranda's. William had announced that he was selling his car, because he was going into the Marines after Christmas. ("Just between you and me, Howie, it needs a ring job, and the transmission is slushy.") Howard bought him a beer, and told him to wash his hands.

Howard envied him.

Save money to buy land. Life in the army had been that simple for Howard. The second night on the troopship, he had stood on deck, a chill in the air, watching clouds moving, like migrating geese, across a blatant moon. The wind changed, and there was a hush, and then a sound that was the sound of the sea as heard in a dream of the sea. And he had known at that moment that he would buy a piece of land when he got back; known that he would make it back. He would not farm. Farmers had no love for land but only for black soil, plants, and timely rain. Farmers, like goats, could be admired but not loved. Howard wanted land for religious reasons. He would hold the land like a Bible to be studied, interpreted, and mulled over on Sunday mornings, he a priest with priestly duties toward it. The land would have a house, a field, and a thick wood. There would be boulders. Some of the land would have steepness. There would be giant moths, giant spiders, and flowers as a delicate as a child's tear. Owls would hoot at night. He saved his pay.

When the war ended, he had two thousand dollars, which he protected as though it could buy the salvation of his soul. Death to the man who tried to rob him. No one did, although a supply clerk, a Kentuckian named Hodgkins, watched him for a year, hoping he'd be killed. Hodgkins died choking in his own spit from a bad cough in France. When Howard came home, Charlene was already walking and didn't know who he was. He bought fifty acres of land with a house and barn from that crazy farmer Piken. Even as the years passed, he kept his dream of the land. These days the thought of his land glowed with increased intensity, as every morning on his trip to Keene he saw the unspeakable ugliness of old snow dirtied by a city. Indeed, the thought of the land was stronger the farther he was from it. It was almost as if he drove to Keene each day not to find a job but to think about his land. The black design of apple trees in winter, their lordships the boulders, queenly ferns—how was one to explain these things?

He had tried to enlist in the army the day after he saw William. He stopped at the recruiter's office, paused to sniff the wind, marched smartly to a desk where a young second lieutenant with a college-boy face sat, hands folded in his lap. Howard snapped to, arms at his sides, head and shoulders straight to the front, chin tucked in, and shouted, "Sir!" The lieutenant smiled as once Mr. Lodge had smiled. It was not until Howard was in the street again that he realized that the lieutenant pitied him, and that Mr. Lodge had known from the start that the shop was going to be moved out of New Hampshire.

The streets in Keene were full of kids, oddballs, police, and old people who seemed on the verge of weeping. Girls did not wear bras anymore and you could see their breasts bouncing when they walked. Interesting. Boys had long hair, beards, mustaches; for the life of him he could not figure out why, for they spent a good deal of time pulling whiskers, fidgeting with greasy curls, and tossing their heads to keep the hair out of their faces. Without realizing it, he had come to accept long hair as normal, as one accepts a gas station where once a house had stood because the gas station is there and the house is gone. He had already forgotten that it was Freddy's beard that had triggered the argument that led to their final estrangement.

The oddballs all seemed to want to avoid going to wherever home was. There were drunks and dried-out drunks, and women with stunned looks on their faces, and out-of-work men like himself who had stupid ideas about politics and who spent those ideas at Miranda's like paychecks, and old people walking in the road hoping, it seemed, to get hit by cars.

He was very conscious of police cruisers. Being out of work made him feel hunted, as though the unemployed were a species of game. Someday the police would arrest him. Mr. Elman, you are charged with chronic unemployment, impersonating a husband and father, and looking cross-eyed at a police car. How do you plead? Guilty. Twenty years in state prison. Take him away.

Miranda's Bar was a continual disappointment to him, though he went there every afternoon. The walls threw off a bad smell, like a hospital full of sick children. The room was dense with the muffled bragging of middle-aged men who spoke with great conviction on subjects they knew nothing about—government, God, and football games—full of irritating youths who played a bowling machine with much skill and little purpose. The beer was flat. Howard sat each day at a table for two by the window that faced the street. He imagined he was waiting for someone, though he could not say for whom, nor why the thought should be in his head. Once, one of the youths playing the bowling machine sat at his table, saying, "Qué pasa, man?" and pulling his sparse chin whiskers. "Somebody ask you to sit here?" said Howard. "Touch-y," said the youth, moving off, while his friends laughed at him. After that Howard noticed that Nick, the bartender, watched him carefully. Nick had a wide Greek face and the dark, suspicious eyes of a man who knows a great deal without ever thinking.

First beer: The people in the street dragged themselves along the slushy sidewalks, their faces as pale as the dim afternoon light. They seemed to go nowhere, come from nowhere. None of their activity, Howard judged, mattered; that is, if they all vanished from the street, the street would be no less interesting for their loss. To a god, the weathering of a boulder over a thousand years certainly must be more pleasing than this going to and coming from, this endless repetition, endless, tiring parade.

Second beer: One repeated the same old mistakes. Each of us has a blind spot in his thinking that defeats him time and again against all teaching and experience and pain. He thought of a wasp that exhausts itself buzzing against a screen when freedom lies at an open door a foot away.

Third beer: Yesterday two blacks entered the bar. "You know . . . you know . . . you know . . . you know . . ." they repeated as they glided by like barking otters. Again he faced the street, watching for the woman who walked past the bar each day, a bank-deposit bag in her hand. She had a great and bouncing ass and thick calves with spatters of brown water decorating the backs of her stockings. She reminded him of Fralla Pratt. . . . Life was not so bad. Life could be good. He ceased to think. He felt sad and yet exalted, as if he were the last man on earth setting out in quest of the last woman. His brow was warm.

He returned home, as if from a day's work—tired, irritable, thoughts unpleasant and badly ordered because the effect of the beers was wearing off. Elenore would glare at him, and he would ask, "What the hell are you looking at?" "You know," she would reply. After supper, eaten without talk—the only sound the machinery of their teeth and mouths, and the gentle humming of Heather and her cat—his mood would improve, and by way of repentance he would help Elenore with the dishes.

Every day she reported what Freddy had told her that afternoon, and Howard listened intently.

Freddy is stripping paint. He looks good, but he has a cold. That black thing (beard) catches some of the cold. Mr. Thorpe is out of work for the time being, and he is depressed. Freddy promised to spend Christmas with the family at Charlene's. He promised. You leave him alone. He don't want no trouble.

Don't yell at him. Mrs. Cutter and Mr. Thorpe are flying on an airplane to New York to be with their mother for Christmas. She is in a nursing home. Freddy is doing good in school. He talks about school more than anything. He has a friend who plays drums in a band in Boston.

Elenore didn't know what Freddy was taking in school. He had told her, but she hadn't understood and had forgotten. He had picked up some crazy ideas. He said Columbus didn't discover America.

The previous night, while Elenore was delivering her report on Freddy, the phone rang. Howard answered. He recalled the incident, trying to put it in perspective.

"Mr. Elman, this is Bert Reason, of Reason Real Estate—in Keene? How are you this evening?"

Silence.

"A lovely evening. Maybe not so lovely, kinda cold. Good weather for the skiers, though...."

Silence.

"Mr. Elman, I was driving by your place today. Pretty spot in that field. Nice barn. In fact—"

Howard hung up. Moments later the phone rang again.

"What do you want?"

"Surprise! We were cut off." Laughter. "I'll come to the point. I'm a man of few words myself. I'd like to get together, the two of us. Like to talk to you about your house. Now, I know you're busy. God knows *I'm* busy, trying to make a buck just like everybody else. Bucks—that's why I'm calling you tonight. If I was in your shoes, I'd be dancing right now. You listen now...."

Howard hung up.

"Who is it?" asked Elenore.

"Some nut."

The phone rang.

Howard answered.

"A few minutes of your time can pay you big bucks." A laugh and a shriek, both at once.

Elenore and Heather gathered around the phone as though it were a television.

When the phone rang again, Howard ordered Elenore to answer it.

Very troubling. Trouble from the wires. Howard was full of war anxiety—controllable, almost pleasurable—but he wished there were someone to fight, wished the voice over the phone, a voice cracking with deathly good cheer, would materialize into a man.

"Hello," said Elenore with some formality. She put her hand over the mouthpiece. "It's a Mr. Reezey. He wants to talk to you."

Howard waved her off, put his hands behind his back, and paced.

"Can I listen?" Heather asked.

Howard quieted her with a hand on her shoulder.

"Howie, he wants to buy this house," said Elenore, a hint of relief, a hint of elation, in her voice.

They wanted to take his house.

He couldn't remember exactly what happened after that. He grabbed the phone and said something, and the man talked and wouldn't stop talking. He mentioned "thirty thousand," but most of what he said was garbled to Howard. Finally, Howard hung up and then took the phone off the hook before it could ring again. Heather said she heard a wail, like babies' crying, coming from the phone. She and Elenore listened to the wail until Howard told them to go into the other room. Elenore became sullen and angry, and he tried to explain ... well, he couldn't remember what he tried to explain. He put a pillow over the phone to muffle the wail. He wondered whether the telephone company could have him arrested if he disconnected the wires. He had better not touch them, he decided.

Thirty thousand dollars? It didn't make sense, he thought now, in the cold light of morning. He didn't want to think about it. You can't think about everything and still dig post-holes straight and eight feet apart. Who had said that to him? Uncle Jack? Colored dawn washed over the Cutter house. The bird, the early bird, Howard's bird, was silent; but other birds chirped with annoying amiability. Reedy, Reeney, Weezey? What the hell was his name? *This is Hirk Weezey of Weezey Real Estate.* Something like that.

Thirty thousand dollars. Admit it: It would be nice. He could buy a brand-new Cadillac, thus fulfilling a lifelong dream. He could buy a nice little over-and-under .410 shotgun, which he had always wanted, for no particular reason other than that it was cute. He could buy a new fly rod and a radial-arm saw and a Rototiller for Elenore's garden and a four-wheel-drive Jap jeep to take into the woods. He could drive Elenore and Heather on a trip in the Cadillac to Niagara Falls, someplace like that. Or maybe Moosehead Lake. Or Canada, to look at the Frenchmen. Or wherever women wanted to go. You could never tell. He'd buy Heather a guitar or a piccolo. Hell, he'd buy her a hundred piccolos.

Thirty thousand dollars. It was something to think about.

After the telephone encounter with Mr. Weezey, he had taken down the .308. He had laid the parts out on the blanket on the floor and cleaned them. It was a game of solitaire with him. He arranged the parts in a certain order, than rearranged them. The parts had to match a preconceived pattern that he carried in his mind. Sometimes, no matter what he did, the pieces didn't look right, and he would put the rifle back together and take it down again. Last night he had taken down the rifle four times before the parts lay as they should and he felt a sense of satisfaction, a slowing of his clock so that he might sleep.

He had awakened this morning at four in a bad dream, a war dream. Someone was in Freddy's room; he was sure of it. He put on his pants, took the .308, which he kept in a corner of the bedroom, and crept like a commando down the hall. The door to Freddy's room was open. He waited a few long minutes for a sound, but none came. With great caution, he reached into the room with his left hand, snapped on the light switch, and whirled the rifle to bear with his right hand. There was no one in the room. He searched the entire house, and the only odd thing he found was a jar of Elenore's preserves on the cellar steps. Dill pickles. A moist but cool summer that year. Cucumbers, greens, and squash thrived, but the tomatoes never ripened. So it goes with gardens—victories and defeats; the Lord giveth and the Lord taketh away to keep a man healthy, sane, and poor: Ollie Jordan's Law.

Back in bed, Howard lay on his back with his eyes closed lightly. A parade of animals came trooping across his field, weaving their way amidst his junk cars and appliances, like Legionnaires on a narrow city street on the Fourth of July: a deer with an apple in its mouth, a bear standing arrogantly, a turtle carrying a sleeping cat on its moss-green back, a skunk running with all the grace of an obese woman, a hundred silver dogs with human faces grinning without intelligence, an owl with a perfectly round face, ducks quacking in unison and waddling in step, and among them a robed shepherd with a chain saw for a staff. Howard's eyes sprang open. The owl was not an owl but the alarm clock. The quacking was not quacking but the alarm clock's ringing. Another day begun.

Now Mrs. Cutter's hound appeared out of the shadows up the hill. It bounded into the birches and bounded back into the field. Howard had to admit that the animal had a unique and admirable way of running, embodying somehow qualities of both genders, nose to the ground but rear end high, legs long but powerful, body shaggy yet sleek, tail curved, erect, and stiff. Hm. He saw an insult in the tail. Could such an insult be deliberate, a trick taught by the clever and malicious owner? A dog trained to tell someone to go fuck himself. Brilliant. Well, fuck you too, he thought. The animal raced down the hill to the stone wall, where it stopped abruptly. Then, sniffing here and there, it made its way slowly along the boundary.

A picture formed in his mind of shooting the dog, accepting

its bewildered look like a bill, skinning it, opening it, gutting it, dissecting it, as though deep in its tissues it held some precious secret.

Smoke began to curl upward from the south chimney of the Cutter house, the column growing fatter and thinner at the same time as it rose.

Still sitting in the rocking chair, he took aim at the beer cans on the Chevy. He could see them very clearly in the morning light. He shot well that day, knocking each of the beer cans off the hood with one shot. He then set the cans up again, and this time hit five out of six. Then he wasted four shots on an old stove because he liked the metallic *thunk* of the bullets' ripping through the oven door.

Then he went to the De Soto. It started with more than its usual complaint. It was going to need a new battery before winter's end. Leaving the engine running, he went into the house to put his gun away.

"I'm going now," he shouted to Elenore, who was in the living room eating her breakfast in front of the television.

"Call me if you get anything," she said.

He thought for a moment she meant deer; he thought for a moment he was going deer hunting; but of course, he realized quickly, she meant a job.

Outside he paused. It was ... what? Wednesday? Yes. Every Wednesday he made his weekly inspection of the looms, looking at them, touching them, listening to their clatter—*work-for-pay, work-for-pay, work-for-pay*—listening for noises within noises. Then, at noontime, when the weavers sat on wooden benches eating their egg-salad sandwiches and canned peaches from plastic dishes, when the machines were silent and he could hear his own footsteps on the pitted concrete floor, he would oil all the looms, and then, confident that they were in perfect working condition, he would walk among them feeling wise, tall, and oddly triumphant. Lost in this thought, he got into the De Soto and drove off.

8 : NEW YEAR'S EVE

It was snowing harder now, and Elenore Elman watched the flakes swirl in the glow of the outside spotlights shining from Mrs. Cutter's house. She didn't like this kind of snow; it was too wild, out of control. She liked snow that sifted down from the heavens without the violence of wind.

She was determined to sit out the party in the kitchen. She was here out of duty, not pleasure. She didn't like parties, didn't like any event that was an excuse for drinking. She was here because Freddy had asked her to come and because she wanted to keep an eye on Heather—who couldn't be denied this adventure—and because, well, she was curious to see what Mrs. Cutter had done to the inside of Ann Rae Swett's house. At first she was surprised that Howard had agreed to the party, but of course it gave him an excuse to see Freddy, and of course, like herself, he was curious. She didn't like the boy's staying at Mrs. Cutter's house. People were talking. Once Arlene Flagg had some information, it was all over town. But Elenore said nothing. The boy was becoming a man and therefore a part-time fool. Bear it, she told herself. Men built the crosses in this world and women carried them, she believed.

This was a bad time, worse even than it seemed, she suspected. When Howard lost his job, some vein of common sense had drained out of him. She was working these days to gather some strength, some purity, to pray for . . . what? She wasn't sure yet. Pray for order. Something like that. At any rate, she had spiritual debts to pay and more spiritual loans to take out. The burden weighed on her.

For a few minutes Elenore was comfortably morose. Then the party began to pick up, and she was aware that the alcohol was taking effect on the drinkers.

Zoe Cutter came into the room. "May I get you a drink?" she asked, mildly insistent. She didn't like her guests turning introspective.

"I don't want no drink," Elenore said.

"Well, have some ginger ale, then," said Zoe, and after some persuasion she steered Elenore to a chair in the living room.

The increasing gaiety of the party, which Elenore perceived as exaggerated and grotesque noises, fell upon her now: Mr. Thorpe laughing like a villain in a scary movie—"Bru-ha-ha-ha-ha-ha!"—as Arlene Flagg tickled his ears with harsh whispers; Freddy and Mrs. Cutter chatting and standing too close; beside them Harold Flagg making pleasant but meaningless talk, like a waterfall; Heather striking a piano key over and over, intruding upon the music coming from speakers that seemed to be all over the house. Elenore remembered the drinking episodes of her father and uncles. They began with the same kind of noises as these, noises she hated, an inevitable progression that began with stupid jokes and pointless conversation that soon exploded into rabid opinions rabidly expressed; she hated the slurred speech of men who seemed to doze as they spoke; she hated their weeping and their self-pity and their dirty talk; above all she hated the violence, the ridiculous accusations, the awkward, slow-motion tussling, the fists in the faces of the innocents as well as the combatants; she hated the heavy silence that followed, the drinkers in a black, dreamless sleep amidst spilled and stinking ashtrays, clods of vomit in their hair, shoes askew on the floor, bits of food on the table, bottles everywhere, so that the room looked like the laboratory of some insane scientist in one of those stupid science-fiction movies. In the morning they would tell you about the fun they had had the night before and how Leon had shit his pants again and how today—poor dears!—they were suffering with big heads.

It was nine o'clock.

Only Howard was silent, Elenore noticed. Hands folded behind his head, he sat by the fireplace, huge and motionless, content for now. He made her uneasy these days. She could feel his thinking like bad weather coming on, could feel it when he prowled the hidden corners of the house late at night, and when he maneuvered the parts of his guns on the floor like the pieces of a puzzle with no solution. The house itself was ill with his thinking, and when he left in the morning, she was relieved and grateful. Poor man, poor everybody. No wonder you needed a God the Father, a Jesus Christ, a Holy Ghost, a Mother Mary, and forty thousand saints to help you through the day.

Mrs. Cutter brought her a glass of ginger ale with some ice and smiled at her. Elenore, as though on command, returned the smile. She was impressed with Mrs. Cutter's golden skin and thick, yellow-gray hair and the rings she wore and her long, plaid wool skirt, but it was what she had done to this house that made Elenore come to regard her with awe.

Ann Rae Swett had been a molelike woman who, Elenore deduced, was frightened of the sky and everything up there. The shades were always drawn in the Swett house. A few forty-watt bulbs in overhead fixtures cast a dirty glow in the gloomy house. The rooms were filled with too much furniture—bookcases stacked with shoe boxes full of God knows what, magazines and letters piled on tables, numerous overstuffed chairs upon which no one sat. The wallpaper was faded and torn. It was a large house, bigger than her own, yet it seemed cramped and small. Ann Rae Swett had a favorite expression: "You stupid." Wagging her bony index finger, she yelled constantly at her children and the foster children the county shuffled in and out of the farm: "Come over here, you stupid." "Pick that up, you stupid." "Don't do that, you stupid." And yet she was not a mean woman. She was edgy from overwork and confusion, and besides, she just didn't know any better. Everett Swett—now there was a mean man. He hid his moods and intentions like a shoplifter concealing cheap goods. His face would be calm, his voice jovial, when suddenly he would smack the nearest child or animal. He hit with his right hand, a short, quick, arcing slap with the palm. He reminded Elenore of her uncle Sims. The Swett house and family were grossly exaggerated versions of her own house and family. The value of Ann Rae was that Elenore could compare her own life with Ann Rae's and feel she had made some progress, and so she was sad when Everett Swett died and lonely when Ann Rae sold out and left the farm.

Mrs. Cutter had changed everything about the farm. Except in the bedrooms, the shades were gone. The linoleum was gone. The old wallpaper was gone. The overhead light fixtures were gone. The very smell of the Swetts was gone. Even their spirit, which Elenore thought might linger for generations, was gone, as though deposited at the dump by the legions of workmen who came and went these days. Part of the house had been remodeled already. The wide pine floorboards were sanded and finished until they were as golden as Mrs. Cutter's skin. Bright, intricately designed rugs decorated the floors. The kitchen was full of new appliances, a Franklin stove, numerous electrical outlets, the walls painted white, with wood trim. In the living room, strange birds played on the strange trees of the new wallpaper; and the fireplace, which had been bricked, a closet built around it, now warmed the room, the closet gone. The wainscoting that Freddy had been painstakingly liberating from layers of dull paint was now down to the old bare wood and glowed softly, like a buffed boot. This was just the beginning, Mrs. Cutter had announced. All the rooms would be remodeled. Walls would come down. Sliding glass doors would be installed for a house that craved light. In the spring the barn would be converted into a boutique and antique shop. A New York architect at this moment was completing the plans for the barn's renovation: the great hand-hewn beams to be left untouched; the loft, which Elenore knew to be matted with layers of straw and chicken manure, to be removed and rebuilt so that one could view the great cathedral ceiling. (Elenore thrilled to the phrase "cathedral ceiling.")

She sipped her ginger ale cautiously without quite knowing why, and then she told Mrs. Cutter, "I got business," and went to the bathroom.

Zoe marveled at the Elman woman's skin. It was as smooth as a girl's and white to the extreme, like the skin of Victorian women who took small doses of arsenic to keep their complexions pale.

She heard Ronald laugh. He was conversing with Elman. Whatever Ronald's defects, snobbery was not among them. He would drink with anyone.

They had returned from Mother's after a depressing Christmas. Mother complained for the entire day—complained about her pills, which made her dopey; complained about not being able to taste food; complained about neighbors in Kansas City she hadn't seen in years; complained about Daddy, whom she called the Flying Dutchman, because after a period of ghosting in and out of his family's life, he disappeared. Zoe wondered whether her father had ever seen her in the few bit roles she played in the movies. If he were still alive, he certainly must have seen Ronald on television; and he must have been flattered, for Ronald had his same weak good looks, though he was much taller. Mother alternately doted upon and badgered her son, as she had her husband. ("My six-foot-four-inch movie star...." "Stand up straight...." "He's a senator on television...." "God, Mother, he's forty-two years old...." "You've always been critical...." "Don't let's start, you two...." "Dear Ronald. . . ." "I'm sorry to be critical, but . . ." "You take advantage because I'm an old woman. . . ." "Do you know how much this place costs? . . ." "Oh, I'm getting a headache. . . ." "Dear Ronald . . . wear a hat.")

Finally they left the old woman to Dr. Fiver and his excellent staff.

But the whining did not end. Ronald took over, as he always did after a visit with Mother. On the drive to New Hampshire he complained about his headache, about Morris Lipshitz' firing him from *Love of Life*, about his thinning hair, about the impoliteness of everyone everywhere these days. In fact, he was miffed at Zoe for not allowing him to bring one of his bitchy boys up to Darby. Once in the house, he sulked, sitting by the window and looking at the Vermont hills in the distance. (He thought they were the Catskills.) Then she hit upon the idea of the party. It would cheer him up, give him an audience to perform for. The party had worked; for the moment Ronald was happy yammering with Elman. Zoe was pleased.

"Hotfoot, Connect-ti-cut, is not a bad place," Ronald Thorpe told Howard Elman. "Hotfoot is nice—veddy veddy cultural, veddy veddy historical, veddy veddy dull." Laughter. "Cigarette, *mon ami?*" And he quickly produced a Gauloise before Howard could open a fresh pack of Camels.

Howard returned the pack to his green work-shirt pocket, buttoned it, lit the Gauloise, inhaled, and made a face. "I can't say I envy you for your smokes."

"They're Fronsh," said Ronald.

"Well, viva la fucking Fronce," said Howard, recalling an expression from his army days.

Both men laughed uproariously, all out of proportion to the joke. Then Thorpe went off to get some champagne, stopping on his way to entertain Freddy with a story about an actor who forgot to zip up his fly before going onstage.

Howard studiously avoided Freddy, refusing to look at him or speak to him. He was afraid of . . . an incident; the word came to his mind with grave import. From Ronald Thorpe he learned that Freddy had decided to take a course in poetry writing next semester. Very mysterious. *Back your ass against the wall/Here I come balls and all*—he could not imagine his son taking a course in college to learn to write poems like that. Nor could he imagine Freddy composing little verses about flowers. He remembered a feminine voice long ago, reciting, *The summer heat romances the rosebush and* . . . and something about a girl with dapples or dimples who gets kissed by a stranger, or maybe only thinks she gets kissed, and breaks into a blush. *Here's spring, a boy with a pocketful/of marbles* . . . and something something something until eventually the kid loses all the marbles and cries so hard he turns into a cloud, and flowers grow from the marbles scattered in the fields. Impossible, absolutely impossible. He was outraged that someone should suggest such a thing. But who? The question rang in his defective memory.

"Have some hors d'oeuvres," said Zoe, holding a tray of snacks that looked like tiny smiles.

"Sure," said Howard, and took the tray.

The woman left, startled or amused at something he couldn't catch. He put the tray on his lap, took one of the whichamacallits, "odd doors," inspected it—it was a chunk of something wrapped in bacon—ate it, and washed it down with a guzzle of champagne. Not bad. Interesting how the odd door slips off the toothpick onto the tongue. He tossed the toothpick into the fire.

A wood fire was all right, he supposed, as long as you didn't have to depend on it. He had a lot of bad memories of wood stoves whose fires went out in the night, so that you could see your breath in the house when you got up. A fireplace was worse, a waste of wood, because most of the heat went up the chimney. Still, he had to admit, an open fire pleased a variety of senses, its warmth as soothing as a woman's touch, its hiss as simple as rain, and the sight of the flames uplifting yet sad, like migrating birds.

He watched Zoe, wrinkled and golden—almost shining—

talking with Elenore, who by comparison seemed fat and featureless. She looked at Elenore with the steady, confident eyes of a full colonel; and yet she stood on dainty feet with the pretty, painted toes of a whore. She was the kind of woman, he believed, who would arouse a man, then not give him any satisfaction. He had an urge to do something to impress her, bend iron or whistle "Alouette." Because she was throwing this party, he credited her with great creative and managerial powers, as though she had invented the whole concept of asking friends over on New Year's Eve. He was strangely content, strangely allied with her. The party—perhaps any party—was a truce, a temporary cessation of hostilities in return for this: the exchange of useless and unsought information, the tit-for-tat of polite insults, the vague suspicion that everyone in the room was slightly horny.

Howard was struck with a brilliant idea. He rose with his tray of odd doors and marched to the kitchen. There he located a loaf of bread and some mayonnaise. He stripped a dozen odd doors from the toothpicks and packed them on the bread. After he had made a satisfactory sandwich, he filled a water glass with champagne and returned to his chair by the fireplace. He took a long drink of champagne. Sneaky stuff. He bit into his sandwich of odd doors. Delicious.

It was ten o'clock.

Ronald Thorpe returned, and Howard was glad to see him. The man was good company.

"Zoe talks about raising horses next year," said Ronald. "I told her this isn't good country for horses; I mean, I said, 'You think this is Kentucky?' She pooh-poohed that like she does when you're right and she's wrong."

"Ain't no good place to raise horses," said Howard. "They ain't nothing but trouble."

"Glad you agree," said Ronald, launching into an anecdote. "Only time I was on a horse was in 'fifty-six. I was doing an Autry movie. They wouldn't film us together—he's short, you see. Short leading men—the bane of my existence. Well, they brought this horse in, and they said, 'Thorpe, you rob the bank, shoot the teller, back toward the door, grab the reins of the horse, snap off a couple of shots, and the stunt man takes over from there.' Well, I robbed the bank all right, and I shot the teller, and I backed up and grabbed the reins, and that horse had the worst breath. Oh, gawd, I couldn't stand it. 'Closer to the mount,' shouts the director. It was Bobby Fredericksen—dead now, emphysema. So I got closer, and that horse's breath was so bad, I swear my eyes began to water. I was afraid my makeup would run. Anyway, the horse must have sensed my revulsion, because darned if he didn't pick the hat right off my head. We struggled for the thing, and I won in the end. They used that scene, fitted it in. 'Brilliant,' they said. But I never did a Western again."

"Ain't no horse ever took my hat, but I had one step on my toe," said Howard.

"Indeed, and how did that happen?" asked Ronald.

"I was helping him mount a mare," Howard replied.

"You were what?"

"You mean you never seen horses do it?" said Howard, launching into his own anecdote.

"Must be quite an event," said Ronald.

"I'll say," said Howard. "They show lots of effort, no doubt, but they got to have some help so's they do it right. I mean the mare's cooperative enough, but the stallion generally don't have any aim. This time I got my toe stepped on, I was helping out getting my daughter's mare settled. She was breeding age, and I brung her up the road to this family of Winstens, or Winstels, or something like that. Can't remember. They left these parts. Didn't like the weather. Who can blame 'em? This Winsten girl had this stallion, and she was going to breed him to my daughter's mare, and we was going to split the profits from the sale of the foal. She was just a little thing, maybe eighteen, and she says, 'You are going to have to help out; my daddy ain't here.' So we got the mare in the humping stall. She was in heat, and the stallion got a whiff of her and he begun to act up, ripping and snorting in his stall. He was a big black fella, but young still. We fetched him and led him to the humping stall. Didn't take no persuasion—he was ready. Ought to seen the whang on him." Howard doubled his fist, grabbed his forearm, and shook it in Ronald's face.

"My, oh, my. My, oh, my," said Ronald.

"So I tells the Winsten girl I'm in favor of letting 'em go at it," said Howard. "I mean, who am I to hump horses? But the little girl says no. 'This has got to be done right,' she says. Meaning, it's got to be done her way. Meanwhile, that big fella is ripping and snorting, and it's all the two of us can do to hold him back. You'll never guess what happens next. That little girl produces a bucket of water she's had on hand and a bar of soap, and sudses up that stallion's whang. I ain't sure why, to this day, but she seemed to know what she was doing. The soapsuds was flying. She gets it all clean and then steers it into the mare. And then me and her get in the back and push on the flanks of the big fella. 'Push,' says that little girl. She was fearless; it was dangerous in that stall. Then, bang! That big fella was off in sixteen seconds, and—wouldn't you know it—he goes right at it agin, except this time he misses, because there ain't nobody to help him. Anyway, when things begin to calm down, the mare all of a sudden decides she's had enough of this, and she kicks and bucks, and the stallion comes falling back and steps on my toe. Hurt like hades. The upshot of all this is that it went for nought. The big fella put on a good show, but he was too young. The mare didn't settle."

Zoe wondered where Reason was. Maybe the storm had kept him home, though he had insisted (curiously) that he loved to drive in the snow. The flakes were smaller now, blowing wildly and—it seemed from inside the warm house—silently. She didn't like this kind of snow, because it reminded her of a Midwestern blizzard. She preferred the fat, wet snowflakes of certain cities in the East—say, Washington. Why hadn't Reason called? Rude man. Briskly she headed upstairs to phone his house.

The light was on in her room, and she was certain she had shut it off not ten minutes ago. She was never wrong about these things. An image came to her of a bed full of the guests' tossed coats, lying there like exhausted lovers. The door was open about six inches, and here she paused, bracing herself as if to face an enemy. In the room stood the Elman girl, Heather—now knock-kneed, now bowlegged—in a pair of her high-heeled boots. The girl hugged herself in the cashmere sweater with fur cuffs that Edward had given Zoe in Italy. Expensive tastes, little girl, thought Zoe, but she was touched, taken by surprise. The girl was at the peak of childhood, at that age just before the first glandular disturbances of adolescence, at that age when one has achieved certain goals—security in the playground, confidence that childhood cannot last forever, knowledge of the geography one moves in. In six months none of that would matter, and there would be only the incomplete awareness that one was on the bottom rung of adulthood and that childhood was not so much gone forever as immaterial; that the world was full of new things to worry about—the size of one's feet, the development of one's breasts, pimples, sweat, periods, childbirth, the price of forty-five-rpm records, the blacks in Africa, straight hair, curly hair, Russia and the atomic bomb, and of course transportation to dances. This one, this nearly perfect model of a child, thought Zoe, will have an added despair—her teeth. Heather's upper front teeth, like her mother's, were large and discolored (they were two shades of white, one shiny and one dull), and they protruded over her lower lip when her mouth was shut. The effect was to make her look stupid, inattentive, laughable. Zoe remembered that Murry Staples had once told a dancer, "Good God's sake, you can't play Lady Macbeth—you can't even play Mary Poppins—with teeth like that. Get them fixed." He had also told Zoe, "Gladys, you're smart enough, and you're tough enough, and you're not bad-looking, but you haven't shown me you want to act. Find out what you want and then come back and see me. And for God's sake, change that name. It doesn't fit you. For God's sake, maybe if you change the name, you'll find an identity." Such was Murry—big on truth, big on identity, big on mental cruelty.

Let the child have her good moment, thought Zoe, and she backed away from the bedroom door and went downstairs to call Reason.

Drunk perhaps, rocking slightly on the balls of his feet but mind delectably in control, blowing a tiny bubble of spit, Harold Flagg watched Zoe Cutter in the hallway, pacing slowly back and forth as she made a phone call. He focused on her feet. The toes were little and helpless, like piglets, and—he bet—there were intricate red welts on the flesh where the thongs of her sandals bit in. Still, it was not just the feet that aroused him; it was the woman's social position, her wealth, her fiscal clout. He had reached a new sexual plateau: Money made him horny. The tiny bubble of spit burst, and he began another. He mused on the possibility of marrying her. "Dear Zoe, start the New Year right and do a good turn for a lonely widower." Too simpering. "Mrs. Cutter, how would you like to be the better half of the chairman of the Darby board of selectmen?" Too bold. "Mrs. Cutter, one thing about us New Englanders, we don't mince words. Marry me." No, no, no. How had he proposed to Celia? He couldn't quite remember. The bubble burst. Now he remembered. He hadn't proposed. It had just sort of happened. Indeed, he'd heard about their engagement before it had been a fact. He and Celia had been holding hands at the square dance, when Kate Starkey, who was an ally of Arlene's—yes, that was the right word, "ally"—asked Celia, just as frankly as a twelve-year-old can, when Celia was going to get her ring. And they had both known at that moment they would marry, would have to marry. He didn't care about money then. He was pure. Well, nearly pure.

Zoe hung up the phone and came swiftly toward him. My God, she's read my mind, he thought. He brought his fat fingers to the rims of his eyeglasses and stood absolutely still, like a predator poised. She stopped very close to him, and he could smell her perfume, could smell her alarm. He was tremendously aroused.

"It's possible," she said, "that one of my guests is marooned in the snowstorm. I think we should take the four-wheel-drive and look for him."

"Of course," Harold said.

Zoe rounded up Howard and Freddy, and they followed her, Harold in his rubber boots lagging behind. Elenore said it was going to be a cruel January. Arlene recalled the time the bodies of Esther Wallace and Garland Stevens were found locked in an embrace in the Stevenses' family car on Rifle Range Road. "The monoxide crept in and killed 'em." Ronald Thorpe hid in the room Zoe called Miami. (She would say, "If the phone rings, dear, tell them to call back in half an hour. I'm going to Miami to get some sun.") Arlene must have seen him slip away, because when he emerged, she condemned him with a look. Later he told Zoe he had said to Arlene, "I wouldn't be of much help. I'm a pansy." But in fact he had said nothing. He didn't know why he had lied to Zoe over something so trivial, unless from habit.

Zoe insisted on driving, over the objections of Harold, who sat beside her in the front seat and launched into a lecture on the severity of New Hampshire winters. Zoe switched on the radio, and the three of them—Zoe, Harold, the radio—chattered loudly, as if in competition.

Freddy and Howard sat in the back seat. Freddy, looking straight ahead at the snowflakes darting into and then suddenly away from the windshield, watched his father out of the corner of his eye. Approvingly as a bear in garbage, Howard sniffed in the new-car smell of the big Chevy power wagon. He peered over Zoe's shoulder at the speedometer and nodded to himself. He touched the cold vinyl seats with his palms. Satisfied, hands on his knees, deeply meditative, he settled into the vibrations of the car.

For Freddy, it was time to speak. It was a good storm, he said. Yes, Howard answered, his voice low for a change. Something blue about snow falling at night. Did Freddy remember the time they had seen the ducks skidding comically on the ice at Boulder Pond? No, Freddy had forgotten. That was all right. He was very small then, a fingerling, and he had ridden atop his father's shoulders and pretended he was driving a truck. A tank, corrected Freddy. Yes, a tank. Much better. Now Freddy was a man; well, almost a man. Then Howard grunted, and Freddy supposed that was a form of apology for saying he was anything but a man. Freddy wanted to say that he had made great strides in understanding his father, but of course he did not. A pause. Did Mrs. Cutter pay well? his father wanted to know, his voice lower still. Yes, but she was finicky. You had to know when to stay out of her way. Howard said he knew a supervisor at the shop like that, a fellow named Napper, who had been a prisoner of war in Germany and who later went to Manchester to work for the telephone company. Mrs. Cutter used the telephone a lot, said Freddy, who now felt compelled to talk about her. She was going to buy more land, build things. She had ideas. She promised Freddy a job all summer. Good, very good, said Howard with sad finality, as though something had come to account. But how in hell, he whispered, was she going to sell dresses and hats and furniture out of a barn, and who the hell was going to buy them? The barn would be fixed up, and she would advertise in *The New York Times, The Washington Post,* and in certain magazines, Freddy answered. The people would come, no doubt. Didn't Howard realize there was a great migration rushing north, plus countless visitors with many dollars in their pockets? Well, no, not exactly. Well, yes, now that he thought about it. A pause. Cunning in his voice, Howard asked Freddy if he would stay if all those people were coming here. They say you have to go away before home means anything, Freddy said. Yes. After all, Howard had been in the army, to distant shores, and home had looked good from far away. And yet the statement was not strictly true, Howard said; but when he tried to explain what he meant, he found he couldn't. First he searched for words; then, finding none, he resorted to gestures, and, those failing, he settled deeper into his seat, like an old man taking a nap. Freddy said he wanted to go to Colorado or New Mexico, or perhaps California or Oregon. He didn't tell his father he dreamed of women with beauty unheard of in the East. The land out west, Howard said, was like North Africa, like the back of a gold watch. But how did he know, asked Freddy, since he had never been west? He remembered somehow. A pause. Freddy asked his father how job hunting was going, and Howard, showing a trace of anger, told him not to get smart about that.... There was something mad and beautiful about the snow, Freddy thought. Perhaps the mad thing was the car and its headlights plunging ahead, while the snow was merely beautiful. Sitting beside his father, he felt great love yet great distance and, mysteriously, at peace.

They found Reason's car in a snowbank five miles from the house on the highway. It was a green Oldsmobile station wagon with signs of rust showing along the fenders. There was no one in the car, and the keys were not in the ignition, but the door on the driver's side was half open, and snow filled part of the front seat in a pretty dune. The back seat was folded down, and the entire rear compartment was crammed with cardboard boxes full of papers and magazines, as though, Howard thought, the man was on his way to the dump.

For once Zoe was stymied. "What do we do now?" she asked.

"Reason must have hitched a ride back to Keene," said Harold.

Reason ... Reason ... where had he heard that name? Howard wondered. A song on the radio?

They drove back to the house, Howard and Freddy sitting apart like strangers.

Back in Zoe's living room, Howard found Elenore and Ronald Thorpe talking and the Afghan hound reclining by the fireplace in the chair Howard had claimed as his own. The dog bared its teeth, watching him with defiant yellow eyes. Ronald, glancing to make sure that Zoe was still in the kitchen, whispered, "Kick the cur." Howard stood over the animal and glared at it. The dog growled deeply, almost soundlessly. Then with a deft move Howard picked it up by the scruff of the neck and the tail and flipped it onto the floor. The Afghan yipped and slunk toward the kitchen just as Zoe, startled by the noise, hustled into the living room.

What she saw was the dog at her feet, tail wagging uncertainly, Elenore watching her blankly, Elman in a chair by the fireplace, his legs crossed, his hands folded on his lap, the look on his face faraway, like a man in a deck chair on an ocean liner measuring the curvature of the earth, and Ronald grinning, shrugging, somehow in league with Elman. She marched the dog to the shed off the kitchen, feeling she was locking up the wrong beast.

Howard and Ronald resumed their conversation. There was something about Ronald Thorpe that reminded Howard of Cooty Patterson, a childlike quality that in the adult world was a disability. An image passed through his mind of his carrying first Cooty, then Ronald out of a burning building.

"Cigarette, *mon ami?*" offered the actor. Howard declined.

"I'm so depressed," said Ronald. "I haven't worked in three weeks."

"They lay you off?" asked Howard.

"Worse. Morris Lipshitz."

Howard nodded wisely, waiting for more.

"Morris doesn't like me. He thinks I'm a schmuck. I'll tell you who's the schmuck. Morris is the schmuck. Part of the problem is me, I suppose." Sigh. "I've always been too tall to be a second banana, and too something or other to be a top banana. Now I'm at that awkward age, thirty-eight." He lied. "Too old to be young, too young to be old. I'm not a good market. I'm going to have to change my image. Do more commercials. Maybe some summer stock this year. Gad!"

Howard listened, fascinated by all those strange, trivial words, like things one stumbled upon in someone else's garage.

It was eleven-thirty P.M.

Heather lay curled on the couch.

"Sleepy?" whispered Zoe.

"Not sleepy. I want to stay up for the Happy New Year," said Heather.

"Tired," whispered Zoe, almost as though giving a command. And again, "Tired."

"Not tired. There's a Happy New Year on the television." And in a moment, the child was asleep, her two front teeth still showing over her lower lip.

Zoe, insomnia prone, marveled.

The party had fragmented, was winding down, Zoe thought: Freddy mumbling something about the mental health of J. Alfred Prufrock; Ronald and Howard carrying on their mysterious friendship, in which neither understood the other; Harold (who was being such a dear old walrus) digging in her deed to find her exact boundaries; Arlene and Elenore talking maliciously about something. "Small party, Happy New Year," Zoe toasted silently.

Arlene was drunk. Zoe had hoped for some change in her behavior, some hint of some past pain that had caused her to hide her natural beauty. But Arlene drunk was merely an exaggerated version of Arlene sober—a gossip. Zoe had overheard her telling Elenore, "She married fourteen million dollars." Amazing how close she had come to the actual figure, a figure Zoe was certain she had never mentioned in New Hampshire, a figure not even Ronald was aware of.

"It's time they locked him up," Arlene said, raising her voice now as if she wished to be heard across the room where Ronald and Howard gabbed.

Elenore nodded.

"None of those Jordans is worth anything," said Arlene.

Elenore said something.

"Just between you and me," Arlene said, "that Ollie Jordan is in for trouble. His sign . . ." And at that point, Zoe heard the dog begin to bark loudly from the shed.

Moments later there was a banging on the front door—loud, insistent, outraged, like the pounding of a man locked out of his own house by his wife. The hound in the shed began to howl with a similar kind of frustration.

"Someone get the door while I calm that stupid animal," ordered Zoe.

"Don't go away," Ronald Thorpe said to his champagne glass. He got up. Howard, charged by some intuitive unrest, followed.

Ronald cupped his hand to his ear and said to Howard, "I believe someone's at the door." With the flourish of a butler in an old English movie, he opened the door, saying, "It could be mur-der. Bru-ha-ha-ha-ha-ha!"

White. Messenger. White as maggots on the wounds of the dead. Howard tipped forward, then checked himself from leaping on the creature in the doorway and tearing it to pieces. *A man. A mere man.*

"Bru-ha-ha-ha-ha-ha!"

Clearly a man. Medium size. Wearing an overcoat, trousers, boots, hat, scarf wrapped around his face. His entire body white with snow, driven into him as if by powerful blowers. Drafts of cold coming out of him into the room.

Clearly a man. With spectacles and enormous, chilly blue eyes, looking at him now.

The man did a little dance and shook the snow off, and the feeling in Howard that the man was an apparition started to shake away as the snow fell to the floor.

"Jesum Crow, it's cold out there." The man was off in a mile-a-minute monologue. "Snow blowing like the furies of hell. Must have walked five mile into the teeth of it, and, he-he, it bit my head off. Course I bit back. Punishment is all the devil respects, don't you know. Same with your average lawyer.... Ronald, you handsome bastard, how are you?"

"Bru-ha-ha-ha-ha-ha-ha!"

"Ah, and who might this be?" said the man to Howard, as though turning to a child. "Let me guess, now. Mr. Elman, I presume?"

He had stopped his dance, and was standing perfectly still in a little pile of sifted snow. He was plump, about thirty-five, with soft young skin and glowing cheeks. He removed his hat and revealed a head of wild red hair, all slanted to one side like a wind-blown grass fire. If before he had given the impression of cold, now he gave the impression of heat.

"Ah-ummm," grunted Howard in an attempt to say nothing yet give the impression of speech. He put his hands behind his back, moved sideways and looked away, all to avoid shaking hands.

From the kitchen Zoe appeared with the dog wagging its tail and quickly making for the man, as though it had just recognized a friend.

"Reason," said Zoe. "Dear Reason."

By this time everyone, including Heather, who had been awakened by the commotion, had gathered in the kitchen, where Bert Reason stood in a little puddle of melting snow and explained, with great elaboration, how he had lost control of his car, spun completely around, and nosed into the snowbank.

"Car drove by, bunch of out-of-staters, a football team of muscle in that car, I swear it, and they wouldn't even stop. Oh, I got hot. I got so hot I couldn't think straight. I'll tell you, if these fingers were lightning, I would have burned those footballers to cinders, I was so hot. Another car went by, woman looking straight ahead as though I were invisible. And another, a trucker with a leer in his eye. I got hotter. Finally, just to keep cool, I started to walk, with the hope that the plow or state police would come by and give me a lift. I was still hot when I got to the cutoff road that comes to Darby. By this time I figured, what the hell? Only three miles to go. Might as well walk. Well, the storm got worse, and the wind picked up, and pretty soon I wasn't hot. I was downright cool. He-he. That old north wind blew into my face and you could see the snowflakes wild and crazy, saying—I swear I heard it, though I knew even then I wasn't hearing it—saying, 'What are you, Man, doing out there in this snow?' " Here he paused, as though indicating that he was only fooling, and then he contradicted the effect of the pause by laughing nervously.

"It's Mr. Reezey," Elenore whispered in Howard's ear.

"Ah-umm."

"Now, Howie, you know who it is. He's the man that wants to buy our house."

"You want to sell the house, you talk to him," Howard whispered, but too loud. Arlene moved close to them.

"I ain't the man of the house," whispered Elenore.

"Well, the man of the house don't want to sell the house." She turned away from him.

At this point Heather interrupted Bert Reason and announced, "It's time for the Happy New Year on the television."

"Of course. Happy New Year, Guy Lumbago," said Ronald.

Harold—returned from a trip to the bathroom—was waving the deed. He had found something interesting, perhaps important. He tried to get Zoe's attention, but he couldn't catch her eye. Reason droned on, and the Elmans squealed in each other's ears.

Harold squeezed through the kitchen door. But when he reached Zoe, she had taken the child's hand and (it seemed) slipped by him somehow, merely smiling at his "Eh—Zoe?" and leaving him holding the deed. He followed her.

They were watching television—Zoe, the little girl, the Elman boy. Flagg could hear the New Year's countdown: ten, nine, eight—"Eh, Zoe?" he tried; "Shhh," she said—four, three, two, one, "Happy New Year!" "Happy New Year!" Zoe was kissing the Elman boy—on the mouth, no less. My word, Harold thought. And then she was kissing Harold on the cheek. Later, daydreaming at the store, Harold would reverse the situation, convincing himself that Zoe had kissed Frederick Elman on the cheek and himself on the mouth.

"Is it really the New Year?" Ronald asked, moving from the kitchen to the television room. "I missed it. Curses. Back to hell with you, Reason, for keeping me away." Ronald went to the piano and began to play, in the manner of Guy Lombardo, "Auld Lang Syne." Freddy produced his harmonica and joined in. Heather led Zoe by the hand to the piano and began to sing, in a loud, clear, country voice, and then the others, too, and then, in its own way, the hound. "Should old acquaintance . . ."

Oh well, the deed can wait, Harold thought, and he folded it and put it in his pocket and, a little envious, watched them: the actor looking at the ceiling as he played; the child looking at the actor; Zoe looking at the child; young Elman looking at Zoe; and, like a row of dominoes, Arlene looking at Elenore Elman, Elenore looking at Reason, Reason looking at Howard Elman, Elman looking at the fire.

Harold shut off the television, and though he didn't actually sing, he did hum along.

9 : CABIN FEVER

The light from the Flaggs' store window didn't cheer Zoe Cutter this afternoon. It was a day without shadows, the air filled with an eerie snow that seemed not to fall but to hang like a kind of pollution. The gloom seemed to come in the store with her. "Five above, and it won't get any warmer," Arlene Flagg said, strumming her fingers on the cash-register keys. Outside, Harold had just finished pumping gas into an aging Audi. Holding his gloves between his teeth, he made change for a woman whose face was hidden by a summery yellow hat with a wide brim. Arlene leaned toward Zoe, who knew she would say something about the woman in the Audi. Yes. She was the eccentric Sara Orne Piper, the widow of Scully Piper, a painter of birds, Arlene whispered self-importantly. Zoe resisted an urge to say something cruel to Arlene and instead dismissed a long-standing annoyance. She removed an obsolete poster—SEND CLAUDE LEAVITT TO WASHINGTON—from the corner of the window, folded it, and laid it on the counter.

"Jimmy Cleveland is still in Congress, and Claude Leavitt is still in Claremont," said Harold Flagg. The store bell rang, *ting-*

a-ling, as he entered. He took the poster and chucked it into the wastebasket.

His glasses fogged immediately, but he didn't remove them. He hung his huge jacket on a hook, the gloves sticking out of the pockets like ears. Finally he removed the glasses, held them at arm's length, and looked at them as though they were something extraordinary. Then he cleaned them with a balled handkerchief from his hip pocket, and with much fussiness fitted them back onto his head.

"Oh dear," said Arlene, as though to the snow.

"Strange weather," said Zoe.

"There's no way to predict it in these parts," Harold bragged. "Tomorrow it might be sixty and the sun shining. The important consideration"—there was something studious about his expression, Zoe noted—"is that there are no typical winters here. No two winters . . ."

". . . like no two snowflakes . . ." said Arlene, as though to warn that this was a standard speech.

". . . are exactly alike," Harold continued, ignoring Arlene, or perhaps unaware she had spoken part of his sentence. "I've seen winters so warm the flies didn't go away. I've seen winters full of thaws and vicious freezes, and winters with blizzards that drifted the barn door shut, and winters where the sun didn't shine all of January, and"—here Harold paused, and he and his sister exchanged intimate looks—"one winter when it didn't snow at all. The cold that winter drove thousands of animals out of their burrows and froze others in their peaceful sleep. Snow, you see, acts as a blanket. . . ." Another pause.

"That was the year that Father died," Arlene said finally.

"It was the following July," said Harold. "A warm summer with much warm rain. The fields were high and thick. Green heaven. One afternoon Father fell—er, was drawn—into a hay baler. His heart was punctured, but he was able to unwrap the wire from himself, as though to spare us the sight, before he collapsed."

"That was what caused Harold to quit the farm," Arlene said. She sighed dramatically. "I can remember the smell of the mowed hay. It sickens me now."

"I opened the store shortly afterwards," said Harold.

Arlene's face was blank and bitter both, like a widow's, thought Zoe. She knew the look well, had seen it in her own mirror. It was the third time they had told her the story of Pater Flagg falling—"er, drawn"—into the hay baler.

"At any rate," Harold went on, breaking the sad spell with a shift in tone, "if it was a bad winter for the creatures, it was a good one for the skaters. The river was like an iced highway from the rapids below Bellows Falls to the dam in Brattleboro."

"Not that you ever skated, Harold," said Arlene.

"Quite so. Sometimes one needs to be reminded of these things." (Impossible to tell whether he was being sarcastic, thought Zoe.) "We raced cars up and down the river all January and February that year. Great fun."

These little afternoon gab sessions had become very important to Zoe. She was, she thought, alone with the weather. Ronald was in New York, struggling to retain the good graces of Morris Lipshitz. Freddy was in school. She missed his pacing around the house with a book in his hand, stammering aloud the thoughts of ancient poets and, in a steadier voice, lines he had apparently composed himself. *When it is quiet, my mind is like a conch, and I hear an ocean.* He mumbled these things as though trying to be discreet and overheard at the same time. Even the dog was no companion. Kinky left each morning on his own business and returned in the evening to sleep. Nothing pleased Zoe these days. The house seemed empty, dark; voices on the telephone inhuman, as though machines were speaking; the light of her sunlamp cold and harsh, like crystals in New Hampshire granite. It was as if her system lacked some key vitamin necessary for health, a substance she craved without knowing what it was.

"Cabin fever," Harold explained, "arrives about this time every year. Drives some people mad. Some kill themselves; some kill a relative. It's because spring comes later here for man than God intended." (He was a closet atheist, Zoe guessed.) "The only month worse than February in this town is March." He chuckled, paused, and chuckled again, saluting his ability—the ability of all good New Hampshiremen—to take it and dish it out in regard to evil.

The man was a walrus, much blubber, much bluff, a big marshmallow. And yet . . . Zoe wondered.

"That's why they hold town meeting the first Tuesday in March," said Arlene.

Of course, thought Zoe. Companionship, argument, decision—signs of spring, spiritual crocuses pushing up through the winter blues. It was while Zoe was thinking about what town meeting might be like that the Jordans entered the store.

First a child. She—it moved like a she—was bundled in what seemed to be dirty bandages, but on second look Zoe could tell they were merely rags. The child clung to her mother's leg until her mother peeled her off, and then she clung to a wooden post and looked at the grocery shelves with awe and fear, as though they were unpleasant and incomprehensible works of art. The mother looked at nothing, her eyes unmoving in her face, itself unmoving over another face—mask on mask on mask, like a desert, the mask of an ancient sea. Two adolescent boys, a pair of Mortimer Snerds, thought Zoe, reached for Coca-Cola. "Don't," said the Ancient Sea. The boys giggled at a joke only they knew. Other Jordans entered in shabby overcoats and felt hats, including a young woman—it moved like a young woman—holding a baby reeking of vomit. The hunchback caught Zoe's eye at the door, stopped, and bowed. Then he adjusted imaginary glasses in mockery of Harold, as though he had been in the room with them a few minutes ago when Harold had cleaned his glasses, and bowed again. Last, a man, Ollie Jordan with the wounded nose, whose fault it all was, or so Arlene said Harold said.

The kind of people you meet in magazine articles on the poor, Zoe thought. Marvels of media. What is new is already familiar.

All humans connected to all other humans. Zoe resented the idea.

The Ancient Sea shopped: hot dogs, milk, margarine, spaghetti, dried beans, a jar of pickles, a fistful of candy bars, Kool-Aid packets, milk of magnesia.... The child, which Zoe had positively identified as a little girl, brought the Ancient Sea a coloring book. The Ancient Sea returned it to the magazine rack, and the child began to cry. The sounds mingled with the seal-bark laughter of the Mortimer Snerds, who must have been on all fours behind the shelves, because Zoe couldn't see them.

More Jordan sounds: Wounded Nose conversing with Harold by the meat counter, where Harold steered people with whom he had serious business; Wounded Nose speaking with bits and pieces of sound instead of whole words. Zoe was reminded of a drawer full of her mother's sewing ends.

The hunchback was looking at her again. She folded her hands in front of her, and he did the same. She brushed her hair with the wave of a hand, and he duplicated the gesture exactly. She played the game another minute until it suddenly sickened her. The hunchback seemed to sense her revulsion before she felt it herself. He stopped the game, sat on the floor, and his face went blank. She pitied him.

A thought passed through her mind of Christmas shopping with her mother. Reflections in windows. Fatigue. Confusion. Zoe looked out the window.

Outside were parked a Jordan car and a Jordan truck, unique in their ugliness, as though manufactured by the Jordan Motor Works. In the Jordan car a figure moved nervously. This would be Jordan-the-Mad, Willow, who killed the cow with the chain saw.

Arlene totaled the goods brought to the cash register by the Ancient Sea, who watched nothing through the window and didn't speak. The Mortimer Snerds went out the door, taking their laughter with them. Ollie Jordan searched Zoe with a look before he left, a curious, detached, mildly interested look.

They rarely came in all at once like this, Arlene explained; usually they appeared in ones and twos. It was the time of year. Like everybody else, the Jordans were nervous in their houses.

Zoe asked about the strange, dull shine on their faces, which looked like old plastic toys.

"Simple dirt."

"Not your usual precise answer, Arlene," said Harold. "In fact, it's kitchen grease and wood smoke. The shanty people all take on that complexion in winter. Wood-stove tan."

"Ignorance," accused Arlene.

"Deep ignorance," said Harold. "Ignorance upon ignorance, like rocks in a rock wall."

"And, of course, Howard Elman is right down there with them," said Arlene. Zoe wondered whether that was a bone thrown her way.

"At least Elman washes his face," Zoe teased.

"Add to lack of education lack of plumbing," said Harold. "Elman has running water, and Jordan doesn't." His tone indicated that Ollie Jordan ought to be punished for not providing the equipment necessary for cleanliness.

They gossiped awhile longer, and then the store fell silent again. Zoe felt a need for radio music. She went outside into the snowy mist and started for home, walking fast to keep warm.

After Zoe left, Harold Flagg cashed up the money drawer, taking the charge slips and the big bills to the back of the store. He counted the tens and twenties and recorded the sum in a large green account book, which he valued as another man might value a pair of deerskin gloves. He laid the charge slips and the book on the white enamel top of the meat case and paused for a moment. He took his time at this work because it gave him pleasure. "Quit grunting!" (Arlene shouting, he barely hearing her.) The ball-point pen felt slim and feminine in his fat fingers. He wrote as boldly as a doctor and as legibly as a school-teacher. He was vain about his handwriting, and gently reproachful to himself for this vanity. The debtors, locked in this green book, meant more to him than the money they owed him. He felt somehow triumphant over them, benevolently kingly, as he knew he had no right to feel over his peers. The creditor, by law, by tradition, by the biomechanics of the human brain, was allowed to judge the debtor beyond the debt itself, he believed. And so when he came to the Jordans' account (today's bill of $33.62 was added to a previous balance of $112.26 for a new balance of $145.88), he was almost grateful. A man's enemies, he mused, provided him with a major source of stimulation ("Quit grunting!"), and should an enemy also be beholden to him, well, so much the better. One-four-five-eight-eight. He memorized the sum; he would chant it to himself from time to time like a mantra.

Harold had never trusted Ollie Jordan. The man mystified him; he was sly; he carried secrets. After Willow Jordan killed Harold's steer, all Harold's suspicions about Ollie Jordan came to a head. The incident had made him feel strange, haunted, as though he were the butt of jokes by unknowable cosmic creatures. The problem stayed with him for two days, until he finally resolved it. Willow Jordan was crazy, that was for certain. But he was also stupid, and incapable of inventing the many pranks he had pulled all these years. It must be, Harold reasoned, that the father was the real instigator, the son merely an agent. All these years Ollie Jordan had been an evil man, and for the good of the town he must be separated from his fellows. Once he had come to this conclusion, Harold was comforted, calmed, the thing settled in his mind. He assigned himself the task of destroying Ollie Jordan. Not that he was going to shoot his adversary, like some brain-injured anarchist shooting a president. No, Harold was sane, law-abiding—intensely law-abiding—and patient. He had told himself simply, The time will come. In fact, there were dozens of people in town whom Harold had sentenced to final ruin. A few he had managed to damage seriously—Dr. Ackely, for example, whom Flagg blamed for the death of his wife. But most remained untouched, even unaware they were doomed. One did not force these grave issues. ("Puh-lease quit grunting!") One waited for that almost mystical moment when events, mood, an intellectual accounting of facts, perhaps a quirk of law, joined in a leap of the imagination. It had happened. Ollie Jordan's time had come.

For a while Harold had forgotten the sight of his severed steer. Oh, he had sent Ollie Jordan a bill—recorded in the green book under a different section from that of the grocery bill—but, as he had told Arlene after she nagged him that he should prosecute Willow Jordan, "The matter is on the back burner." It had stayed there until Mrs. Cutter suggested last week that the town needed an ordinance banning junk cars from sight on public roads. He had wavered. Philosophically, he opposed laws that told a man what he ought to do with his property. He didn't like zoning, or as Arch Sawyer would put it, "any such things as that."

Mrs. Cutter's petition for a junk-car ordinance followed. Tough woman. Anyway, he had thought about it. The new people would like the ordinance. They were concerned with trees, stone walls, cemeteries full of strange names, fields, and the blue sky over the river. They did not seem to understand that it was easier to get used to ugliness than, say, to the discomfort of cold or the pangs of loneliness. Still, in the long view, he admitted that if the junk cars were hauled off or hidden behind tall wood fences, the value of the town would rise, and the value of the people who moved in would rise. He wavered. Then it struck him that Ollie Jordan's yard was littered with junk cars. If the language of the ordinance were phrased properly, it might cut both ways, against Ollie Jordan and against the absentee land-lord who owned the property, an Italian from Rhode Island who, as far as Harold knew, had never laid eyes on the town of Darby. Once the process of law had begun to work on Ollie Jordan, it might continue to cut until there was nothing left of the man. The law would ask why Jordan didn't send his children to school; why he didn't have a driver's license; why he didn't pay income taxes; where the guns came from in his business. (It was rumored the guns were stolen, reaching Ollie through his cousins in other towns.) Eventually the county would put the children in foster homes, which were not—face it—palaces, but which were better than unsanitary shacks. Willow would be sent to Concord. Good riddance, fool. A queer future lay ahead for the hunchback, Harold imagined. The social-service agencies in Keene would love him. He was everything they had dreamed of—deaf, dumb, deformed, and trainable. Why, the boy had so many things wrong with him, there were probably enough federal funds available under various programs to canonize him. St. Turtle Jordan, patron saint of U.S. Obfuscatory Agencies in Southwestern New Hampshire. "Quit chuckling!" (Arlene moving up front, waiting nervously for someone to come in.) Ollie Jordan would be sent to state prison, where presumably his criminality would harden, perhaps making him more efficient. *I'm doing you a favor, Ollie.* Without their leader, the rest of the Jordans would disappear from the town. He guessed most would end up in Winchester, where, it was said, some Jordans actually prospered. There was a chance of violence somewhere in this process. Men with an easy familiarity with guns were likely to turn to them as tools when threatened. The prospect of danger made Harold instantly hungry. He thought about the sandwich he would make after the accounts were finished—baloney drenched in mustard on rye bread, potato chips, two bottles of orange soda.

Tonight at the selectmen's meeting he would argue that the selectmen ought to support Mrs. Cutter's petition article at town meeting. He didn't worry about Frank Bridges, who was a fine, decent man, an architectural draftsman. Frank liked to think he was a progressive, and therefore he could easily be persuaded if you put things to him right. Archibald Sawyer was something else. You never could tell what he was going to do since his second stroke two years ago. He was now eighty-two, and he had spent half of those years as a Darby selectman. He carried forty votes in his pocket at town meeting. Still, Harold was aware, it was being whispered these days that Harold Flagg ran the town and that poor Arch Sawyer didn't know where he was half the time. You couldn't predict what the voters would do. You could find out exactly what they thought; then town meeting would come, and they would change their minds. Voters were like the old—sentimental, moody, and forgetful.

He recorded the last entry for this fiscal day in the green book and shut it with a satisfying slap.

"Arlene, want a sandwich?"

"Not an hour before supper. No, I do not want a sandwich. And I wish you wouldn't make all those noises when you do your books; it gives me the willies."

Harold sliced a half pound of baloney and began constructing a triple-decker sandwich. He was entertained by an image in his mind of Mrs. Cutter walking home. There was something vulnerable, charming, yet cheap about a woman alone on a road. He must visit her, court her. "Do you remember how?" he asked himself with a chuckle. He'd get to it one of these days.

Mrs. Macadam came in; he could tell without looking. Arlene would be happy now. For reasons he did not understand, or bother thinking about, Arlene became jumpy and irritable late in the afternoon. She was normal again once the rush of customers started, about four P.M. He bit into the sandwich, the food almost melting in his mouth. Arlene was telling Mrs. Macadam about the Piper woman's hat. He couldn't recall whether she had worn a hat today, and he didn't get Arlene's point. . . . He would never find out. He stuffed some potato chips into his mouth, and the sounds of his chewing drowned out the conversation.

The Jordans were home, piling out of the car and truck to the barking of dogs. It was a moment before Ollie Jordan realized what was odd about the sound. The deep, rumbling, heavy-equipment bark of the half-basset hound was missing. He had shot the dog yesterday after catching it running deer. It seemed to Ollie that life was carried on by a series of murders.

It was odd that the dog had been running deer so early in the season. It seemed like an evil portent to him. Every year domestic dogs formed loose packs and killed hundreds of deer throughout the state. But usually the dogs did not begin their work until late winter, when the deer were most vulnerable. The dogs were pets, well fed and fit, and most of their owners never knew they ran deer. The dogs intuitively adopted one of the ways of men—the secret life enveloped by the public life. But Ollie Jordan knew the signs—a happy tiredness, sore paws, clods of hair in vomit. He killed the dog out of principle rather than necessity, for he could easily have kept the dog tied. Ollie and men of his ilk might hunt with dogs themselves on occasion, but it was repugnant to them that the dogs hunted on their own, because of the awful carnage they made and because the dogs hunted for the same reason as the men—sport—and thus the men were angry, as priests might be angry to see lesser men imitate their rites.

He unlocked a padlock that fastened a chain around the steering column of the car. The other end of the chain was secured by another padlock around the waist of Ollie's son Willow. Ollie stepped out of the car on the driver's side and tugged the chain for Willow to follow. Then he led him toward the dark shacks in the snowy mist.

The chain was the final solution. All one night Ollie Jordan had pondered the problem that Willow's behavior posed, while the boy (God, he was twenty-four) lay dreaming fitfully at his feet, as though he were aware that the laws governing his freedom were about to be revised. Ollie Jordan was not a man to whom truth came in sudden insights. Truth came slowly, he told himself, and inevitably, with the heavy reasoning of the cosmos, and almost always too late. Willow, left to his own ways, would eventually become a prisoner of the state or be killed by somebody. Therefore, he must be removed from his ways. Ollie tried locking Willow up, but that didn't work; the boy screamed and cried and butted his head bloody against the walls. Ollie tied him with ropes, and Willow bit through them. Finally he put him in chains. They kept Willow restrained, and he didn't seem to mind too much. But he couldn't be left alone in chains, because he became entangled in them. At night Ollie chained Willow to himself, and the boy slept on the floor on a mattress beside the bed where his mother and father lay. The solution meant that Willow must be kept restrained and in sight all the time. This would be done, Ollie told himself, and was at peace.

Willow now tugged at his chain. He wanted to walk to the great sign to the west of the shacks. "C'mon and fix the lights," he said. He spoke very little these days and made less and less sense.

Willow wanted to climb the frame of the sign, but Ollie wouldn't let him. "You're not a goddamn monkey. You're a goddamn man," he said, but he knew he was speaking to himself. They walked between the supports of the sign to the other side, and immediately, as though they had stepped into another room, the sounds and the feeling in the air were different. They could hear the rush of cars and a truck gearing down on the interstate highway, although it was more than a mile away. The sign, like an ocean or a mountain, created its own weather. The wind swirled the snow crazily here, building huge drifts in some places and leaving others bare. In the summer the sign threw off heat like a radiator, and the Jordans could feel its hot wind at night. Sometimes, when it rained, a small fog grew around the sign. The hill was steep below, almost a cliff. Somehow a few hemlocks clung to rocks, growing out of the hill in the shape of a man's arm with the biceps flexed, the green fist of the foliage defiant in the sun. Hemlocks were good trees, thought Ollie. Willow was looking as though at a vista, yet the white, sifting snow obscured the purple hills in Vermont. They couldn't even see the river, white and frozen in the valley. "What is it, Willow? What's out there?" But again Ollie was speaking to himself. Soon Willow began to shiver, but he didn't want to leave. Then he began to cry, and they went back into the house to strong, familiar smells.

Zoe walked in the road on her way home. The skimobile trail in the woods, which she normally used, made her uneasy today. She read somewhere about cold fogs that rolled over mountain climbers and destroyed their ability to discern direction or the passing of time. Such a fog was extremely unlikely here, she realized, but still she yielded to the idea and walked in the road because it seemed safer.

In the oak tree in front of the parsonage perched hundreds of birds—dark, unmoving, silent, as though they all had some strange disease. The snowflakes themselves seemed strange, floating on imperceptible air currents. Again she remembered something she had read about how one day the stars in the universe would burn out and all matter be reduced to junk. She thought now of Elman's yard. The joke cheered her somewhat, and she wished there were someone there to share it with.

When she reached home, she turned on most of the lights downstairs and started a fire. The dog hadn't returned yet, and she resented him for his freedom, his pleasure. She phoned Ronald. A lisping voice answered. "Ronnie isn't here. . . . No, I don't know where he is. . . . I'm not his keeper." She hung up, fuming. She despised Ronald's companions. They were stupid and bitchy. She called Reason. Mister, what is holding you up? She wanted results. Mister, talk is cheap. She hung up and felt no better. She played the radio, and then the stereo, and still the rooms seemed empty and full of echoes. She switched on the television, and today was the one in seven when reception was poor. She couldn't understand how Elman, down the hill, with an antenna up a tree, got better reception than she did up here with a new, expensive rotary antenna on the house. It didn't make sense. Nothing made sense. Not Elenore Elman, who went through life like a zombie; not Elman, with his reverse Midas touch; not dear Ronald (big brother, you're all I have), who wasted himself entertaining nasty young men; not Harold Flagg, suffocating in his own fat. She called the antenna company: "This is Charley Powers of Powers Television Service, your approved Zenith dealer in the twin-state region. I will be out of the office until tomorrow morning at eight o'clock. This conversation is being recorded. If you wish to leave a message, speak at the beep. . . ."

"Beep you!" said Zoe, and slammed down the phone.

The dog returned home at nine P.M. and immediately went to sleep on the chair by the fireplace. By this time Zoe's mood had improved greatly. She had decided on the right medicine to cure her touch of cabin fever, and, her plans made, she relaxed by the fire reading the *Wall Street Journal* and sipping wine. Tomorrow she would drive Kinky to the Keene kennels and leave him there for ten days. By nine A.M. she'd be on a plane headed south. And by evening she'd be having dinner with her old friends Natalie and Brooks Acheson in Key West.

10 : SUNDAY MORNING

Howard Elman could just barely hear his wife whispering her prayers in the living room, while a bald-headed priest on the television chanted something about mercy. *Lord have mercy. Christ have mercy.* He imagined he could hear her thump her chest with her small, fleshy fist. Every Sunday at nine-thirty A.M., as if through Elenore's will, their house was transformed into a church, the couch a pew, the scatter rug a kneeler, the television an altar. She was standing now. Soon she would kneel, then sit, and stand again, in a kind of slow-motion exercise for a God who did not like to rush. Well, he had his own version of the Sabbath to celebrate, and he went to the barn, where a V-8 engine hung from a chain like some martyred saint.

Father Francis Joseph Bell was indeed bald. The Channel 22 producer had told him his head would shine like a halo unless he powdered it before Mass. Father Bell had refused with haughty dignity. Eventually Father Bell's bishop intervened and ordered him to powder his head. And so, every Sunday, while he laid out his vestments in the sacristy, Father Bell powdered his head— and was filled with shame. Life was not easy, even for a priest—

especially for a priest—and he prayed to God that He accept his suffering as a small credit against the time he would spend in purgatory.

Elenore suspected none of this and would not have believed it if it had been laid before her eyes. Priests were not prey to petty human emotions, she believed. Priests could suffer and sin and love, but only on a grand scale. She ranked them a step below the saints and lower angels on her hierarchy of divinity. Father Bell was part of that crew of Holies who brought her the sacrifice of the Mass every Sunday, not from Greenfield, Massachusetts, but from heaven itself.

The idea of attending Mass in person, of officially converting to the Roman Catholic faith, frightened her, as the idea of riding a bicycle might frighten a child not yet ready for the experience. Her hybrid Catholicism was sufficient. She had reached a certain level of worship and was content with it—for now. She baptized each of her children herself but sent none of them to church. They too were not yet ready, she believed, because they had come out of her unworthy belly. She tried to make up for her fundamental inferiority by praying extra hard.

Today she would pray even harder than usual. Today she had a special favor to ask.

"Hail Mary, full of grace, the Lord is with Thee," she prayed, as Father Bell moved stiffly about the altar arranging the holy utensils for the holy repast.

For years Elenore Elman had been making secret deals with saints, the Blessed Virgin, and members of the Holy Trinity themselves. She asked for favors in return for devotions, good acts, and personal sacrifices. For herself she asked little—silence at suppertime, big red tomatoes in the garden, sunshine. For her family she asked for safe arrivals, reliable transportation, some harmony among them, pork without worms, a commitment to daily baths, and grace—always grace. "Saint Mary Magdalene," she prayed, "I ask that you pray to our Savior today to grant my Sherry Ann grace." And in return Elenore offered a rosary to

Christ to aid fallen women everywhere. And so it went usually, small devotions for small requests. Elenore did not insult heaven by asking for the impossible—wealth, personal beauty, happiness. She did not ask for the return of her Sherry Ann, the daughter who was so beautiful she made her mother shy.

Elenore tried to pick the right saint for the right job, but this was not always possible. She knew very little about them. They all lived so long ago, in times both holy and horrible, when men bashed one another's brains out in ceaseless combat and women washed clothes along rivers and bore children without the help of doctors or hypos, and the children died young in their mothers' arms. She wondered how the mothers did their dishes and how anyone went to the toilet without tissue. Vast mysteries. There were more saints then, she figured, because there was more need for the divine presence.

Most of Elenore's requests were granted, and she spent a good deal of energy paying off spiritual debts—saying prayers at odd hours of the day, kneeling on hard floors until the tears came to her eyes from the strain. Those requests that were never granted made the rounds from saint to saint, finally ending with the Blessed Virgin, until they were dropped with a small prayer of apology for wasting the time of the Holies. Sometimes, long after she had dropped a request, it would be granted, and she would think it was a miracle and feel sentimental.

She bothered the Trinity only for major requests, and then only by way of a grand plan involving lesser Holies. For example, when she prayed that Freddy would receive his scholarship, she asked that the Blessed Virgin Mary speak about the matter to her son, Jesus, who in turn might influence another member of the Trinity, the Holy Ghost, who, in Elenore's view, was charged with deciding matters relating to education. She also prayed to Saint Thomas Aquinas, who, as a great Catholic intellectual, perhaps had the ear of the Holy Ghost. And she prayed directly to the Holy Ghost Himself, explaining that Freddy was a good and deserving boy. She promised Him a novena a month for all the ignorant souls in purgatory for every month that Freddy remained in college under the scholarship.

Father Bell read the gospel in a sweet Irish voice. Then he announced that the Catholic Daughters were sponsoring a Nevada night Wednesday. Then he told the congregation that the fuel bills were higher than expected this year and that today there would be a special collection for heating oil. Then he gave a short sermon on love. In his sweet Irish voice he said that when you got right down to it, there wasn't much worth living for after love. He made distinctions between carnal love and divine love, between love of money and possessions and love of God; he explained that love of family, love of children, was simply part of divine love. He started to talk about love of self but changed his mind, and for a moment he couldn't think of anything to say. He raised the subject of the Sacred Heart and quickly switched to the communion of saints. He then forgot what the subject of his sermon was, and he talked on about the saints and their good works and how they were servants of Christ, all the while trying to remember what he was supposed to be talking about. Pride, perhaps. He thought about his powdered bald head. He invented an anecdote (or maybe he had heard it years ago in the seminary) about a monk with four rings; but he never finished the anecdote, because he remembered that now he was talking about love. He told the people that you could bear even blindness or the pain of cancer if you had love. And then he wished them all God's love and went back to saying the Mass. It was a typical Father Bell sermon. And typically, Elenore, like the congregation, didn't listen to it, although her spirit was somewhat massaged by the priest's voice.

Today Elenore Elman intended to make a deal with Jesus Christ.

But she was troubled, because she didn't know what to ask for—a reconciliation between her son and husband, a job for Howard, health for herself, a stroke of luck out of the blue to save their home. It seemed to her that evil was everywhere around her house. She had nightmares that her family was coming apart. She half expected to wake up one morning and find Howard gone, Heather gone, the house gone, herself alone in bed on a windy hillside, everything lost between a dream and dawn. She prayed first to the Virgin and then to the Savior. She prayed for grace.

If Elenore did not know precisely what to pray for, she knew what to offer as her part of the bargain. She had been thinking about it all week, and she had made up her mind. Some requests called for devotion and some for good works, but important and difficult ones called for sacrifice. Both her knees had been operated on at great cost for varicose veins. They looked like stacks of putty today. It was as if God had wanted her legs all along. And so, as her part of the bargain, she offered her legs to Christ, explaining that in the eternal, cosmic balance of things He could take what strength remained in her legs and bestow it on some deserving, paralyzed child. She asked that God seriously consider that bargain, and she prayed to the Virgin and to Jesus.

"Go in peace," Father Bell told the congregation, and, himself at peace—that is, relieved—he left the television screen.

Elenore rubbed the soreness from her knees. She was exhausted, wrung out, from praying and thinking, from negotiating. Divinity must come from within herself. She nodded off.

The engine that hung from a chain in the barn had come from a Dodge sedan wrecked in an accident two years ago. The car, bloodstains still visible on the front seats, had sat in Howard's yard since the accident. Today he would drop the engine in the chassis of a two-and-a-half-ton International truck he had just bought. It had high wooden sides, gray and unpainted, on a homemade dump body. The fenders and hood were faded green with flecks of rust working through. It was parked half in, half out of the barn, like some huge, curious animal peeking inside. Its used-up engine lay on the old barn floor. Howard had removed it and forgotten it, and it might sit there for years, until it was in the way of something else or until he decided to resurrect it. He had got the truck in a trade for his Ford wagon plus three hundred dollars in cash. A mad act, he knew. He needed the money; he needed the car; he did not need the truck. *A mad act.* He pushed the thought into the depths of his mind. This was not a matter to brood about on Sunday morning. He had a vision of unexploded World War Two bombs buried in harbor mud. He began work on the Dodge engine. He was determined to have it installed in the truck by the end of the day. (Years later Freddy Elman would remember those moments when he watched his father work on cars with his swift and dexterous hands, and it would strike him that most of his father's IQ was in his hands.)

In Howard Elman's view a man couldn't have too many old cars in his yard. Cars were full of metal, glass, fabric, gears, rods, screws, nuts, bolts, levers, locks, mirrors, springs, valves, hoses, rubber, plastic, wires, plugs, lights—which needed only a man with tools, imagination, and skill to fashion them into something useful. The furnishings in the Elman house could best be described as Detroit Baroque. When the Elman children were growing up, Howard rigged two rearview mirrors in the kitchen so Elenore could keep an eye on the children in the living room. The mirrors were still there. The sofa and Howard's favorite chair were covered with the upholstery from a Pontiac's seats. Howard's favorite ashtray was a hubcap. Outside, the Elmans grew potatoes inside old tires.

Howard had an idea he could build a house—yea, a castle, a city, a civilization—from the parts in junked cars. The idea made him feel priestly.

The truck had saved his soul—temporarily, anyway. On the wooden side, facing in toward the dump body, the words "Charlie's truck" had been elegantly carved. The truck had made Charlie—whoever he was—a happy man. Perhaps today Charlie was dead, or down on his luck, or perhaps he had given up the truck for a new one, the way a man tires of the things he once loved. Howard hoped Charlie approved of his work. The project had kept him busy all last week. At the finish there would be that moment of triumph as he started the engine and backed the truck down the driveway. And then the sadness would come over him—briefly, delicately, like a cool wind in September that hints of winter—and it would strike him that the truck would never mean quite as much to him as it did now, while he was working on it. And then, nothing. The nothingness of looking for a job that didn't exist. *But no, Howard,* the choirs sang in his head, *this is Sunday morning, no time to brood.*

He had no idea what he'd do with the truck once he had fixed it. The thing was a huge, mechanical angel sent to save his soul. But how this would be done, or even why he should think it would be done, he did not know. Have faith, the choirs sang. This is Sunday, and this old barn is your cathedral. Listen, now, as the wind prays for you.

Everything depended on luck, Ollie Jordan would say, and yet the nature of luck was as elusive as the nature of trout. There's good luck in horseshit for the flies and the grass, Ollie preached, but not for you and me. There's good luck in a pint of whiskey for you, but bad luck in the same whiskey for your old woman. When all the creatures agree on who the devil is, why, we'll all be friends.

As this thought faded, the image of Bert Reason, white with driven snow, appeared in Howard's mind.

Friday, on the telephone: "I see the only progress we've made is that you've learned my name."

Silence.

"Now, Howie, I know you're not going to say anything, but I can read you by the way you breathe into the phone. Ha-ha. There, you pulled it away. Put it back. That's better. Now, listen up. Consider, now, your options. Call them one, two, and three. Option one, live on. Hear no evil, see no evil. An illusion, Howie. Option one is no option at all. The old days are gone forever. Elenore can't work. She's tired; sick, maybe. Who can tell? And as for yourself?—able-bodied and unemployable. It's a darn shame, ain't it? Oh, one of these days you're going to find a job, but by that time it'll be too late. Option two will already be operative. That is, Howie, they will have taken the property. Option two, let 'em take the goddamn house." Reason had mimicked Howard's voice badly. "Call all those payments so much rent. Move to Keene and live with your daughter and son-in-law until you're on your feet. You know how easygoing Parker is." A pause to let it sink in. "Option three, sell the house. The only real option you've got, Howie. Thirty-six thousand dollars, our latest offer from you know who. I will repeat, three-six, zero-zero-zero. Something to think about. . . ."

"I ain't going to sell my house to nobody," Howard had replied.

"Oh Howie, Howie. There is a certain similarity, Howie, between an earthquake and a man having a heart attack; a similarity between the anticipation of the hunter and the desperation of the hunted. You see now what I'm driving at? All things are repeated on greater and lesser scales."

None of this was to the point, as Howard remembered it. Perhaps Reason had not spoken the words at all, but Howard had heard them somewhere long ago, or perhaps he had heard them recently from Freddy.

Thirty-six thousand dollars. They would take his house and bury him with money.

"Take the money, Howie, and run. Run for your life. Buy time, buy pride, buy peace of mind." On and on Reason tempted him. "Thirty-six thousand dollars, the price of freedom. The price of a new life. Take the money and get the hell out. There's nothing here for you. Go somewhere where they appreciate a working man. Go where the jobs are. Go west. Let your imagination roam, like the buffalo on the range."

Howard, speechless, breathing into the telephone like an asthmatic, had done what he was told—let his imagination roam. He pictured a place of high mountains with snowy tops and rich green meadows on their lower slopes. He pictured deer in endless orchards and trout as abundant as minnows in clear, cold streams. And he pictured a log cabin nestled on a south-sloping hump, bordered by fencing, the Elman residence, thank you. He pictured himself laying a trap line in the winter along his stream. He enlarged the picture to include a tiny town with a gas station, a general store, and perhaps a movie theater for Heather and a pay-telephone station, because, well, because every place ought to have a telephone booth. He enlarged the picture further to include a state, but here he ran into trouble. Which Western state? Not California. It was more populous than New York, and smoke hung in the air over the cities. Not Colorado. It was full of skiers, fear-provoking creatures with sunglasses, oily brown faces, and strange boots. Not Texas. Texas was full of Texans, bragging incessantly about Texas. He could not, for the moment, think of any more Western states. His mental picture of the United States was incomplete, like some half-made machine from a kit. Iowa. The name sprang to his head. Iowa, Iowa—it had a good sound. He didn't know anyone from Iowa, had not met anyone from Iowa, had never heard anything unusual about Iowa. All this was to the good, he concluded, because it meant that the few people in the state minded their own business. He decided that Iowa must lie between California and Colorado, somewhat north of each. There now, it was taking shape in his mind, a state with a humped back and the northwest corner jutting outward so that the state resembled a bear on all fours. Near the head would be a desert; along the belly, plains; and following the spine, mountains. A good state. Iowa, Iowa, where the deer and the antelope play, the choirs sang.

He would pack his family into the International truck and move to Iowa. He would find work, but not in a factory. Never again. He was too old for the sweat and the lint sticking to his face like leeches and the loud, beastly machines roaring like a stormy sea and shaking the floor so that sometimes his toes itched from the vibrations. He considered. He would work for himself. He would start his own trucking company: "Elman Trucking, West of the Pecos." It had a good ring. *What are you going to truck, Howie?* Not Reason's voice, but the voice in his own mind sounding like Reason. Apples, goddammit; he'd truck apples and tons of salmon from the river and pigs to market and horseshit if they wanted him to. He'd truck anything. He took a moment from working on the engine and stood by the door on the driver's side, imagining the sign he would paint on the door: ELMAN TRUCKING, WEST OF THE PECOS. WE TRUCK ANYTHING. *But, Howie, you said "we." Who is we?* Reason's voice in his head. A fair question. He pondered it. The "we" would be himself and Freddy. And the moment the thought came into his mind, he realized it was unrealistic. The entire sequence of thinking had been unrealistic. He wasn't going to Iowa. He was going to stay here, because he was what he was, like a rock or a bunch of berries.

Rage.

He plotted to kill Reason. Murder was medicine, aspirin for brain fever ... the bullet a suppository for the constipated thinker. ... He would back Reason against the wall, grab him by the throat, lift him off his feet, and feel his twitchings as he dangled there—the twitchings of evil—crush his windpipe with his thumbs and butt him in the mouth with his head, butt him until he gagged on his own blood and broken teeth, butt him speechless. The image alternately pleased him and disgusted him, stirred him and settled him; and then it vanished as his thoughts shifted to the requirements of working on the engine.

He worked faster and faster. He could feel the rhythm of his tools. He might die, but parts of him would work on, the way the heart of a turtle beats on hours after its head has been cut off. If need be, he could work himself into a stupor. Work was his strength, his manliness, his very pride, as another man's might be his name or his profession or his prick.

Finally it dawned on Howard that he was hungry. He had been working for three hours without a break. He needed some lunch, a bowl of Habitant pea soup, a couple of English muffins, juice, coffee. Elenore would be finished with her Sunday worship. She would be calm, almost cheerful. They would sit at the kitchen table and talk intimately about something neither would remember in ten minutes. He wondered whether he loved her. Whether she loved him. Or whether the question meant anything. He could love. He loved the truck. The truck was keeping him from violence, though it took his money. In the long run, it would ruin him. As one was saved, one was ruined. Was it Ollie who had given him that idea? He couldn't remember. He wondered now what he had been thinking about for the three hours while he worked. Something about bears? Once again he had lost track of time. Rage started to return, but he shook it off.

He quit work and headed for the house, pausing in the driveway to scan his properties, a quick mental inventory—land, vehicles, house, rock wall, apple trees, fifty acres of blue sky above, and the tail of a cloud about to dissolve, the frozen field, the dry leaves beneath. All his.

II : A BUNDLE OF LAUNDRY

Hold on, Friend, to the only friend you've got.

Howard felt tricked into reading the words, written (this week, probably, judging by the freshness of the pencil markings) over the urinal in the men's room of Miranda's Bar. He could still see the words in his mind as he walked back to his table. You couldn't get away from words; they were everywhere, like black flies in the spring. He didn't mind the black flies. All they wanted was your blood. The words wanted your brain. Both the barroom and the men's room smelled of beer and piss to greater and lesser degrees, and he tried to make something of the relationship but couldn't. He filed the thought away.

Outside, the street was black in the dim afternoon light, with patches of dirty plowed snow between the street and the sidewalk. Howard Elman began to think. Here walked the human race: going places, coming from places, going and coming in straight lines and at right angles like the gears, pulleys, and levers of a great machine; concerned with looking good and living long, concerned with loving and being loved, concerned with getting rich, or richer than their neighbors, anyway; busy creatures with never enough sleep, never enough time; inventors of gears, pulleys, and levers after their own image to do better what was not necessary in the first place; speechmakers, hunters, homemakers, riggers, agents, merchants, pursuing happiness like a pack of hounds after some poor frightened rabbit. He could sit here at the window of Miranda's Bar thinking and watching the street, but he couldn't move. A man had to have a job to move, and then he could stop thinking.

He wondered whether Elenore knew that he no longer searched for a job, that he stood in front of the employment office but did not enter, that he walked the streets like a man lost in the woods, that he stood on the city common and watched his footprints in the slush, that he had no idea, even, why he came to the city each day or why he felt false to himself and yet secure in that falseness. She knew, he thought.

He tried now to picture her as she must be at this moment—a dewdrop draped in rosary beads in a chair in front of the television's cool light. But the image wouldn't form. When they married, her eyes were blue, but they had changed; and now he could not remember what color they were. He opened his wallet, searching for the frayed photo of Elenore in the garden holding a tomato. She was beautiful; the tomato was beautiful; everything was beautiful that year.

He remembered now that she had been surprised, even shocked, at the first labor pains for the birth of all her children, because the babies had not come when she expected them to. ("Your mother ain't never sure how pregnant she is," he would say, introducing one of the few family jokes. "That's why I married him—to remind me," she would reply.) He smiled now, thinking of it. He was her clock, and she had married him to toll the time of day. He wondered why he could bear to think of her only as one thinks of someone who has died long ago.

Usually in the afternoon he sat in Miranda's, brooding, or seeming to brood—often his mind was completely vacant for minutes at a time. But sometimes he felt the need for conversation, and he would talk with the drunks at the bar, almost always making a speech that led to an argument that was never concluded, and the reason for which he could not remember clearly later. Once, the Greek behind the bar had told him to leave (in tones so hushed that at first Howard thought he had misunderstood). And it seemed to him the Greek had said as he left, "Someday that one will do something bad with his hands." Probably, though, the Greek had said something else, and he had only imagined he had heard the words.

Once, he had impressed the drunks at Miranda's by giving a speech about education: "A man's mind is like a good engine—you can't improve it by souping it up with books. Oh, it may look better, sound better, run faster; but it won't run longer, and it will break down when you least expect it. You soup up a good engine, and something happens"—here he lacked a word, "integrity," and substituted in its place "life"—"to its life; I mean the lifeblood, the . . ." He did not complete the speech, because the thought in his mind never fully developed. No matter; the drunks were impressed. For a moment he was triumphant. Later, after he had worked out the idea in his mind, he had blurted out, "See, there ain't no such thing as education. For every thing you learn, you unlearn another." But they had looked at him dully, and he realized that whatever had touched them earlier was something in his voice and not what he said, and that now he had lost it. They were not interested in meaning. They were interested in amusement, in relief.

Another time he had told the drunks, in an argument about religion whose substance he could not now remember, that the pope was a Christian; and it was not until later that night, in bed, sweating in the cold after awakening from a bad dream and then to the reality of the sound of dogs' running deer in the woods, that he had realized how stupid the comment had been, and he had wanted to explain to the drunks, and to the world, that he was not stupid, at least not unrelentingly stupid like some men, but selectively stupid like most men.

Hold on, Friend, to the only friend you've got. The thought surfaced in his mind. Everywhere men were writing in books, in newspapers, on billboards, and, yes, on shit-house walls, telling other men what to think, putting things in their heads and pushing other, probably finer things out. There ought to be a law, he thought. And then, contradicting his own outrage, he figured if he could write well, clearly and beautifully as a stream flows, he would write over the urinal "A man wastes his life with 70,000 trips to the bathroom." He watched the street and brooded.

There were certain facts he had to face up to. He had not been a good father. Oh, he had some strengths—he had provided (to a point), had loved (to a point), had been fair with them; but in the important areas—setting an example, understanding their problems, and deciphering the secret code of each child in order to guide that child—he had been a failure. The role of father had always been strange, unnatural to him. Elenore seemed to sense it, too. There were times when she insisted he keep away from the babies, as though she feared he would eat them. And there were times when he might, in a way, have eaten them, when they did not seem to him to be human, or even worth any-thing—as, say, a chicken is worth something—but merely an-other useless burden to the earth. He guessed they would taste like veal. The girls especially did not seem human to him, be-cause they reacted in unreasonable ways, holding up in the face of disaster and breaking down at the sight of a crushed flower petal; having neither the sense nor the instinct to kill; demand-ing for the sake of demanding. And then there was the mysteri-ous anger of women. The anger of a boy or a man could be understood. It was rooted in wounds to his pride; it sought con-frontation; it passed with victory, or with apparent victory. Fe-male anger was different. It was rooted in wounds to the soul; it was anger at God. He remembered Sherry Ann, in his arms dur-ing one of her rages, wrestling, shaking, twisting, with all the tricks and doggedness of a brook trout on a hook. At sixteen she had run away, and never returned. And he had been wounded, not so much by the loss but because he had never understood what the loss was, only that it was there.

Elenore had been relieved when Sherry Ann left, as though freed from her main competition: a secret revealed—he didn't like it. How should a man react when confronted with knowledge only God should have?

He wished then that Ollie Jordan were there so he could explain some of these problems while they were still clear in his mind. Intelligence, in a man, is up and down like a river, he would tell Ollie; and usually with the same result, he would add. It flowed best when it was high and swift; it was harmless when it was low; and it was at its worst when it overflowed its banks and covered the country around it with muck. But, of course, he would not say these things, because though the thoughts were there, the words were not. And, too, Ollie Jordan had changed. He was stricken with a sense of duty toward his mad son, Willow. Ollie's friendship, like Cooty Patterson's, had slipped away.

Certain facts to face. Howard had not been a good father, especially to his son. He had been absolutely certain, right from the start, that the boy's prime talent and his future lay in his ability to shoot a rifle. He had never stopped to ask the boy whether he liked to hunt. He had expected him to be a younger, perhaps bookish version of himself—the new model, an improvement of the old model. He had committed the basic mistake of parents everywhere. Now, having realized his mistake, he also realized that he had no idea what his son really wanted, and that despite knowing better, he, Howard, was not going to change; he would still insist that his son be like himself, only a little better—not a great deal better. Sad, he thought. Even his love was a mistake.

Heather was the happiest of his children. And why? he asked himself. Because he and Elenore had largely ignored her. A child needed food, cover, safety, and free time. A child did not need instruction. Instruction was destruction that had already been incurred by the parents, passed on to the child under the guise of instruction.

None of this was true, he thought. It was only thinking.

The problem was, he had not known a father himself, unless he counted Uncle Jack, the possessor of a small range of smart-alecky wisdom and nothing else; a farmer, and a poor farmer at that. Only the bear, whom he did not know, could he think of as a father. Not a particular bear, but the spirit bear that was the remaining spirit of his youth. Maybe if he weren't so ignorant. Maybe if, like Freddy, he had some education, he could roam libraries and pull together enough facts to go with his thoughts and create . . . what? Well, he didn't know.

And so Howard brooded, considering the great problems, the deep problems, but not the immediate problem, the real problem—the fact that he was running out of money, and that because of taxes, insurance, oil bills, and debts, the day would come when he could not afford to live in his own house.

"Take time, Howie, but not too much time," Reason had said only last night on the telephone. "Things of value take time, you'll say, and by the Christ, you'll be right most of the time. But not always. I mean, a man can fall for a woman in thirty seconds and can fall on his ass even quicker—or maybe they're the same thing. Ha-ha. . . . Too much and too little time, hey, Howie? Let's get to what's real now—real estate. My latest offer on behalf of my client—you know who!—and my last offer, I might add, is thirty-nine thousand nine hundred. I believe my client has a prejudice against going over forty thousand. And why not? The whole piece is only worth twenty-five thousand and you know it. Howie, I know you well enough by now to know you are not being cagy. You are being stubborn. Child stubborn, bear stubborn. See, we're talking like friends now. Have you looked at—in the legal parlance, searched—your deed of late? Probably not. Because, like most men, you thought you owned what you thought you owned. I'm sure it has never occurred to you that the stone-wall boundary on your north border may be in some dispute, not as a stone wall, mind you—ha-ha, of that there is no reasonable doubt—but as a boundary. . . ."

He was looking into the green-brown sun-flecked woods that were the eyes of Fralla Pratt.

"Howie," she said, "you awake?"

"Course I'm awake. Sit down and take the load off your feet," he shouted, loud even to him, and the drunks turned to look at him, and the Greek behind the bar moved to the Little League baseball bat he kept under the bar to calm the tumultuous. The smooth silver ball of the pinball machine was the only thing in the room moving with its original purpose.

Fralla jumped back, fear on her face—hunted, sexual. "Howie, you ain't drunk, are you?"

He got ahold of himself.

"No," he said normally, if not softly, "I ain't drunk. I was here thinking, and you surprised me."

She sat down and lit a Kent. He saw now that she was nervous, pained, and that she was going to tell him something. But not yet. First they must indulge in some chitchat. Rule of life, he thought.

She told him she was glad the shop had closed, because she had found work for which she was better suited. She was a waitress at the Jade Dragon. Had he been there? Well, he ought to try it. The food was strange but tasty, and the prices more reasonable than you'd expect. And it wasn't true what they said about Chinese serving rats from the cellar. Those were chickens. The tips were, well, not great, but okay. The place was bathed in green light, like trees, if—that is—trees could be like jewels. Well, never mind. It was hard to explain. Anyway, it was very restful.

Howard explained that he was not working, but—without lying outright—he made it sound as though his unemployment were by choice, and as though he had no money worries, was in fact a kind of playboy, dallying here at Miranda's and ... He didn't finish. Didn't have to. Fralla wasn't listening. The chitchat was over, and she had interrupted him and was telling him about her son.

"I don't come here, usually—at least not without an escort," she said. "I ain't that kind. It's my Porky. I've got to find him.

He's got a gun. I saw it in his pants. He can't fool his mummy. Howie, I'm so scared."

She explained that someone had gypped Porky (someone was always gypping Porky), had sold him a car with a sawdust transmission, and now she was afraid Porky would do something bad and go to jail. Jails were terrible places, she said, full of criminals and police. Porky was sensitive; he was unaware; he was trusting. Did Howard know what they would do to Porky in jail? Howard didn't answer, as indeed he was not expected to. He looked deeply into Fralla's eyes. They were a forest unto themselves, deep, deep, deep with stone walls, rich green ferns, towering oaks, and sugar maples with streams, and a pond of still brown and white water, with the dimple of a single trout, feeding on the surface, the pattern repeated on the bark of a giant pine, and in the sunlight here and there, butterflies. I love you, he thought he said. But of course he had said nothing. In a single second, as he looked at her eyes, he felt his gloomy mood turn inside out. He was young; he was optimistic.

"Do you see, Howie? Do you see?" she pleaded.

"Oh, yes, yes. Yes indeed."

"I knew you would." She was holding his hand.

She ordered a beer. She hoped that Lloyd Hills would come in and tell her where Porky was. Lloyd was Porky's only friend. Not a friend, really—a companion. And a bad companion at that. (He had served time.) But Porky looked up to him and might confide in him. They waited five minutes, and Fralla began to cry. It was hopeless, she said. Porky must be driving around (he had taken her car), drinking, and building himself up to be hurt. "Help me, Howie."

With a six-pack of beer between them, Howard and Fralla drove the streets of Keene searching for Porky Pratt. Howard was happy. The beer was making him mellow. He felt as though he had been given something useful to do—find Porky and bring him home to his mother. His only regret was that he had not brought the De Soto to Keene today. He explained to Fralla that he owned many vehicles, several of them registered, and she appeared to be impressed.

Porky was twenty-five, Fralla's only child. She was a failure, she said, for producing only one child and not raising it to be fit to survive in a hard world. She cried. Howard gave her beer. It was the only thing he could think of to do. She seemed grateful, and blew her nose. Porky was the product of Fralla's second marriage, Howard gathered, but he couldn't be sure, because although Fralla talked at length about her private life, she left out key facts and dates, disguised others, and mixed events in time. Porky had worked briefly at the shop, and Howard remembered him as lazy, stupid, unpredictable, destined for trouble.

It was hard to see, she realized, but Porky was saintlike. He had bad dreams; he was frightened of his own bed. Very beautiful. Did Howie understand? No. No, of course not. Only a mother could understand. She cried some more and then lit a Kent.

She asked about his own children, and Howard told her about Freddy's liking college. "College." She spoke the word reverently. She explained that Porky might have gone to college, but his teachers in high school had never given him a chance and had forced him to quit at age sixteen. Howard must be very proud of Freddy. Yes, very proud, Howard said, and, saying it, believed it, understanding that he had been proud all along.

They drove around town for almost an hour until it was dark. They stopped at a gas station to get some fuel and to let Howard go to the bathroom. The six-pack was gone, the empties shoved under the front seat. Fralla called her apartment from the gas station, but Porky had not returned. She called the Jade Dragon and told Paul Hui that she was sick and wouldn't be in tonight.

Then, abruptly, she announced that she was hungry, and Howard understood he was to take her out to eat.

He called Elenore. She was a long time coming to the phone. He told her he had met an old friend from the shop and they were having a few beers and not to worry. The half truth dried his mouth. He waited for her to speak. *Ask me no questions and I'll tell you no lies:* a favorite expression of Uncle Jack's. Elenore said she had no intention of worrying and hung up. He was troubled for a moment. It had been too easy. Deception ought to come for some price.

Still, he put the phone call out of his mind. Events were washing over him, and he was very calm. It was as if he had been swimming against a current for days, and now he had given up and let the sea take him where it would.

Howard and Fralla ate supper at the Chrysalis Restaurant, in downtown Keene. It was the oldest restaurant in the city. Years ago it had giant chandeliers that vaguely resembled the pupae of monarch butterflies, but they were gone now, although much of the restaurant was still painted in patterns of orange and black, which most people in town believed to be in honor of the colors of the local high school—specifically, in honor of the football team. In fact, the reverse was true. The founder of the Chrysalis Restaurant, a Yankee named Nathaniel Vernon, had also been a butterfly collector, specializing in monarchs. He had bequeathed the high school a great deal of money in 1880, the only condition being that the school colors henceforth be orange and black. Howard Elman was ignorant of these facts now, but one day he would read them and rejoice inexplicably.

Fralla wept and talked, talked and wept, between bites of a hamburger and some coleslaw on the side. She talked about the wonders of her only son, branching out to include comments about her various husbands and boyfriends.

"I used to dream that Porky would grow up and become a doctor," she said. "God, he was cute. He had fat, smooth hands, soft as flowers. I was so sweet on the idea of doctors that—Christ forgive me—I married a man for his nickname, 'Doc' Pratt. Let me assure you, he wasn't no doctor, unless you could call him Doctor of Difficulty. Well, 'Good-bye, Doctor,' I says. By that time it was too late. The good doctor had a way of making Porky jealous, and he poisoned the idea of a father in Porky no matter who I went with after that. Oh, I admit I spoiled him, but what could I do? He was all I had. When Porky was five years old, he was as touchy as a poodle. 'You shouldn't blame yourself,' they tell me. But I can't help it; I do. That's the way I am."

Here Fralla wept with such vigor that she couldn't speak for a whole minute and had to take sips of beer to compose herself. When she resumed speaking, she told about a Marine on a train in North Carolina during the Korean War and how it was hot and they couldn't get any ice and they had become separated because of this problem, although she didn't explain how, assuming oddly that Howard already knew, and how even then she was one to laugh loud and cry often, and why was it that the more feelings you had, the harder life was, and the harder life was, the more feelings you had. . . .

Howard nodded, grunted, gestured meaninglessly at her, as though fascinated. In fact, he wasn't listening or remembering or feeling; he was eating. In his tippy-bird fashion he downed a Western, home fries, pumpkin pie, and a beer, served in a long, elegant restaurant bottle, which he imagined made it taste lighter, bubblier, less alcoholic.

After supper they drove back to Miranda's in the hope that Porky—or perhaps Lloyd—would show up there. Every few minutes Fralla called her apartment, hoping her son would answer. Howard brought her a handful of dimes, and she put them in front of her on the table, arranging them and rearranging them—nervously, yes, but with some apparent purpose in mind, too, thought Howard, until it struck him that there was a relationship between Fralla's playing with the dimes and his own cleaning the .308 on the living-room floor. It seemed for a second that he was on the verge of a revelation, but he was not. He verified the connection between arranging dimes and arranging gun parts over and over in his mind, but the significance of it escaped him, indeed seemed farther away than ever.

There was a certain pleasure in discovering relationships, but it didn't mean you learned anything, he tried to explain to Fralla. She touched his hand and said that Porky had grown up lacking in something. He was like those Indians—not real Indians but India Indians—who never got enough food and felt sick all the time. Porky was starved for a father's love and his strong hand. She blamed herself. She was always falling in love with "doctors of difficulty."

Howard bought a cigar. Sometimes, when he reached a certain stage of drinking, a certain pleasure in living that he knew would be short, he bought a cigar.

He thought about the gun. Porky was carrying it in his pants. He didn't know how yet, but he would trick Porky into turning it over to him. It could be done, he assured himself. After all, everyone else had tricked Porky.

Later Howard would remember that he had said little, that he had listened patiently as Fralla went on and on about Porky and her troubles. In fact, as Howard began to get drunk, he said much, bragging a great deal about his house, his cars, even his trees.

Up the hill from the house there was a flat, boggy spot, he told her. Here grew a stand of old spruce, useless for lumber but valuable in its own way, as a cemetery is valuable. Here moss lay over the ground like a green shroud, and the sun was just a nickel of light through the trees. Here the wind could be heard but not felt. Few animals or plants thrived under those trees. It was a place to visit, but not to live in.

Fralla had a plan, she explained. When Porky slept, she would take the gun outside and drop it in a storm drain. . . .

He had bought a house from a farmer after the war, he said, interrupting her. He used to think the farmer was too stupid to know its true value. But now he had changed his mind. The farmer had simply tired of the place, as one can tire of any-thing—an old watch, the sound of crows, dust in August, a wife. You could see the fatigue of the farmer in the farm itself. He, Howard Elman, returning GI, dogface, had awakened it, freshened it. He had installed an oil furnace, insulated the attic, put on storm windows, covered the worn, unpainted clapboards with colorful asphalt shingles, added a new roof, which (face it) would have to be replaced soon (this summer, maybe next summer), cleaned out the barn and dumped all the shit in the pigsty and the next spring plowed it under for a vegetable garden (not a truck garden), and prayed to the boulders in the field (the boulders that had conspired to wear out the farmer) and promised them that he would never farm. Never. Did she understand? Did Fralla understand?

Why sure, Howie. She continued where she'd left off. It would be difficult to take the gun from Porky. He didn't sleep the way normal people did. He had nightmares, fought in his sleep, always losing, it seemed; he was frightened of his bed, the way little children are sometimes. (Howard was nodding, nodding, thinking about how he would tell her of his new truck and how he had dropped a rebuilt engine into it.) After the gun was disposed of, Fralla continued, Porky would be grateful, but not at once. First he would be hurt, and he would want to hurt her, because he would know that she had taken his gun. Once, when he was drunk, she had taken the keys to his motorcycle and he had slapped her and she had cried. And then he had done a beautiful thing—he cried, too. Wasn't that beautiful?

Yes, yes it was, Howard said. Did he tell her he had a new truck?

It was at this point that Lloyd Hills entered Miranda's Bar. He failed to see Fralla Pratt before she was upon him, demanding to know where her Porky was. Where was Porky? Where? Fralla demanded. Lloyd, backed against the wall, at first denied having seen Porky that night and then abruptly admitted that yes, he had been with Porky, driving around, having a few beers, and that Porky had gone to Winchester to the Rhythm Ranch to listen to Raymond and Carla Stone and the Seven Little Pebbles. Fralla believed it, and she was calmed. But a moment later she started in again, asking Lloyd about the gun. And Lloyd was scared. Almost kindly he asked her to shut up, explaining that he didn't know anything about a gun, that he didn't want to know anything about a gun, because he was on probation and they could send him back to jail. Fralla was satisfied that Porky would do no harm that night. Lloyd left hurriedly, and Fralla gave Howard a big kiss and ordered a beer.

Howard knew they would make love, although even then something in the back of his mind bothered him. Lloyd was lying. And Fralla knew he was lying, and had lied to herself in believing him. It would not be until the next summer that Howard figured out what Lloyd and Porky were up to that night, when he read in the newspaper that they had been arrested for a series of burglaries in the winter.

Howard drove Fralla to her apartment, which was just a short walk from Miranda's Bar. It had a small kitchen with grease stains on the ceiling. In the living room was a couch, used by Porky as a bed when he was home, a television, a hi-fi, and a dresser. Howard sat on the only easy chair in the room, and Fralla sat on his lap. She kissed him. "I love cheek to cheek," she said.

She was bigger than Elenore, yet less soft, with more bones, more muscles.

She would not let him see her in the light. She went into the bedroom and closed the door; she ordered him to undress in the bathroom. When he returned, the bedroom was dark, and she was under the covers. He groped for her with all the hunger of a miner groping in a dark mine for what he thinks is gold.

Afterward she made him look away while she put on her clothes. Then she went to the bathroom, staying a long time. She returned fully dressed, holding his pants and a beer. The two of them sat up in bed and watched television.

She put her head on his shoulder, and he could feel her breathing lightly. He was extremely happy. Well, as happy as you can be while drunk, he thought he told her. But she didn't seem to understand him. He let it pass. They watched a program about African animals, which, Howard gathered, lived in a zoo that went on for miles. Then he was looking at the doorway, filled with a shape.

Porky Pratt was standing there holding a forty-five-caliber service pistol.

"Get away from my mother," he whispered. Even from across the room, Howard could smell the nervous sweat of the man. He thought immediately of Cooty Patterson and the woman in Cooty's room. He lurched forward to his feet, almost falling, outraged.

"Your mother is a grown-up woman, a decent woman. And you've done nothing better than worry her sick. . . ."

"Shhhhutup." Fralla stepped in front of him. "Bay-beee, bay-bee," she said, changing her tone.

Howard understood now that Porky was prepared to kill him.

"Bay-bee, it ain't nothing. He didn't hurt Mummy. He didn't do nothing to Mummy." She picked up Howard's shoes, shirt, and coat, and put them in Howard's hands. Keeping herself between the gun and Howard, she guided him toward the door.

"You get out of here and don't you come back," Fralla shouted. He was standing barefoot in the snow, wind crawling along his back like cold insects. It struck him that moments ago he had been drunk and now he was sober.

He drove for a block before stopping to put on his clothes. He was agitated—not nervous exactly, nor shaky, but anxious for combat, full of a lover's jealousy.

He stopped at the Beaver Street Market and bought a quart of beer. It was almost midnight, and it felt strange to be in the city so late. The streetlights made everything blue. Bay-bee, she had said. It was clear she was protecting not him but the son. He tried now to remember the sex act with her, but it seemed long ago in his mind. The darkness the woman insisted upon had made the act incomplete. It would never be complete. He felt unpleasantly chaste. He drove home, drinking.

The effect of the beer came upon him very suddenly, and by

the time he reached home, he was very drunk. He could not negotiate the curve into his driveway, and the pickup came to rest over an old snowbank and then would not move. The tail of the truck was in the road a little. He thought that was funny. He stepped out of the truck and fell down. The sky above whirled blackly. He threw up in the driveway, stood breathing loudly. Then he went back to the pickup and gulped down the last of the beer. It seemed important to dispose of the bottle, as though it were evidence against him. He stood holding it. Finally he pissed into it. (The next day he discovered he had put the bottle in the middle of the road. It was still there, the urine frozen.)

He staggered into the house, too drunk for remorse or guilt or even caution. He began to sing: "Piss in the field, piss on old Mrs. Cutter! Piss in the grave. Horse piss, Jesus H. Christ, piss. Piss on 'em all."

Still singing, he shut off the lights and walked up the stairs. He checked Freddy's room—he was gone. He checked Heather's room—she was asleep. He checked the other rooms—empty, all. He went back to Freddy's room. "I, ah . . ." He started to say something, but no words came. So he resumed singing. "Piss in the grass, piss in the grave, piss on the stars. Dee dum, do dee."

He retired to his bed. It was moments before he realized that Elenore was not in the bed. Hm. He giggled. He looked under the bed. "Dee dum, do dee." He checked the closet, running his hands through the clothes and knocking down a row of hangers. Strange. Had he drunk so much that she had vanished? It seemed like a sound idea, and he pondered it.

He snapped on the light in the hallway. "Elenorrr? Where are you?" No answer.

He went downstairs and paused at the bottom. There he discovered that there was a bundle of laundry on the floor. He pushed at it with his foot and found that it was not laundry but his wife, crumpled up on the floor as though her bones had suddenly turned to water. He wondered whether in his drunkenness he had knocked her down the stairs and killed her.

12 : THE FILBIN RITES

Freddy in a chilly phone booth at the University of New Hampshire, listening to his sister Charlene:

"They don't know what done it to her, and they're going to send her to Hanover to find out. Course they found sugar in her blood, you know. Not that I was surprised. Just last month I says to her, 'Mummy, you got to stop eating all those sweets—they ain't good for your blood.' Remember last year when she had those blackouts? I tried then to get her over to the clinic. Course she wouldn't go. She's as stubborn as *he* is in her own way. Whole family is stubborn. Includes you, little brother. They say the sugar in her blood's got nothing to do with the paralysis in her legs, but I don't believe it. They think she fell down the stairs, but there ain't no broken bones. She says she don't remember. She said she was sitting there praying, and Daddy come home drunker than a fart—pardon my French—and she couldn't get up. Sounds fishy to me. I asked her if she was scared, and she said she ain't never scared when the Blessed Virgin is in the house. Poor Mummy, happy in her ignorance. All for the best, I suppose. You'd think she'd be suffering, but

159

she ain't. She seems downright at peace. I don't know how they're going to pay all them bills. Her hospital room costs a hundred-odd dollars a day, and if they ship her to Hanover, well, you take it from there. He ain't had no medical insurance since the shop closed; he ain't had no ambition since the shop closed. You can't tell me he can't find a job somewhere. I know he don't read so good, but he's able-bodied, and he ain't witless, though sometimes I wonder. You know what his problem is? He's ignorant and stubborn. I don't mean for you to be pleased by these remarks, knowing how you two get along. Just because you had the opportunity to go to college don't make you the know-all and be-all. He ain't as bad as you make out. Course, I've got to admit he ain't perfect, either, especially these days. Truthfully, Freddy, I worry about Heather being brought up by that bear in that house on that back road. I says to him, 'Your children are about grown. Why don't you sell that house with its big oil bills and high taxes? Ain't nothing there but a yard full of junk and hill full of trees not good for anything but scenery, which you can get plenty of by taking a ride to Mount Monadnock.'" At that point, Freddy had interrupted, but Charlene had gone on talking anyway and silenced him. He had felt cold and slightly nauseated, like the time he had been in an automobile accident. "He wouldn't listen. You know he never listens. 'This is my house,' he says, 'and I came here to live until I die, and here I'll live until I die.' Why can't anybody in this family be good-humored, like Parker? Anyway, I says, 'You ain't got a job. Mummy's going to need care when she gets out of the hospital. How you going to get by, living out in the country?' He says, 'That's for me to know and you to find out.' So I says . . ."

Freddy calling home, collect, listening now to Heather:

"Daddy's not home. He went to Mr. Filbin's funeral. Mr. Filbin killed himself. Daddy promised to buy me a new guitar for my birthday. I learned a new song, 'Crying in the Classroom,' and I don't like school no more. I'm going to quit when I'm sixteen. Priscilla Simon has tooties now, and she's getting stuck-up. Brian Walters has a new pig. Named him Squeally." A horrible thought passed through Freddy's mind: News of Elenore's paralysis has destroyed Heather's brain. Absurd thought, he knew. Destroyed brains occurred only on college campuses and only temporarily and only as part of one's education. Still, the thought was there, jumping around in his head. "Mummy is better. She has a new rosary that the sisters brought her. It has red beads. In the bed beside her is an old lady with tubes in her nose. I don't like the hospital, because the elevator makes my stomach feel funny...."

Freddy was upset. It was bad enough his mother was in the hospital, but she'd pull through, he was confident, without quite knowing why. What upset him more than anything else was the thought of his sister Heather, alone with his father. Already, it seemed to him from talking with her on the phone, she had regressed. Howard just isn't competent to raise her, Freddy thought.

Next he called Zoe Cutter.

Zoe Cutter was rejuvenated by her Florida vacation. She returned to Darby enthusiastic, energetic, and full of plans. She bought a huge chunk of hilly, wooded land that joined her property up the hill and spilled over into the next town, Donaldson. She now had frontage in two towns, on two sides of the ridge. For all practical purposes she owned the hill. After some study of timber practices, she hired a forester to prepare a master plan for harvesting her trees. It was clear that wise timber management would provide her with enough income to pay the taxes on her properties and, as a bonus, improve the forest itself. She learned to view her forest as a great, wild garden of trees that needed weeding. She still flirted with the idea of raising horses, but for this year she would lease her fields to local farmers. She would watch them, learn from them. She hired woodcutters to clear trees grown in along one of her stone walls. She already had enough firewood stacked in the woods for two years. Next year she planned a maple-sugaring operation. She wouldn't sell the syrup locally, she decided, but in New York, where it would fetch a higher price.

Darby, and indeed all the towns that surrounded Keene, provided a wonderful labor pool, she discovered. People in the area were driven both by some remnant of the Puritan work ethic and the need to make ends meet. Wages were so low that both husbands and wives had to work, and the husbands often worked two jobs. Trade unions were noticeably lacking, a situation that suited Zoe. She could count on a willing, honest, hardworking labor force that came cheap.

The basic problem with the area, she decided, was a lack of marketable resources. Even with wise management, her land would produce only subsistence living. More was needed to turn a profit. She concluded that to thrive, Darby and the other towns must capture dollars from tourists who prowled the country roads. She could see that the country would thrive only if the city were brought to it, and she was surprised and puzzled that local farmers could live on the land and not recognize this simple economic fact of life. They must assume that life has to be hard for it to be good, she thought. Well, she was going to do her part to change all that. The boutique would do for starters. Eventually she'd make this land pay and make it pay so that people could see how it paid.

She wasn't sure what her next step would be. Condominiums, perhaps. A ski area, maybe. At any rate, she coveted the Elman land. It had good frontage on a town road, and once it was cleaned up, it would delight the eye. Reason promised her it was only a matter of a week or so before Elman agreed to sell. But she didn't trust Reason, and she didn't understand Elman. He might be stalling to get the price up, but she didn't think so. No, there was something strange, violent, inscrutable, about the man and his motives. It was hard to deal with a man who was too dense to be greedy. She'd give Reason a month, and if he didn't produce by then, she'd come up with another plan.

On another front, she had decided to involve herself directly and deeply in town politics. Hence, she had launched a petition to require owners of junk cars to screen them from the sight of the road. She believed in her proposed ordinance, which would be acted on at town meeting the first Tuesday in March, but beyond that, circulating the petition gave her an opportunity to meet the townspeople. She was an outsider, but they seemed persuaded by her main argument, which was that junk cars lower property values. Property was everything here, she knew. She met a surprising number of new people, most of them young and well educated, liberal in politics but anxious to preserve the beauty of the land. Further, she had the support of Harold Flagg, known as the most influential figure in town. The insider and the outsider in league—she didn't see how she could lose with that combination. Already she had more than enough signatures to place the junk-car question on the warrant for town meeting.

The phone rang. It was Frederick, calling collect.

"Hello, darling," she said. "When are you going to come and see me? I've been having wicked thoughts about you."

She could sense him blushing. He had a deep Puritan streak in him, and he didn't like such talk, which made him all the more attractive, perhaps because he was so open to corruption.

"I want to come down and talk," Freddy said gravely.

"About chucking it all and going to California?" She didn't understand.

"No, about family."

"Are you worried about your mother?" asked Zoe. "I've just heard, myself. I've been on vacation—escape from your dreadful climate. Doesn't spring ever arrive here? Anyway, Arlene filled me in. Elenore's going to be all right, I guess."

"I think Mom will be okay," said Freddy. "I mean, she's had a million operations. She seems to thrive on ill health, on suffering. . . ."

"Amen," Zoe interrupted. "Story of mothers all."

"I'm worried about Heather. I think my father is becoming . . . unstable." He let the word hang there.

"Your father and I do not speak these days," said Zoe. "I don't know what's going through his mind. But I've seen Heather at the store. She seems all right. I wouldn't worry."

"She needs to get her teeth fixed," said Freddy.

"Yes," said Zoe. She'd heard that one before—Frederick's concern for his sister's crooked teeth. She could hardly take it seriously, and yet he took it seriously. He was getting at something.

"Dear, what are you driving at?" she asked. She could feel his discomfort at the other end of the line.

"I want to talk," he said.

"All right," she said. "Later in the week. I'm busy today with this petition business, and I've got to run down to New York tomorrow."

Freddy hung up the phone. He was shivering. He had spent the last forty-five minutes in an outside phone booth. It had snowed last night, and the plows had pushed the snow up on the sidewalks so you had to walk in the road. The wind was gusty and hard from the north, and the sky bright and, like the wind, hard. "When will the melting come?" he asked himself. He began to jump up and down to keep warm, and then he broke into a run and headed for the dormitory. What was it about Zoe Cutter that held him close and yet kept him at a distance? He had thought (fantasized) that somehow she would make a man of the world out of him. But he still felt like a boy searching, searching. . . . It occurred to him that for her part Zoe wanted something from him besides sex. Something to do with his father, perhaps. He knew she was trying to buy him out, a move he, Freddy, wholly approved of for all concerned. But he suspected that some strange game was going on between them, a bond somehow, with himself as . . . what? A knot? A prize? No, that wasn't right. He didn't understand. It would not occur to him until years later, after he had begun to write, that the struggle for property was at the root of the war between his father and Zoe Cutter. And he would never solve the problem of Zoe in his mind.

He began to jog to get warm, and his mind was blank for a while, and then he was thinking about California, or what he imagined to be California, for he had never been there: sunlight that turned everything to gold, warm sand on the soles of the feet, beautiful girls. It was a lovely mind picture, and then it vanished. A name had jumped into his mind. Filbin? Filbin? Oh, yes, he remembered now. Filbin was one of the men who had worked at the shop with his father. Killed himself? Was that what Heather had said? It seemed strange to him. He had come to believe, without really thinking about it, that you had to have a college education to get up the will to kill yourself. Men of his father's ilk killed others, not themselves, when they went off the deep end.

Howard got spiffed up for Filbin's funeral. He broke out his blue suit from the attic. The suit smelled of mothballs and the jacket was a little snug around the chest, but otherwise it was all right. He found a white shirt and ironed it, discovering that ironing wasn't all that hard. Indeed, he felt a certain instant satisfaction as the wrinkles vanished and the cotton flattened. He applied a modest spit shine to his black shoes and put on a clean pair of white socks. He wet his thinning hair and combed it, but he didn't shave the two-day growth of beard on his pocked face, because it just didn't occur to him. He rummaged in the dresser for a tie. Elenore had a place for ties, but he couldn't remember where it was. He found them, finally, hanging on a hook inside the closet. "Right in front of your goddamn nose," he said to himself. He wished he had a tie with dolphins on it like Mr. O'Brian at the unemployment office. Such a tie, he believed, would speak more respectably to the memory of Filbin. Howard chose a gray tie with glittering red dots. The middle part of the tie was navy blue, so that if you tied it properly, the knot would be blue and play off against the gray and red. Although Howard rarely wore a tie, he could tie a Windsor knot. Someone had taught him to years ago, and it was the kind of thing he never forgot. He looked at himself in the mirror. The bottom of the tie reached about to the middle of his chest. A bit short, he thought. He buttoned the three buttons of the suit coat, just covering the end of the tie. Better, he thought. In fact, pretty good. Hell, he could dress up with the best of them, if he had to.

Howard could not understand Filbin's suicide. Killing he understood. Taking life, he believed, was somehow normal. Earth was a war mother. Trees robbed light from other trees and killed them. Animals preyed upon one another for food. Insects ate everything, and everything ate insects. Men killed for more complex but apparent reasons—power, revenge, righteousness. But suicide was something else. It was beyond him; it baffled him. There was something dirty, perverted, un-American, about it. Suicide did not shut the door on death. "Why Filbin?" he asked himself. "Why?" He did not wonder so much about the reasons that made the act necessary. But why the show of it? Why leave us with the unanswered questions? Why not just drive your car into the river? Filbin, finicky Filbin, had built himself an elaborate death machine. He had hooked a hose from the exhaust pipe of his car to a well-crafted port he had built into the front side window of his Pontiac. He even included weatherstripping. He started the car and climbed into the back seat and padlocked himself in chains, lest his resolve fail. His wife found him hours later when she returned home from bingo.

Early for the memorial service, Howard met some of the boys from the shop—Carsons, Talbot, Stillings. Carsons was a wreck. Like Howard, he had not been able to find a job since the shop closed. Talbot was working part-time, pumping gas. Stillings was working full-time at the hospital. They were training him to be an orderly.

"Charley Kruger done the right thing; he packed up and moved to Florida," said Talbot.

"Kruger always done the right thing—that son of a bitch," said Howard.

The four men nodded. They were envious of Kruger.

"When that Mr. Gordon come, I knew the handwriting was on the wall," said Stillings.

"If you knew, why didn't you tell us?" asked Howard.

"Why? I wonder why he done it," said Carsons, and it took a moment for the other men to realize he was not talking about Kruger or Mr. Gordon but about Filbin.

"Must have been crazy," said Stillings.

"I heard they locked up poor old Cooty Patterson," said Talbot, looking for affirmation.

"You heard right," said Howard.

"Well, I heard they let him out," said Stillings.

Unaccountably, Howard began to feel rage boil up inside himself. It seemed wrong that Cooty had been locked up, wrong that he had been released, wrong that Stillings should be allowed to speak of Cooty.

"They don't let nobody out of that place," said Howard, the edge of his rage in his voice.

Stillings pressed on. He had a job. He had confidence. He had knowledge of the world and felt obliged to disseminate it.

"People come out of there right and left, Howie," said Stillings.

"He must of been sick inside," said Carsons, again talking about Filbin.

They sat in the back, four men in ill-fitting, out-of-date suits, erect in the pews like old soldiers at a Fourth of July parade.

Howard tried to shake off his rage. It just wasn't fitting that a man should want to murder at a funeral. Carsons beside him smelled of booze, not so much from his breath as from the pores of his skin, the smell of a nervous man taken to drink. Talbot was strumming his fingers on something (Howard dared not turn to see what). He imagined that Stillings was smiling. He thought about Charley Kruger, fishing in Florida. "That son of a bitch," he mumbled to himself.

"What's that, Howie?" whispered Carsons.

"Nothing," he whispered. "When you suppose they going to wheel the body in here?"

"Ain't going to be a body," whispered Carsons. "This is a memorial service."

Howard settled back, folding his arms. So a memorial service was a funeral without a body. He felt cheated. Well, when I die, he thought, I hope they parade me up and down the street bald-acky-bareass. At least then everybody will know I'm dead and they're alive. Memorial service. Jesus H. Christ, what a farce. At least with Swett, they put him in a box, and they let you see him in the box, and they let you watch while they put the box in the goddamn ground, and if you wanted to hang around, you could watch 'em put dirt over it. But this? This was a farce. The only way you knew Filbin was dead was from the newspaper and the gossips. For all he knew, Filbin was in Florida catching large-mouth bass.

Mr. Lodge came in. He was wearing a dark tie and a striped suit. He sat with Filbin's family, a frozen, grim look on his face. He looks good, Howard thought. He looks rich and fine. Filbin's widow was dressed in black, her face hooded in a veil. She was holding the arm of Filbin's son, Richard, who looked as if he wanted the service to be over with. Howard suppressed an urge to call out to him.

The minister had entered the pulpit and was speaking. Howard could hear the voice, but the words were mumbled, like a radio blaring in the next house. Something about Filbin's family, something about his work, his devotion to . . . what was it? God? Something or other. And then there was an organ playing in the balcony, and then singing, soft and beautiful. Filbin's cousin Merwin, Howard guessed. And then the minister read from the Scriptures. More music. And, goddamn, he could feel Carsons quivering beside him, could feel him begin to weep before he heard the strained hiccupping sounds. He was both sympathetic to Carsons and enraged at him. Carsons, he wanted to say, what the hell are you doing breaking down at a goddamn memorial service? There ain't even a body here. You don't even know if there is a body. Smarten up. That Filbin, who the hell does he think he is? What kind of goddamn joke does he think he's pulling? . . . And Howard found that he too was sobbing.

13 : TOWN MEETING

Article 12: By petition. To see if the Town will adopt the so-called Junk Car Ordinance to require owners of unregistered automobiles, trucks, buses, and the like, with the exception of those vehicles in current use for agricultural or forestry purposes, to screen said machines from sight of public roads and places where the public normally gathers, such screening to be effected by means of trees, shrubs, and/or wood fencing as per guidelines set forth in U.S. Publication 50473028272012. (Recommended by Selectmen.)

The De Soto flew southward in the fog on Interstate 91. The snow had settled from warmth, and now, warmer still, it seemed to rise in the form of vapors, cool again, and snake along the highway in malevolent coils.

Howard and Heather were returning from Mary Hitchcock Hospital, in Hanover, where Elenore had been transferred. Her legs were still paralyzed, but she was cheerful, and the color in her cheeks, pale for years, had returned to a girlish pink. Heather, in the front seat with Howard, now sang, now counted license plates, now complained that the ride was long and she wanted to go home. Howard swelled with love for her. It was as if the small amount of love he carried for his other children had come together to form a large love for Heather. He cooked meals for her, did her laundry, and carted her around. He gave her whatever she wanted. (Last week they ate hot dogs for three days.) He treated her, taking her to McDonald's or to the movies. He took her for rides. He let her skip school when she wanted. They rarely talked. Heather sang, and Howard listened. He felt relieved from the effort of making conversation. He was forgetful, mildly detached.

Her legs were dead, Elenore told Howard, but it was all for the best. They had been full of knots that gave her pain. They moved her about with difficulty. She liked the wheelchair better. It could do nearly everything legs could do, and it didn't make you pay. The therapist had shown her how to get into and out of a car, how to go to the bathroom, how to do housework. She asked Howard to rearrange the cabinets in the kitchen so she could reach everything, and to build a little platform in front of the sink so she could do dishes. Instantly he pictured a ramp along the counters and sink. He saw two-by-fours and plywood and nails and red paint and his table saw buzzing and himself swinging a hammer. She was going through the change of life, she said, and yet she seemed younger, more alert, more radiant. Above all, she seemed holy. She kissed his hands and called for Heather to sing "O Come All Ye Faithful." Her eyes grew moist, and she whispered that she had a secret that gave her joy and would save them, and the tears ran down her cheeks and fell onto his hands. He realized he loved her, that he had always loved her, and he did not know what the love meant, and that something soft in her was getting into him.

The fog crept out of the snow-filled woods and slithered onto the highway. The De Soto plunged into it, displacing it, passing on. Without being aware of it, he drove faster. Heather began to sing. Once—it was summer and he could remember the smell of heat and someone's wrapping him in something clean and white—a woman had sung to him, "The Mediterranean is ultra blue, and there is heat there and no fear of cold winter, and the babies lie in the sand." For a long time, as they shifted him from foster home to foster home, his records lost somewhere, he believed he was an orphan; but slowly it came to him that this was not true: he was a bastard. The De Soto was now going eighty-five miles per hour.

They'd be home in time for supper. He'd have a beer and watch *The Lone Ranger* with Heather. (He envied the masked man for his good luck.) After that he wasn't sure what he'd do. He wanted to work on his dump truck. But tonight was town meeting, and he had half a notion to pick up Ollie Jordan and go to the meeting and rail against the new law proposed to make people fence in their junk cars. It didn't make much sense to him. "Cars ain't like cows that go wandering off soiling other people's yards," he said. Heather ignored him; she could tell when he was talking to himself. He could not imagine that anyone was actually offended by the sight of his derelict cars. They were as natural and varied and pretty to him as trees. He was convinced that Mrs. Cutter had circulated the petition for the junk-car law for no other reason than to harass him; furthermore, he was convinced she wanted his land merely to deprive him of it. He carried a picture in his mind of himself shouting her down at the meeting, and it was this picture that tempted him to attend his first town meeting in many years.

He didn't believe that anything he could say would change the outcome of the meeting. Indeed, he believed that the meeting was rigged. The world was run by certain powers—committees of communists, big businessmen, and the Vatican—which, though they might seem to be at odds, in fact were in league. Issues, debates, wars, great movements, governmental changes—all were elaborate shows put on by the powers to keep ordinary men like himself busy. Howard's conspiracy theory did not upset him; rather, it set his mind at ease, because it answered a question he sometimes posed for himself: If the world were run the way it appeared to be run, by governments and leaders who were seemingly as baffled, wrong-thinking, blind, stupid, and greedy as ordinary men like himself, why had it not destroyed itself by now? It was either believe in the "powers" or in the hand of God. He rejected the second alternative because it didn't make sense to him that a superior being should want to invent a world based on chance and struggle. The idea was as absurd as building a car that drove only backward or an elevator that went in only one direction or a ball that did not bounce.

Town meeting was a silly game, Howard believed: long, pointless speeches by men sweetened by the sounds of their own voices; old ladies complaining about the road agent; the moderator—was it Vic Copley?—rapping for order on a wooden table; farmers smelling faintly of their barns; their wives crocheting, stopping only to vote. Still, he was tempted to make an appearance. He could see the Cutter woman flush with anger as he stood over her, shouting, and then they were taking him away and he was fighting them and they were falling and he was strangling the woman.

"I'm crying in the classroom / Since teacher erased my heart from the blackboard," sang Heather. "Don't erase my heart."

Howard wondered whether Ollie would go with him to town meeting. Ollie was becoming lost to him, as Cooty Patterson had become lost to him. Ollie was preoccupied these days with a mad devotion to his son Willow, who was now like a baby, needing to be fed, stroked, and assisted on the toilet. Ollie was always at his side and neglected the rest of his family. The result was startling changes in the Jordan scene. Many Jordans had left, taking with them various pieces of equipment—a tractor, a lawn mower (never used, as far as Howard knew), and pieces of furniture. Those who remained huddled around the wood stove, looking stunned, like the refugees Howard had seen during the war. The last time he had visited Ollie, the hunchback lay on his side in front of a mirror, making faces. Willow, shackled to a chair, ate a pie while Ollie bathed his feet in a pan. ("Gets corns so bad he wants to cry, this boy does," Ollie had said to Howard.) Willow's power over Ollie was clearly as complete as Ollie's power over Willow. Howard considered talking to Ollie about Willow, but he abandoned the idea. He had nothing practical to tell him except to break Willow's head.

. . . And then they were upon the car, driven by an old man smoking a briar pipe, treating the interstate highway like a country road. Howard jerked the steering wheel to the left. The De Soto balanced on two wheels and did a frightening little dance, its tires squealing, Heather squealing in concert, from terror or perhaps joy—he couldn't tell at the time—and then the car settled back down on four wheels, and there was silence, and the precious feeling of control once again.

An erection. Unsummoned. In the daytime.

A good sign, thought Harold Flagg. He had come to ask Zoe for her hand in marriage.

She offered him tea.

"Tea is fine," Harold said, his hands folded demurely in his lap, his bottom splayed over one of the antique bentwood chairs. "And, ah, don't forget, two sugars and don't spare the cow."

"Two sugars—Har-old!" She shook her head.

Lately she had been lecturing him about his weight. He took that as another sign that she felt affection for him.

She put the cup on the table in front of him, pausing for a moment, as though for him to admire her hand. Fingers to sip, he thought, and was further aroused. She wore a sun-yellow jump suit, which fit her like a not-tight, not-loose middle-aged skin. Her behind was as small as a boy's, and her breasts were as tidy in their cups as peaches wrapped in soft yellow paper. Her feet were gripped by the thongs of brown sandals with two-inch heels, and it was there that Harold concentrated his attention. That a woman would wear such shoes on a winter afternoon was to Harold a matter of considerable erotic importance. The deep-red slashes of toenail polish conjured up images in his mind of whip welts, of tiny, pulsating vulvas, of blood itself, which to Harold was the symbol of ever-giving, ever-suffering, ever-wounded womanhood. He avoided looking at her face. Not that it wasn't beautiful. But there was a toughness there, a worldliness, a reflection of intelligence, that he admired but that did not arouse him; indeed it threatened his own sexuality. He reminded himself that when the day came that they would make love, he must not look at her face.

She sipped her tea silently. An impressive feat in itself, he thought. Now was the time to propose.

"Zoe?" he said.

"Yes, Harold," Zoe answered.

The dog came over from the braided rug by the fireplace and belched. "Awful dog," Zoe said.

A bad sign, Harold decided. He put off the proposal for a few minutes.

They went over the deed again, Zoe at once believing and skeptical, like a good student, Harold in his glory.

"It had been assumed by recent owners of the properties that the north-south border between them was a wall roughly bisecting a field and clearly visible. 'And thence northerly from a pine and along a wall to Taylor Road.'" Harold made a great show of reading from the deed, but actually he was reciting from memory, his eyes examining Zoe's crossed ankles. "It is the very simplicity of the deed that deceived various owners. In fact, there is not one wall but two walls. . . ." And Harold went on to explain his research in great detail. "The point is, you own the entire field from this house to within twenty feet of Elman's house. No court would dispute it."

"So the lawyer tells me," said Zoe. She moved her ankles under the table so he couldn't see them, and then he found that she was smiling at him. Had she guessed his lust for her, and if so, was the smile in his favor? He pondered the question.

"I wonder," said Zoe, "if I claim the property, can Elman sue me, or the town, for the taxes he's paid on it over the years? And further, could I then sue the town for not taxing me properly in the first place?"

"In fact, I have thought about those possibilities"—in fact, he had not—"and I'm no lawyer, but as far as I know, there is no legal precedent for either action."

"I'm sure you're right about that," Zoe said.

He didn't like her tone. Discussions of land brought out a certain sarcasm in her. Once they were married, he would carry on land negotiations, he decided.

He shifted the conversation to put her in a better mood.

"This house is always a delight, because every time I come here, there is something new," he said.

Zoe's legions of carpenters, plumbers, electricians, architects, and decorators had transformed Swett's run-down farm into a showplace. Among other things, it now had two and a half baths, plus a sauna. (Harold bathed every other day, and he couldn't understand what one woman—granted, she entertained—would do with two and a half baths. He reasoned that the baths were an attempt to demonstrate financial clout, and on that basis he approved. As for the sauna, once they were married, he would see that it was removed. Ten years ago a Finn had built a shacky sauna on Mill Pond, and he and other Finns baked themselves in it and then jumped half mad and naked into the water. Later the Finn hanged himself from an oak tree from which kids used to swing into the water. Harold came to the conclusion that the sauna had driven the Finn crazy by overheating his brain.)

The house was nearly finished, Zoe said. It would have been cheaper to build new, she joked. The barn would be ready by June, just in time for the summer-tourist season. Downstairs would be the craft shop, a potpourri (she emphasized the word's Frenchness) of stalls for local woodworkers, silversmiths, glass blowers, and potters; upstairs would be a dress shop, the Loft Boutique. She had given up the idea of the antique shop. Once the snow had melted, she would build a geodesic-dome greenhouse, for no other reason than that she wanted one. Still, she'd bet she'd find a use for it, and it would make money. Invest in quality and you make money, she told Harold, who imagined he heard in the remark the voice of Zoe's departed husband, Edward. Soon she would be mouthing his own sayings, Harold told himself. She brought more tea, and Harold wished he had a couple of doughnuts to go with it, but inexplicably he dared not tell her he was hungry. Zoe confided that she was eyeing a certain piece of property in town for a special project. She looked closely at Harold to see if he knew which property she meant. Of course, Harold knew she was trying to buy the Elman place—it was all over town—but he didn't let on. The special project included renovating an eyesore property into executive-office suites, workday retreats for city workaholics. Why not New Hampshire as a center of finance? She winked.

Was she winking at her own comment or flirting with him? Harold wondered.

Harold now lectured Zoe on his theory of small New England towns. Expenses were increasing faster than the tax base. Towns were losing their identities to the cities, which held the wealth in the state because they held the industry. With the decline of farming as an industry, the towns were becoming bedroom communities. What was needed in the towns was light industry and moderate commercial undertakings, which would provide them with necessary funds without disfiguring them.

A pause. Harold and Zoe basked in a moment of shared ideals. It struck Harold that now was the time to ask for her hand.

"Mrs. Cutter, I have something to request," he said gravely.

"Why, Harold," Zoe said, touching his hand, "that's the first time in weeks you've called me Mrs. Cutter."

She was teasing him, he thought. If he asked her to marry him now, she might think he was kidding. He must be patient and bide his time.

"I think your junk-car ordinance has a good chance of being carried at tonight's meeting," he said. Actually, he had no idea whether the ordinance would be approved by the voters. He had long since given up anticipating how they would act. So much depended on luck, on weather, on where people sat in relation to one another, on the mood of the moderator, on chance comment, on an overheard phrase, on a joke. All these and a hundred other things could swing a question one way or another. Democracy was at once predictable and as fickle as a flock of birds.

"It will pass easily if all those who signed the petition vote for it at the meeting," she said.

"They won't," said Harold. "They'll sign any damn thing somebody puts in front of them, and then they'll vote the other way, or more likely, they won't even bother to show up."

"Then what makes you think the ordinance will carry?" Zoe pressed.

"Intuition."

Zoe now asked a series of questions on the running of the meeting, and Harold saw that that was the reason she had asked him over today. He advised her that if she wished to speak on the petition, she should phone the moderator, Victor Copley— "Shout; he's a bit deaf"—and arrange to be recognized to speak. Harold then launched into a lecture on the history of town meetings. He explained that once, they had run the state, but that because wealth had left the town governments, power had left too and now resided in the State House in Concord and— worse—in the White House in Washington. He talked on, until unexpectedly he found himself standing by the door, Zoe apologizing, saying that it was three-thirty and that she had to make an important call to New York.

"Harold," she asked, helping him on with his coat, "was there something else you wanted? You seemed so on the verge of something all during our visit."

"No, nothing," Harold replied.

Once in his car, he thought about her toes, and his erection returned.

About two hours before town meeting, Harold stopped by the town hall to make sure everything was ready. He set the thermostat at sixty, the idea being to make people slightly uncomfortable and thus remind them of the frugality of their officials. He straightened the wooden folding chairs into rows, because the town's part-time custodian, Bob Crawford (Bob the Boozer), could make only wavy rows. Harold scattered rock salt on the cut-granite steps, moist with condensation but free of ice. He snapped on the outside lights. At last year's town meeting, after a fierce debate, the voters narrowly passed a measure to keep the floodlights shut off except on special occasions. Too bad. Under lights the town hall was clean, monumental, a house made by and for gods. In the saner light of day one could see the paint peeling, the bird droppings spattered in the eave corners, the rot in the carved wooden vines at the top of the Corinthian pillars, the broken slates on the roof, and the weather vane that said the wind blew from the southwest, perpetually. While the outside of the town hall had remained relatively unchanged since it was built, more than two hundred years ago, the builders wouldn't recognize the interior. Changes had been made for two hundred years, and now it was an architectural stew of styles and materials. Harold had hunted through the town records to see what the town hall had been like on the inside when it was built, but the original floor plan was lost. He brooded about the sadness of history—much lost, much forgotten, much changed without a remembered purpose. The building now housed a cheerless hall, a tiny town library, a records room with a safe, three rooms used for storage, a huge, drafty entry, an attic full of bats, a cellar where a church pulpit lay rotting amidst wild mushrooms on the earthen floor, and a meeting room where no one met, because it couldn't be heated properly in the winter and was hot and stuffy in the summer. The selectmen had their office across the road from the town hall, in the loft over the fire station, a situation that caused ill will between the selectmen and the firemen.

Once, church services were conducted in the hall from the pulpit, which was now stored in the cellar. The hall had been renovated to accommodate stage plays and, later, basketball games. Now both plays and games were held in the elementary school, and the hall had fallen into disrepair. Wire mesh covered the huge arched windows, and a netless basketball hoop hung at an oblique angle to the floor. The backboard itself was cockeyed. Harold reminded himself to see that the wire and backboards were taken down. Same reminder as last year. Long ago the varnish had worn off the hardwood floors, and the wood paneling was caked with layers of old paint. A cold dust hung in the air, mingled with the faint smell of some dead animal. The hall's acoustics were strange. You couldn't hold a small meeting there, because when it was nearly empty, every tiny sound was magnified, so that words came out distorted, as though spoken by madmen. But when the hall was full, the sounds were mellow and clear. The place was lonely, Harold thought; it needed people to bring it to life.

Harold hated schools. The selectmen had no power over them, and every year, it seemed to Harold, the school board demanded—and got—more power and more money, while the town government got less. The state and federal governments provided funds to help pay for new schools, with cafeterias and gymnasiums, but not to fix the town hall. Even with outside help, the schools took sixty-four percent of the local tax dollars. The drain the schools made on the local economy was unnecessary, in Harold's view. Children these days knew no more than children of his generation, who learned to read and write in one-room schoolhouses heated with wood stoves. If children today were more sophisticated and worldly (and why should that be good?), it was because they watched television, not because they went to school. Furthermore, Harold was appalled with schoolteachers these days. They were obsessed with the methodology of teaching and with the emotional problems of children, but they knew practically nothing about subject matter. They had no sense of history or language, or even of how to think. Despite their college degrees, they were ignorant.

He shook with love for the town hall and hatred for schools. He could feel his heart pounding.

Harold went across the road into the fire station and climbed the steep stairs to the loft where the selectmen's office was. He sat at an oak rolltop desk, a gift to the town in the will of Homer Brady, who began his political career as a Darby selectman and ended it as a federal judge. Harold went over the town report for perhaps the hundredth time. He knew it better than anyone else in town, and yet someone would manage to ask him a question about it tonight that he couldn't answer. It happened every year. He spent a few minutes at the window. He could see wisps of fog move in the lights, where in the summer moths gathered in wild death dances. There, on the stone steps of the town hall, after the meeting, he would ask Mrs. Cutter to marry him.

Every year on the first Tuesday of March about one hundred of the town's four hundred registered voters crowded the chilly town hall for the annual ritual of town meeting. They included ...

Farmers: whose families had been in Darby for generations and whose attendance at town meeting was habitual. The farmers were plain, frugal, independent, literate, deep, and as narrow as the furrow made by a plow. They distrusted the governments of New Hampshire, the United States of America, and all foreign countries, the United Nations, and any movement that promised world order and the betterment of mankind. They trusted only town government—which is not to say town officials. Although they could see that their way of life amidst the stony soil was being destroyed, oddly enough they believed in machines, in roads, in factories, in tourism, in the very encroachment that was causing their destruction, because those were the marks of progress, and progress relieved the farmer and his mate of the drudgery of work. The farmers were slaves to work, and like slaves, they had a love-hate relationship with their masters.

They worked to be free from work, when in fact they were defined by it. They invented ways of relieving work, and then they invented ways of creating work. They were crazy—and productive in their craziness. In short, they were American. Their chief concerns at town meeting had to do with land and land taxes. Other issues were secondary. Many of the farmers were rich men who lived like poor men, some because they didn't know any better, some—despite scars, missing appendages, rheumatism, tendonitis—because they were happy the way they were. Every year there were fewer farmers at town meeting, and the ones who came were among the ones who came last year. Many were old men who took aspirin in the daytime and drank whiskey at night to ease their pains. Few were young. Some, while performing some cherished chore—pruning apple trees or boiling off maple sap—were suddenly taken with grief because their sons wanted nothing to do with the farm and would sell it after the farmers died. A few were considering selling out. They tried to picture their acres, fields, timber, barns, animals, fences, wells, machines, translated into cash, into big cars, into retirement in Florida. Some had already sold out and moved and were content driving their Cadillacs with deliberation along an ocean boulevard. Others who had sold out paced endlessly along the Florida beaches, as though waiting for some creature to be born from a stall in the suffering sea. The farmers could remember when everyone in town went to the Congregational Church. Now some of the farmers themselves had stopped attending services, not because the new minister had been in the civil-rights movement (although that was bad enough) but because it was clear that he didn't believe in God, and thus he reminded them that they no longer believed in God either. The farmers could remember when vast tracts of land, now forested, were pastures, wavering oceanlike from season to season, green to brown to white and green again. The farmers sat at the meeting with their hands on their knees; the hands looked like potatoes fresh from the earth. Some wore out-of-date suits and ties. Most wore heavy cotton work clothes. Clothes meant nothing to them. They put more value on a good pocketknife, not only for its utility but for its grace and style.

Commuters: whose homes were in Darby but whose work and play were in the city and whose family roots might be anywhere, and who, as a group, were made uneasy by a vague awareness of the divisions in their lives. Unlike the farmers, whose comportment, for good or evil, was the same regardless of the occasion, the commuters carried different standards, values, and amenities for work, family, friends, and hobbies. Commuters made fine adjustments to their psyches from hour to hour, minute to minute. This was evident in the clothes they wore. Commuters owned clothes for every occasion—clothes for work, clothes for house sitting, clothes for entertaining, clothes for going out, clothes for raking leaves, clothes for meetings, clothes for golf; above all, clothes for golf. Clothes they dared not wear on the street, clothes they might otherwise associate contemptuously with blacks, they wore at golf. Commuters never had enough clothes, as they never had enough occasions. The commuters' women begged their men for more clothes and talked endlessly among themselves about clothes. The men bragged that they always knew what they wanted when they entered the sacred vestry of the haberdashery. Commuters never had enough closet space in their houses. Clothes not being worn were to be hidden; commuters couldn't bear to hang a pair of pants in full view. They wore their best clothes to church, but they weren't sure they believed in God. Not being sure of anything was a sign of sophistication, they believed. They feared and despised avowed atheists; or, if they were extremely well educated, they feared and despised unabashed Christians. They judged others by their dress and manners. In dealings with their fellow citizens, they were often vicious, but never rude. They were sexy. They read about sex, thought about sex, and practiced sex. But, as in everything else, they were not satisfied with the sex they got. They saw nothing abnormal about their dissatisfaction. Indeed, they believed dissatisfaction was an ally to the survival of the species, an expression of humanity, perhaps the one single constant in human behavior. They believed that to be human was to march forever onward in quest of . . . something, anything. Because of this belief, they were obsessed with making their children more capable of great rather than small dissatisfactions. They accomplished this end by sending their children to a succession of schools, each farther and farther from home, until, when the children graduated from the last school, they were totally separated from the place of their upbringing and must themselves go questing. When some of their children rebelled, preferring to sit in a modified lotus position instead of marching, the parents were sad and bitter and—sometimes late at night—terrified, as though they had walked around the globe and found at the place of their beginning their own visages in a shallow grave. The commuters built their houses on the highest points of ground they could afford, and they gazed at the hills beyond through sliding glass doors. They made up a majority of the voters in the community, but only a handful showed up for town meeting. They were used to being governed at various levels.

Shack people: who lived in shacks and trailers and nice houses they had transformed into shacks out of a kind of reverse interior-decorator mentality. The shack people had no taste, meaning not bad taste but simply no taste. From the rough, complex order of the forest floor they derived spiritual sustenance and messy habits. Shack people were stunted trees. They feared and despised farmers, who they sensed were their natural bosses. But they gave little thought to commuters, whom they viewed as almost otherworldly. Shack people were rarely sad or nervous, but often angry and out of control. They married when the girls got pregnant. They filled their shacks with children and spilled them out at age sixteen. They watched television endlessly but were not much influenced by it because it too seemed otherworldly. They were obsessed with country and Western music because it evoked the emotive trinity of their souls—sentimentality, self-pity, and the death of love. A few came to town meeting to make jokes. Most didn't know what town meeting meant.

New people: who were full of vitality, bubbling with ideas, hypnotized by the beauty of the countryside, greedy for the secrets of self-knowledge, self-sufficiency. They came to town meeting to participate in self-government. They lived in handmade houses deep in the woods; they warmed themselves with wood stoves made in Scandinavian countries; they grew gardens without store-bought fertilizer; they wore dungarees, often fancily decorated; they smoked homegrown marijuana, which transformed the bluegrass music they listened to into blue butterflies; they had their babies (at least the first) from books and classes on natural childbirth; they discussed at length such subjects as wood heat, well digging, sunlight as a source of energy, and the errors of American government. They saw their lives as laboratories that would help perfect the lives of future generations. They lived like pioneers and thought of themselves as pioneers. But they were not pioneers. They were the educated and pampered children of commuters from New York, New Jersey, and Connecticut, and this venture into New Hampshire was an extension of their bountiful education, a kind of long-term Outward Bound course. Eventually, most would return home and run the family business, leaving behind dozens of strange, badly made—but often beautiful—houses and perhaps a million wild marijuana plants. Those who remained would carry on, in a way as yet unfathomed even by themselves, the tradition of town meeting.

The selectmen sat at a long folding table on the stage in the town hall. Frank Bridges worried about his wife, who was so strange and nervous these days that they had to give her pills; Arch Sawyer (Old Man Sawyer) was thinking about his will until he wasn't thinking at all; and Harold Flagg, chairman of the board of selectmen (of whom it was said, "If Fatty Flagg decides he don't like you, boy, you got troubles in this town"), drummed his plump fingers.

Harold affected a bored air, but in fact his mind was churning furiously. He watched everyone who came in, marked in his mind where he sat, tried to guess his mood, and plotted ways of gaining advantages.

Ollie Jordan came in. Harold was surprised. It was the first time he had seen any of the Jordans at a town meeting. Ollie stood in the back with his sons, the hunchback and the crazy one, and Howard Elman, who stood with his sleeves rolled up and his arms folded in front of him like the blade of a bulldozer. Harold immediately went over to the rostrum, where Victor Copley slouched, smiling to himself. He asked Copley in grave tones to make sure everyone was seated when the meeting began.

The Jordans reminded Harold of black flies. They were small and pesty, and they had a way of disrupting human activity around them. They lived in shacks that could scarcely be taxed, and all they did in those shacks was breed. God, on a summer night you could hear the shacks panting, could smell the sex from them in the damp evening air. Repulsive. The danger was, they were filling the countryside with their own kind, driving out the nice people—the farmers, the retired couples, the young marrieds with their poodles. They were accomplishing this not by conscious action but merely by being repellent. They were, therefore, a difficult enemy, because they could not be tricked or shamed or damaged psychologically. They had to be completely annihilated.

Harold's heart pounded in his chest like the gavel of a judge.

He watched for Zoe Cutter. She came in just before the meeting was scheduled to start. Harold was annoyed. Somehow he had expected her to arrive early and consult with him and seek advice from him. But she never gave him a look when she entered. A bad sign. She sat in the front row, where only the reporter from Keene sat, and old Mrs. Burr, who was hard of hearing, and Todd (Deacon) Church, who had always sat there for reasons clear only to himself. Mrs. Cutter looked at a paper in front of her, and then she closed her eyes. It came to Harold that she was memorizing lines. Finally he caught her eye and waved tinily, with his fingers only, and she smiled. A good sign.

After the meeting he would speak to her on some pretext and hold her until the hall was empty, and then he would take her onto the village green, where the kids had worn a path through the snow, and they would look at the town hall under the lights, and he would ask her to marry him.

"Fire can turn your house into hell." Harold overheard the flat (fartlike, to him) voice of fire chief Elwyn Bell talking to Mrs. Pippin, who appeared to be trying to walk around him.

"Lobbying already, hey, Elwyn?" Harold shouted from the stage so that he might be heard by those coming in. He glanced at Zoe, but her eyes were closed, and her lips were moving.

Mrs. Pippin blushed and struggled to get away. The chief didn't budge, and he continued to speak as though Harold hadn't interrupted him. Finally Mrs. Pippin excused herself impatiently. Harold was satisfied. He had inflicted a small wound on the chief in a skirmish before the major battle over the issue of the fire truck, which would come later.

Harold counted the volunteer firemen at the meeting. There were thirteen, thirteen votes against him, more than he had expected.

Once, Harold had been deputy chief and Bell a captain in Darby's volunteer fire department. When old Chief Van Orman died, the firemen had elected Bell to lead them. Harold felt betrayed. He was convinced that Bell had rigged the election. Bell was an evil man, he believed. Someday he would destroy Bell, and do the world a favor.

The chief was a large, slow-moving man who could walk calmly, almost tranquilly, into danger, but he stiffened with inner petrifaction when called upon to speak in public.

When that time came, Bell shoved his thumbs into his suspenders, as though holding his great chest from collapsing into his weak knees, and moved that Article Four, which asked the voters to appropriate forty thousand dollars for a new fire truck, be approved as written. He then asked Copley for permission to speak on the motion, turned to his audience, and said, "Fire can turn your house into hell. This pumper we're asking for is going to put this town in the twentieth century."

"And our pocketbooks in the nineteenth century," squeaked a voice from the crowd that everyone recognized as Alexander Keeler's.

Laughter. "I'll have order here," bellowed Copley, rapping the rostrum with his fist. More laughter. Copley's friends knew his wife had given him a wooden gavel at Christmas so that he wouldn't return from the meeting with bruised knuckles as usual. His friends had bet that Vic would forget the gavel, and he had.

The chief was oblivious of everything around him. He talked right through the laughter and Copley's call for order.

"... It's like at Christmastime when Mrs. Chapman's barn burned and the pumper we got, which is twenty-odd years old, broke down on account of it's twenty-odd years old, and fire worked into the house and burnt it to the footings before they got a pumper here from Keene, and if we get this pumper we're asking for, I guarantee one hundred percent we could have saved that house, though of course we'd of let the barn go because it weren't much good to begin with, it being without a good roof to start with, and course that cost the town money, not to say Mrs. Chapman, because every time we call in another town and extra equipment that ain't under the fire-mutual-aid contract, and when a house burns to the footings because your pumper don't work because it's twenty-odd years old, it ain't, and it costs, let's see, ah, ah, Melba?" (He turned to his wife.) "You got that slip of paper?" (Melba didn't.)

The audience was mumbling. The chief was boring them, and even those who knew what he was going to say had a hard time following him. Harold scowled. But actually he was happy. The chief might yet beat himself on this issue.

The chief, who now looked and sounded like a man rehearsing a talk before a mirror, produced an envelope from the pocket under his suspenders and waved it at the audience before putting it back. Then he seemed to have forgotten what he had just done, because he failed to explain what was in the envelope.

"I went up there to Concord just yesterday and talked to a Mr. Martin and he says to me we got a good chance in this town to do you people some good . . ." the chief droned on.

The audience grew edgy. Harold could see what was happening. The chief was trying to build dramatically toward his main point, which was that if the town bought a new fire truck, fire-insurance rates for homeowners would drop. The audience was both way ahead of him and way behind him. Most of them already knew about the break on fire insurance, and most figured that that was what the chief was leading up to, but since he wasn't saying it, they began to think that maybe they had been wrong about the fire insurance, and so the result of the chief's buildup was to lead his audience away from where he thought he was bringing them. When the chief finally detonated his rhetorical bomb, the crowd was stunned with confusion. The chief, now completely out of synchronization with his audience, believed in his own mind that he had made his point with vigor, and, not wanting to belabor it, went on to belabor something else—a repetition of the story of Mrs. Chapman's barn. And then he sat down, triumphant, he thought.

Harold knew that the clever thing to do was nothing, since the chief had already defeated his own case. But Harold couldn't resist rubbing it in.

"Mr. Moderator," he said, "I think now maybe the people can understand why the selectmen cannot support Mr. Bell's efforts to buy a new toy at the taxpayers' expense."

Melba leaped from her seat, blurting something loud but unintelligible. Copley pounded the rostrum with his fist. "I'll have order here."

The chief, as if deaf, remained expressionless, neither intimidated by Harold's sarcasm nor moved by his wife's defense of him.

And therein lay the chief's great sin, in Harold's view. The chief was obtuse, and because he was obtuse, he was unreachable. Harold couldn't bear to see intelligence at work that was unaware of its own machinery. It made him think that God had created man not knowing what man was, that man was part of a cosmic "incident," already abandoned by his Creator. Sometimes Harold dreamed that he had died, and that without flesh, sight, hearing, or taste, he remained aware, full of knowledge. The dream gave him the creeps; it made him hungry. He could feel the power of the chief now coming toward him, insensate and formidable as a glacier.

Someone asked the chief a question. Harold could see his error clearly; his sarcasm had snapped the audience's attention to the issue. Slowly but inexorably, the questioning allowed the chief to present his case so that it could be understood. Eventually it became clear to nearly everyone in the hall that the town needed a new fire truck, and that by buying a new truck, homeowners would reap an insurance benefit. Harold could see that he would only make himself look bad by opposing the new truck. So he took a different tack. He said the selectmen hadn't been briefed by the chief on details about the truck and the fire insurance (a half truth). He asked the voters to table the request for the truck until the selectmen had had time to study the proposal. He suggested that the selectmen might be able to get the town a better bargain for a truck than the fire chief could and indicated that the fire-truck issue could well be settled at a special town meeting later in the spring. (In fact, Harold knew that the issue could not legally be acted upon at a special town meeting without authorization from the superior court.) Harold then amended the chief's motion and asked that a vote on the fire truck be postponed. The amendment failed by one vote.

Within a few minutes, about half of the volunteer firemen had slipped quietly out of the hall. They had voted on the only issue that interested them, and now they were going home to watch television.

Harold was the first one to speak on the next article, asking the people to accept certain federal revenue-sharing funds.

"This is a routine question, which you've answered in the affirmative for the last five years," said Harold, his voice blasé now. "We're urging you to say yes again to Uncle Sam. If you vote this down, they'll give the money to somebody else—it's as simple as that."

The moment Harold sat down, Russell Pegasus was on his feet, shouting in a thin, aged voice. "This town was on its own for two hundred years," Pegasus said. "Now this town is a prisoner of the federal buck. In ten years it will be dead from all that money. You won't recognize it, and your children won't remember it." The voters nodded with sympathy, as though mourning an old friend, and then they voted unanimously to accept the federal funds.

Harold wondered whether Zoe Cutter had caught on to what this was all about, whether she had figured out that the town-meeting form of government was nearly impotent, that it was democracy without real power, that most voters did not even come to town meeting, that the ones who came did so out of nostalgia or because—like herself—they had a special interest or because they were new in town and curious.

She had changed her clothes since this afternoon. She was wearing a Scotch-plaid suit over tights. She had her boots on. He was sad. He lusted to see her feet. Apparently she had walked to the meeting. All the new people—even the infirm ones, it seemed—liked to take walks. It didn't make sense to him. You walked when you had someplace to go where a vehicle wouldn't take you—to the refrigerator, for example. Walking for the sake of walking struck him as wasteful, perhaps even unhealthy. The oddest kind of walking, to Harold, was hiking with a pack on the back. This was not mere eccentricity; it was madness. He didn't like it. And then in a flash of insight he knew why hikers hiked. They felt guilty, and hiking was a form of penance. Hikers were liberals. He was relieved now that the thing was clear in his mind. He decided that once he and Zoe Cutter were married, he would break her of walking, for her own good.

Harold Flagg was well on his way to taking care of his problem with Ollie Jordan, and he no longer needed the junk-car ordinance as a lever against him. However, to show Zoe his clout on the board, he had seen to it that the selectmen recommended it. On the one hand, he was philosophically opposed to a law regulating—in effect—taste. On the other hand, he could see how the law might help bring desirable people into town and discourage undesirable ones. But on the whole, the ordinance struck him as trivial. It probably couldn't be enforced; it served no real purpose; it might even be illegal. He was curious to see how the debate would go. Should Ollie Jordan speak, Harold might be able to embarrass him. The prospect pleased him.

Harold wondered why Elman didn't sell out. Did the land have some value Harold didn't know about? Or was Elman just being stubborn? At any rate, there was no doubt in Harold's mind that eventually Elman would have to sell. He didn't have a job; and if Arlene was right—and she usually was—he didn't have any insurance to pay for his wife's medical bills. If Elman had any sense—which he might not have, which would answer a lot of questions—then he should sell to Zoe, because obviously she was willing to pay the best price. It was harsh but just that the land should pass from the likes of Howard Elman to the likes of Zoe Cutter: Elman had lucked into the place to begin with, and he had failed to improve it, and it had failed to improve him. A man should live in a house that fits his means, his personality, his status, his intelligence. In Elman's case the property exceeded the man.

"This article is by petition," said Copley. "If you pass this, you're saying that a man has to screen his junk cars from the road. You all understand that? I'll give the nays a crack at this in a minute, but first I'll recognize Mrs. Zoe Cutter, who has asked to speak on this article as one of the petitioners."

Zoe walked to the rostrum, dignified and confident.

"Thank you, Mr. Moderator," she said. "I hope you'll forgive me—a newcomer among you—for presuming to tell you what I think is right for this town. But tell you I shall." Harold was surprised by her ease and the strength of her voice, her ability to command. Then he remembered that she had been an actress; the idea that her authority might be an act made her self-assurance sit better with him. "For better or for worse, the people of Darby are changing," she said. "As many of you have told me, often with sadness in your voices, your children are moving on after they grow up. Meanwhile, the children of other concerned parents in other places are moving in. The question all of us must ask ourselves is, Must Darby change? I think the answer is a qualified no. All of us, whether our families have lived here for generations or whether we've been here ten minutes, know what Darby is: a massage for the eye and soul. People will change, styles will change, values will change, parts of the town will change; but what must not change is that first impression as you pull off the highway and drive in amidst the fields, into town, past the birches"—which birches? Harold wondered—"past the meeting house, down the valley road and along the brook, and into the deep woods. It's a scene that will forever change and forever be the same if only we preserve its essence through some small effort. I therefore urge you to vote for this article. Thank you."

A dozen persons were on their feet cheering. Mrs. Cutter, her face expressionless, returned to her seat.

"I like that," said a voice from the audience.

"I'll have order here," said Copley.

Howard Elman was on his feet shouting something.

"I'll have order here," repeated Copley, and Elman, as though he had just understood something, was suddenly speechless, although he remained standing.

Then he began to move. He walked to the front of the hall, turned to Copley, and turned again to the audience. He raised his hands. Christ on the cross. But he seemed struck as dumb as Jordan's hunchback. He flailed with his arms. The crowd became very still.

"Mr. Elman, you wish to speak?" Copley asked, but Elman ignored him.

He moved. Something animallike in the circle he made to

reach Zoe, Harold thought. The man walked clear around the back of the hall, as if he were leaving, and then came up the side and veered suddenly, as if about to make a kill, until he was standing in front of Zoe. She stared straight ahead. Her mouth was set. There were monstrous lines—stabbings—around her eyes. Harold shook his head to make this image go away. Howard began to raise his hands slowly, as though lifting something heavy. The silence was appalling, embarrassing. Harold looked to Copley, but, like everyone else, the moderator seemed temporarily fixed in space. Harold was on his feet now. He sensed danger; somehow he knew Elman was about to strangle Zoe. Then there was a terrible gasp. A tingling ran up Harold's spine. He felt too much alive. And then relief. The gasp came from the back of the hall. It was Willow Jordan. Harold watched Ollie's hand go up and come down, strangely without sound, it seemed, on his son's face.

"Is it possible that we can have order here?" The voice of Copley, sardonic, in command now. "Mr. Elman, if you wish to speak, speak now, and then sit. I can't have people browsing up and down the aisles. This is not a department store."

Harold relaxed. He could see that whatever had come over Howard Elman had passed. Elman was now merely confused. He shook his head, coughed on a word, gestured to no purpose, and finally moved off.

It turned out that a fatuous argument put forth by Russell Pegasus ruined any chance for the ordinance—at least for this year.

"We never had anything like this before," he said. "Why do we need it now? Might as well pass a law that says no pigs allowed in church."

The junk-car ordinance was defeated by voice vote. Only the new people favored it.

Harold had all but forgotten the incident when the meeting ended an hour later. He was pleased with himself. He had got his way more than he had not. His ardor returned. Zoe was heading for the door. He moved to head her off, taking a short-cut by going down the stage stairs in the back, knowing that if he hurried he would reach the exit before she got there. The door to the outside was open, and he breathed cold air, coughed, and waved as she came toward him. "Ah, Zoe . . ." he said. But she walked by him without a glance, her face still sharp with anger over her defeat. And then he was alone—or felt alone. He was so familiar to the people emptying out of the hall that they acknowledged him no more than they acknowledged the Corinthian pillars on the building. Vic Copley walked past him. He remembered now that Copley had not asked those in the back to sit. Copley was cunning. He played the impartial moderator, but in fact he was, it struck Harold at this moment, a political puppeteer. Copley was an evil man. The cold chilled Harold, and he hugged himself. This was a bad time of year to propose marriage, a bad time of year, period. Better wait until spring to pop the question, or at least for a sign of spring.

"I'll have order here."

Harold whirled around, expecting to see Vic Copley. But it was only Jordan's idiot son, Willow.

14 : REASON

Howard lay in bed, a bottle of beer in his hand, his heavy white body surrounded by pillows, substitutes for his wife. He tried to think about the meeting with Reason tomorrow and what he would say, but he couldn't. He had agreed over the phone to discuss the sale of his house. He saw himself standing at the top of the stairs, Elenore tumbling before him. But she hadn't fallen down the stairs; she had no broken bones or bruises, the doctors had said. Still, he could see her, tumbling like a child's toy, something she was wearing tinkling musically. He saw himself sitting at a table with Freddy, a young duplicate of himself, and then the room enormous and empty. He saw Reason at the other end of the phone line, pacing with great effort as though he were dragging a steel ball ("Our latest offer, Howie, and final offer, I might add, is forty-three thousand dollars—more bucks than you ever saw in your life") and then Reason stopping, taken aback, disappointed by his suggestion they meet, as though denied the pleasure of setting the meeting himself. Howard took a last drink of beer and put the bottle on the end table. He huddled among the pillows like a giant baby. In his old age he would be an artist, painting the color of beer in an amber bottle against sunlight. Odd thought. Alcoholic thought. He could see the bottle getting brighter. He fell asleep and was soon dreaming.

That night he dreamed about the shop. It had been painted white, and it was full of women stacking web and chanting mournfully, as though they had lost sons in a war: "The sea is ultra blue, and the birds are the eyes of the government."

He awakened at his usual time, alert and strangely elated, with no memory of the dream. In its place was a strong desire to go to the shop where he had worked for so many years. For a brief time his thoughts took on a gilded quality. *Once there was a tank named for a whore. Her name was Pasha, and she was dark and hard and she churned up the grit of the desert, and the sun turned it to golden dust; she was dark and soft, and the sun turned her smell to perfume.*

"I'm sick; I'm going to puke; I don't want to go to school," Heather whined.

"You ain't sick, and you ain't going to puke, and you are going to school." He chased her out of the bedroom down the stairs into the bathroom, where she slammed the door and slid the bolt. He could hear her giggling. She would obey.

"Poor little girl," he mocked her.

She opened the door, stuck out her tongue, and went off to the kitchen.

Before washing, he paused at the bathroom mirror to look at his ugly face. He brushed his teeth, spitting mightily into the sink. He pissed loudly into the bowl. In the shower he sang, "Day-yo, day-yo, daylight come and me want to go home. Day, hey, hey, yooooo." He felt like a man going to work, and he surrendered to the feeling, knowing it was false. He would drive to the shop this morning just to look around. At breakfast Heather tested him again: "My belly don't feel good."

He looked at her with exaggerated sympathy. "Got to go to

school, got to get your education so you can be smart like your big brother," he said, wounding himself slightly with his own words.

Heather ate a hearty breakfast. She pouted, but inwardly was secure, he knew. He was exerting more authority, expending more enthusiasm than he really felt. He thought of an engine that revs with unaccustomed vigor just before it runs out of gas.

Moving now. Smells in the pickup truck a balm. The sun rising over the black, cauldron-shaped hill known as Abare's Folly. Another crazy Frenchman. Fuck you, Abare, whoever you are, whatever your folly, he thought. Days lengthening. Around him aches of an old season: the black asphalt stained white with wavelets of road salt; snowbanks waning and ugly, like old people nursing ancient grudges; in the woods, the snow still deep and covered with a hard crust that was filthy with debris from the forest. Bad time for deer; what was once a comfort was now a trap. Up yours, Abare.

The parking lot at the shop was empty, save for an aged bucket-of-bolts Pontiac with scarred bumpers. Howard parked the pickup truck in the space once reserved for Mr. Lodge. He imagined the infirm old man, tubes in his nose, penis in a bottle. Howard headed for the employee entrance, then turned abruptly toward the front door. The brass nameplate that had adorned the entrance was gone. He could feel himself at once gloating and grieving for the old man. The door was unlocked, and he entered. The holder for the punch cards was still on the wall, the cards gone. The names under the slots struck him like a sweep of rain—Filbin, Hapgood, Croteau, Patterson, Talbot, Stillings, Carsons, Pratt, Elman. The lunchroom in the shop was bare, desolate, and—somehow—final. He crossed to the "great room," as it seemed to him now, where once the mechanical looms, with a tremendous din, made pretty strips of fabric whose end the weavers never learned. The looms were gone. In their place were wooden crates marked with a word he did not recognize. Some company was using the shop for a warehouse. The imprints of the looms remained on the concrete floor like shadows. He touched the metal plates embedded in the concrete to which the machines had been bolted. They were cold. Invisible coils of cold air slithered along the floor. He went to a steel post in a corner and reached in back of it to a nook caused by a bad weld and found a pack of Camel cigarettes. He had put it there two years ago as a spare, because the company for reasons he never clearly understood—something to do with health—had removed the cigarette machine, temporarily, it turned out. He lit one of the cigarettes. It was hot, dry, intoxicating, complex—even exquisite—in its taste. For a moment he was lost in ecstasy.

At this point he sensed a presence behind him. He turned, deliberately, as though aiming a pistol, and saw a man watching him—a warehouseman, he judged, who was trying to decide what the hell to do about a stranger in the midst of his work. The man looked at him in the tired, cautious way that Quinn used to look at his looms at the end of a night shift. In the early days at the shop, when Howard was a weaver, he and Quinn shared the same looms on different shifts. One week Howard worked days and Quinn nights; the next week they switched. They did that for twelve years. They called each other "partner." The one day Quinn didn't show up for work was the day he died, of a stroke in his sleep. He lay in his living room in a casket, his hands holding rosary beads across his chest, while his widow sat and hiccupped tears by the window. Quinn had long, hard, smooth fingernails, tools of the weaver. The important thing about piecework, Quinn would say, was to work steady but not to hurry. Guys who hurried were guys who worried about bills, about children in the hospital, about gambling debts, about health, about wives who demanded more than their men could give—and eventually they would be carried out with mangled hands while the shuttles in their looms slammed on. All the time Quinn lectured, Howard would be thinking smugly, "I hurry."

He loved the shop in those days. He loved the machines as

one loves a dangerous opponent whom nonetheless one can beat consistently. He worked fast, without letup, without guards on the gears of his machines (until they made him cover them); he tempted the looms to hurt him. He challenged them. In all the years he was a weaver, he never received a scratch. It was well known that he was the best—which is to say, fastest and richest—weaver in the shop. Except for Charley Kruger, of course. Occasionally, when he would feel his power over the looms, he would look up at the beautiful steel trusses holding up the shop roof, and he would listen to the thousands of sounds, all loud and full of ugliness because they made no sense, and he would listen for his own looms, and he would listen for the shuttles slamming through the warps, and he would listen to a particular shuttle—bang, bang, bang, bang, bang—until the shiver of victory ran along his spine.

Howard folded his arms in a kind of slow-motion movement, an act of intimidation that froze the warehouseman into an attitude of indecision. It was a technique that Howard had mastered long before he was conscious of using it. It was a technique of a shop foreman. He first began to hate the job, he realized now, when they promoted him to floor supervisor. The job brought no reward to the hands. It taxed his patience; it set him apart from his fellow workers until he saw them for what they were, stupid and frail; it made him cunning, deceptive; it made him a prick. He would be remembered by most as Howard the foreman, Howard the prick, Howard of the endless prick, from head to toe, from shout to fart, stalking, rampant, mindless, loveless, ever-erect, ever-restless, ever-routing prick, prick without pleasure, prick for the sake of prickness, prickness his pride. Here lies Howard Elman, prick. He would stand before some poor web boy, as he stood now facing the warehouseman, arms folded to accentuate his prickness, and he would be thinking, as he was thinking now, Where does the web come from, and where does it go? Parachute straps? Corsets? Ribbons for the hair of a million pretty women? He never knew. *Goddamn you, William, goddamn you, William, smarten up, goddamn you, goddamn you,*

goddamn you, Freddy, goddamn your goddamn education, goddamn,
goddamn, goddamn, goddamn all of you.

He was walking toward the warehouseman, arms still folded, goose-stepping like some Nazi maniac. He recognized the man's face now, a face he'd seen a hundred times on the street but never spoken to, never missed. The man was quivering, his fists clenched at his sides. Howard felt very much in command. It was still his shop; he was still foreman. The man sensed his authority, feared it.

Just as he was upon the man, Howard said, "Kinda stingy with the heat here, ain't they?" And the man's tension fell away, and he smiled as Howard walked past him out of the building.

He stopped at Dunkin' Donuts for a cup of coffee. A truck driver sat at the counter with his head cradled in his arms, dead asleep. A worn woman wearing a snowmobile suit slapped the face of a child who also wore a snowmobile suit. "That kid has the worst fucking mouth on him," she screamed righteously to the waitress, who—pretty blonde in a pink uniform—smiled and seemed to close in on herself, like a rose touched by frost. Female creatures owned the world, Howard thought. The earth itself was female. The shop was female. The females knew everything of beauty and desolation—he imagined an old maid listening to the sound of distant mirth—and the males had what was in between, violence and lust. Down South somewhere was a duplicate of the shop: looms, dye vats, smelly urinals, weavers in white t-shirts, a Howard Elman foreman telling a web boy to wash his hands and smarten up. "Water," he cried, and the waitress brought him some in a glass full of crushed ice. Her fingers glittered with rings, the nails bitten but pink. Great, strong Howard felt like her old-maid aunt, and he wanted to buy her something nice, a trip to Europe or something. The looms sang, *work-for-pay, work-for-pay, work-for-pay,* a mother's lullaby. He tried to think about what he would do after he had sold his house and land, but there was nothing to think about. He heard the looms singing and squabbling.

Then Howard's mind went blank. When he returned to awareness, fifteen minutes had passed and his coffee cup was empty and he was filled with rage and his belly was full of demons and he wanted to puke. "Your Daddy is going to get you good," the woman in the snowmobile suit said to her child. Howard turned on the pink stool, shouting at the woman, "Why don't you shut up?" The boy began to giggle, then laugh loudly and insanely, as only a confused child can; and the woman, as though judging it would be prudent to ignore the challenge of the man shouting at her, turned what should have been her wrath for Howard onto the boy and smacked him in the face. The blow was aimed for the boy's cheek, but he twisted his head at the last moment, and the butt of her palm caught him in the nose. Blood blew into the woman's face. In an instant the boy's hysterical laughter was transformed into hysterical weeping. "Stupid!" Howard heard himself shout. He made for the door and accidentally bumped the arm of the dozing truck driver, who was jarred into voicing a name from his dream—"Marda, Marda"—although he did not awaken. Just before Howard left, he caught a complete picture of the waitress, a floral display of pink uniform and blond hair quaking with fear. Howard turned to her, but she stepped backward, whispering, "I'll call the police." "Jesus, Jesus H. Christ!" Howard stormed out, the words "Marda, Marda" his last impression as he drove off.

That night:
Click! The sunlamp died. Zoe Cutter lay there for a few minutes until the heat left her and she began to feel cool. She opened her eyes, slowly, so as not to be inundated with light, arose, and stood in the middle of the room to feel the air against her nakedness. She wrapped herself in her robe, shut off the room light, opened the drapes in front of the new picture window, and settled into her easy chair with a finger of sherry to look at the night view, Cleopatra in her tomb, cool, dry, mummified, aware—somehow—of everything. Clouds moved across

the face of the moon as if rushing to keep an appointment. Below, the Elman house—an eyesore in daylight—was pretty. Warm yellow light poured from its windows. In the snow-covered field the junk cars were glittering humps, jovial things. The stars were dim behind the blue-white haze of the moon, and the hills in the distance, the hills, the hills were calling her, for she realized that beauty—beauty that was here when she arrived and would be here when she left, plus the beauty she had brought and built with her wealth and taste—beauty was not enough. Zoe Cutter was lonely.

Where was Edward? She was angry with him for dying. Where was Ronald? She was angry at him for not calling. Evidently he was working again, and—evidently—he was shacking up with some swishy dancer. She missed his gossip, missed somebody to bitch at. She wouldn't hear from him until he needed money. Where was Kinky Afghan? Staying out all night, refusing to follow commands, resting all day by the fire—the dog was becoming less and less hers and more and more the countryside's. Where was Harold? Fat, pompous fool, he had some sort of designs on her, but she couldn't be angry at him, because she couldn't take him seriously. Indeed, she couldn't believe that either of the Flaggs had a libido. They were like plants, capable of reproduction but without pleasure. But, come to me, she thought. Speak to me, storekeeper. Fill the room with your flesh, for flesh is what this room needs tonight. Where was Frederick, her handyman? So serious. So boy-man. Dear Frederick.

She remembered now that this was the night when Reason met with Elman. If Elman turned down her final offer, forty-five thousand dollars, she would take him to court for the piece of land between them. It would be best for all concerned that the family move to Keene, she was certain. Getting Elman off that land was doing him a favor. She couldn't imagine him turning down her offer. It was a darned generous offer. Darned generous. She became so convinced of her generosity that she called her lawyer in Keene and told him to be at Reason's office in the morning for the signing.

It was at this point that she heard what sounded like someone at the door. The idea of a visitor brightened her spirits, and she hurried downstairs. Light from the doorway brushed the stone steps. They were bare. There was no one around. On the barn lay moonlight like a cool benediction. Sounds in the air, sounds of a storm. Yet the maple tree in her yard was as still as a city building. Sway, you bastard, sway, she thought. A shift in the sounds, signifying intelligence. Clouds rushing across the moon in retreat. Clouds howling. Sounds falling out of the sky into the valley below and moving up the hill toward her, as if carried by an unfelt wind. She thought of something she had read: Great sailing ships in space, impelled by light from the sun, would someday carry humans to the borders of the solar system. In a few minutes the sounds—she knew now they were from dogs in the throes of private canine rites; she knew nothing more— moved through her and up the hill to the peak and faded until the only sound was the faint rush of the interstate highway ten miles away. Unaccountably, she was charged with sexual excitement.

Howard Elman went to put on the porch light in anticipation of Reason's arrival, and that's when he heard them—dogs running deer. They were sweeping up the hill, maybe a dozen of them—pets gone wild for the night—spread out over a quarter of a mile. He heard the shift in the sounds, which meant that they had picked up a trail and were coming together to run the deer down. The fight between dog and deer was an old one, designed within the malicious order of things to weed out the weak and preserve the strong among both dog and deer. But men had made the fight unfair by giving the dog the advantage. The dog was well fed, rested, alert; the deer half starved, tired, worn down by winter. Furthermore, the dog, living with men for so long, had become like men: It hunted for sport. March was the time of the dog. The snow was deep but had a hard crust on which the dog could run swiftly and tirelessly, whereas the deer foundered, sharp hoofs plunging through it. Howard fetched the .308 and stood with it on the porch, prepared to shoot dogs. The dogs would run the deer, perhaps for miles, until it was exhausted, and then they would kill it by tearing it to pieces. He felt it was his duty to kill the dogs, and it gave him some guilt that the duty might bring him pleasure. He saw no dogs. The hill, blue and white from the moon, was like a great ocean swell. He stood there listening as one listens to some terrifying but brilliant atonal symphony, as one listens to a storm at sea.

Reason arrived at eight P.M., half an hour late for his appointment. He handed Howard a red parka. He was wearing a red blazer, and his cheeks glowed like burning coals. He made some chatter about the weather, saying he was one of those people whose blood hurt in the cold. Howard stood mutely before him.

"I'll tell you, Howie," he said, as if talking to an old friend, "someday this whole area is going to be a playground for the rich. They'll live up on the hill, and people like you and me, good hardworking people, will be living in the valleys in shacks and trailers. The time to get out is now, Howie, while you can get top dollar."

Howard found himself falling under a spell. The man made a great deal of sense. The time to get out was *now*.

"Look, I know this isn't pleasant for you, Howie," Reason said, as the two men seated themselves at the kitchen table. "And I want you to know that I sympathize with you. I'm just doing my job."

Reason now produced some papers from under his blazer.

"Howie, this is a survey of your land and Mrs. Cutter's land," he said. "Take a gander at it."

"Um," said Howard, seeing nothing but confusing lines.

"You'll note this line here representing the stone wall," Reason said. "It's the boundary line between the two properties, ain't it?"

Howard nodded. The lines were making sense now.

Reason smiled. "No it ain't, Howie," he said. "According to a search of the deed—look up here at this line—there's another wall. Maybe you've seen the tail end of it up on the hill in the woods. Here." He pointed at the line. Howard nodded vigorously. Sure he had seen the wall. It went nowhere. It seemed to him that he and the real-estate man shared some important information. He felt a weird kind of affection for the man, something he couldn't explain.

"Well, that wall," said Reason, pausing for a moment to force a laugh, "that wall once continued down to where this dotted line is, and it is the true boundary marker between the two properties."

"Wha—?" said Howard.

"It means, Howie, you ain't worth what you thought you were worth," Reason said. "It means your fifty-odd acres are only seventeen-odd acres."

The man seemed genuinely distraught to have brought the news. Howard wanted to say something comforting, like "There, there. . . ."

But it was Reason who offered the comfort. "I didn't come here to make you poor, Howie," he said. "I came here to make you rich. Mrs. Cutter is a very impatient woman, and she doesn't want to spend a lot of time in court. She'd just as soon settle up. Howie, we're willing to offer you forty-five thousand dollars for this property. It's a darned generous offer."

"It's my home," said Howard. He was groping for expression.

"Look at it this way," said Reason. "It's her stubborn pride that's driving her to offer you more than this place is worth. It's your pride that's holding you back from saving yourself. The difference is, she can afford her pride; you can't. Swallow it, Howie, before it chokes you."

Howard signed a sale agreement.

"All this says is that with our fifty-dollar deposit, you promise to sell to Mrs. Cutter," said Reason. "The real show comes tomorrow at the signing. Nine A.M. at my office okay with you? Can't miss it. It's the only red house on Court Street."

"Um," said Howard.

"Congratulations, Howie, you old horse trader," said Reason, and put out his hand.

Howard got up from his chair, determined to avoid a handshake.

Reason, too, stood, smiled, still holding out his hand.

Howard thought about the dogs outside running deer on the ridge. Anger surged through him.

"It ain't fair," he said, meaning the drama on the ridge.

"It's fair," said Reason, meaning the proposal.

The situation had turned suddenly menacing to Howard. He noticed that Reason had never stopped smiling.

The handshake came unexpectedly. Reason turned as if to leave and then whipped around, stepped toward Howard, and grabbed his hand. Reason's hand was cold, damp, sluglike. By contrast, a kind of tortured heat seemed to radiate from his red face, as though the skin had been stripped from it. Howard shut his eyes—or it seemed to him later he shut his eyes; he couldn't be sure—and the head glowed and pulsated in the darkness of his mind, growing smaller and brighter until it was a button of fire. As unexpectedly as he had grabbed his hand, Reason released it and backed hurriedly toward the door, saying, "See you in the morning, nine A.M.," repeating, as though to disorient Howard, "in the morning, nine A.M. . . . in the morning, nine A.M. . . ." and was gone.

15 : ROAD MEAT

Howard Elman did not sleep all that night. The button of fire,
like some malevolent Holy Ghost, set him to thinking. He
thought about the point of flame a rifle makes when it is fired,
and he thought about the point of flame a propane torch makes.
He went to the barn and hunted up his torch and some scrap
metal. After almost three hours of work, he had fashioned elegant metal brackets with the point of flame from the torch. He
mounted the brackets in the rear of the cab of the pickup and
then took a moment to admire his handiwork. The brackets reminded him of the cupped hands of African beggars. In the
hands he placed the .308. "See you in the morning, nine A.M.,"
he said to no one.

While he was making the brackets, he was not thinking that
he would kill Mrs. Cutter and Reason. Indeed, it was not even
clear in his mind what he was making until he was halfway
through the process, and then it struck him that he was making
an altar for his weapon. At the same time he realized that he was
going to murder Reason and the woman at their appointment
in the morning. He wished somehow that he could arm

them, make a fight of it. But that was not possible. They fought with words, with law, with psychology, not with guns or knives or fists or anything else he understood. They were part of a vast, evil, nameless, incomprehensible conspiracy to reduce him to dust. They had cut off his finger, taken away his livelihood, stolen the affections of his son, crippled his wife, and they were on the way to stealing his property. It was time to put an end to it. "I needed relief," he would tell the judge, for he certainly expected to be caught—until it occurred to him that the .308 had probably been stolen to begin with and could not be traced to him. He might get away with the killings after all. He thought about fingerprints and alibis; he considered staging a fake robbery to mask his motive. But he could not go far with these thoughts. Eventually they sickened him. He would simply shoot Reason and Mrs. Cutter dead and drive away in broad daylight. It didn't bother him that he planned to deprive two human beings of their lives, because he had ceased to think of Mrs. Cutter and Reason as human. The woman was a high-ranking official in the government of hell, and Reason was her agent, a mere demon.

It was now two A.M. The moon was down and the wind had died. The clouds were gone. It was going to be cold in the morning. The sky was brilliant with stars, and he watched them until it seemed to him the earth under his feet moved slightly just for a moment. It was as if instead of looking up he were on the deck of a troopship looking down at the sea, alive at night with glowing things. The porch light was on at Mrs. Cutter's house up the hill. Inside, it was dark. She had been waiting for someone, he supposed, who had not come; she had forgotten about the light; or maybe she just didn't give much thought to details like electric bills. The woman slept, as generals and congressmen and bankers and gods and devils slept, in security if not peace.

He slid the barn door shut. *Locking the barn door after the pony's out.* The phrase appeared in his head. He didn't know why it came to him, and he did not consider it. It was just there, like a piece of food stuck in the throat. He returned to the house and opened a beer. Then he went upstairs to Heather's room, walking slowly toward her until he could hear her breathing. The cat jumped silently from the bed and fled from him. He paused, sipping his beer, listening. It dawned on him that he didn't hear as well as he used to. Once, he heard birds and crickets, like choruses, in the summer, and the wind brushing the dry grasses of fall, and the harsher wind of winter clacking in the trees. All had become hushed these last few years. He sat on Heather's bed, lightly squeezed her foot, bent to it, and touched it to his lips. Then he went downstairs and sat at the kitchen table, drinking his beer and smoking in the dark. He waited for apparitions of Reason to torment him, but they didn't come. I'm not insane—not completely, anyway, he thought. He dozed with his head on the table until the morning light fell upon his face.

Curiously, he felt no fatigue. His body was greased with something from his uneasy sleep. He washed. He made some toast but discovered that he couldn't eat. Food sickened him. Heather came downstairs. He asked her whether she wanted to skip school. She sensed false cheer in his voice and fell silent. He called Charlene and told her he was dropping Heather off for the day. Normally Charlene would have questioned such a request (God, the girl questioned everything and learned nothing), but something in his tone—even Howard heard it as he was speaking—made her an obedient child. They left for Keene in the pickup, and when Heather saw the gun in the rack, she burst into tears.

"Why are you crying?" he asked.

"I don't know," she replied.

"Sing," he commanded.

Heather sang. She was still singing—and crying—when he let her off at Charlene's. It passed through his mind that he would never see her again. Ridiculous, he told himself. Of course he would see her again.

From a phone booth he tried to call Elenore at the hospital in Hanover, but the thing in his voice that had humbled—no, terrorized—his daughters succeeded only in confusing the lines at long distance. He didn't get through.

It was eight-thirty, half an hour before his appointment, when Howard reached Reason's office-home, a huge wooden frame house with a slate roof, pillars, and turrets, and clapboards painted the same red as Reason's sport coat. Inside, there would be the smell of old varnish, Howard guessed; there would be bent light coming in from curved windows; there would be the well-worked oak of long-dead carpenters. He parked across the street. The woman would come out of the west in her forest-green Mercedes. She would park it in the lot that Reason had blacktopped in the yard, in the embrace of an enormous elm that was only one-twentieth alive. She would be wearing a winter coat, fur perhaps, because although there was a hint of a thaw in the air—the morning wind had shifted from the northwest to the southwest—it was still cold. Businesslike, she would stride to the porch door, and here she would pause to push the doorbell, and here he would shoot her. Reason would open the door and bend toward the body on his step, and Howard would shoot him in the head. All shots would be to the head. Images of the deed marched through his mind with autumnal brilliance.

His mouth filled with vomit. He opened the truck door and threw up. He detected the faint smell of stale beer and vomited again. He laid the rifle on his lap and listened to the radio.

Eventually the police would find him and kill him. All right. Here lies Howard Elman: date of birth unknown, date of death marked for the ages in the newspaper. There was no malice in his heart. His heart was pure. He murdered for relief. (It seemed to him then that his mind was thinking in the voice of Mr.—no, Congressman—Lodge.) He leaves a loving wife, Elenore Appleton, who is a living saint and will pray for his soul; four daughters—Charlene, who will use him as a bad example to train her children; Pegeen, whose troubles are so great that his death will scarcely add to them; Sherry Ann, whom he hopes to meet again in hell; Heather (a blank: he could not bear to think about Heather); one son, Frederick—don't you dare call him Freddy—who has cast off the father of his blood and taken a new father, Higher Education. Let the women in his life dab their eyes with dainty handkerchieves; let his son wonder about him; let the rest read a line about him—lo, be it a shameful one—in the books. Had he his life to live again, he would live it the same way, because of his ignorance and pridefulness. . . .

And so Howard eased with fantasy into the temporary tranquillity of self-pity.

The sun was full upon the Reason house now. The red clapboards seemed to pulsate as if from intense heat inside.

At ten minutes to nine, a small, dark man with a briefcase and a fur-collared overcoat entered Reason's office. Nine o'clock came. Nine-thirty. Howard began to get suspicious. They had found him out. They were waiting for him to make a move. They were going to ambush him. The small, dark man carried guns. Howard was prepared to shoot it out. He steeled himself, even shutting off the radio in the truck. Quarter to ten. And then . . . and then, it dawned upon him.

The woman had stood him up!

Howard replaced the .308 on the gun rack and drove off in a huff. It would not be until later that day that he would figure out the truth of the situation. The small, dark man was a lawyer, hired by Mrs. Cutter to close the deal with Howard, and empowered to sign papers. Mrs. Cutter, like Howard, did not trust Reason.

Howard's feeling of normality, that is, of actually recognizing the emotions within him—disappointment, betrayal, and a certain detached sense of self-mockery at it all—was brief. He drove downtown to Lindy's Diner, parking a short distance away in front of Tilden's, leaving the engine running, like a bank robber. He tried to drink a cup of coffee but discovered his stomach was still crawling with demons. He stood on the street corner for a full five minutes, and then went into the newsstand and bought a candy bar, startling the clerk with that tone in his voice. He would have to go back to Reason's and perform some act, any act. It didn't matter about the woman. It didn't matter about Reason. What mattered was that he got relief. He was afraid if the thing in him kept building up, he would do violence to the nearest stranger. He unwrapped the candy bar—Three Musketeers, he discovered, challenging him to a duel, or, from the looks on their faces, to a drinking contest—and took a bite. The lump flew out of his stomach, and he had the dry heaves in the street.

He was standing there breathing heavily when he smelled something strong and familiar, and a voice said, "Howie, how's your finger?"

He turned and embraced Cooty Patterson. It was all he could do to keep from crying.

He showed Cooty his hand. The old man held it, examining the white jacket of skin snug over the stub of his little finger.

"I been wondering about that," Cooty said, and it was as if the two men had spoken just yesterday. "I was wondering what they done with it. I seen it laying on the floor that day, and I picked it up. It felt kind of alive, like a baby something. I figured I ought to keep it because you'd have need for it, but then you was yelling and I dropped it. I come back later and it was gone."

The old man was bent and frail, thought Howard, and yet there was something zestful about him, as though he had found some money and the secret knowledge of the find had brought him inner health. He wore a tattered green overcoat that hung well below his knees. The tips of a pair of brown mittens peeked from the ends of the coat sleeves. A bright wool cap was pulled over his head and ears, his galoshes were tightly clamped around his ankles, and the collars of several flannel shirts bloomed at his throat like the folds of a flower ready to open.

Cooty was holding a bulging green plastic garbage bag. He had come to town to do his "shopping," he said, putting emphasis on the word to show that he had his own special meaning for it.

They went to the diner, and Howard bought Cooty a piece of apple pie and a cup of coffee. Howard sipped water from a cloudy glass, listening alternately to Cooty and to the voice of his troubled stomach.

Cooty lived in a shack in the woods, he told Howard. The shack was owned by a Frenchman who was locked up in the mental hospital in Concord. The Frenchman had given Cooty the key to the shack.

Cooty said he hitchhiked to Keene once or twice a week to get supplies and to be in the presence of people.

"I hitchhike to town, and I stand in various places, and people talk to me," he said. "It's because they know I don't want to hurt them and because they know their words warm me. I stand at the Salvation Army and they give me clothes and they invite me in the chapel and I listen to them sing, and then I stand on the street in front of the newsstand and Mr. Clarke gives me a paper to read and tells me how the children take candy from him and leave the wrappers on the sidewalk and how it bothers him and I stand at Mr. Underwood's bank and he comes out and sometimes gives me a dollar and asks me to move on, and then I stand in the park with old men who talk about breaking a window so they can do time at the county farm because of the huge radiators there, and then I stand at the bakery and at the grocery store and the men with the aprons put things in my bag and speak to me, telling me about their families or about women they desire or people they hate, and then I stand at the doughnut shop and the Chinaman there gives me doughnuts, but only if I clean his bathrooms, which I like to do because I know he does not like to clean them himself because he is a proud man and I am not ... and I love him and all the rest of them and pity them, and then I walk along the roads looking for road meat. . . ."

The old man's soft blue eyes watered from time to time, and

he wiped them with a restaurant napkin. His hands trembled. Signs of insanity were in the way of his speech, Howard believed, and yet he was amazed that none of this mattered to him, that all his ideas of order were now equally indistinct.

Howard sipped water from the cloudy glass. It seemed to him he could taste individually each of its trace elements, the chlorine the city put in to kill germs, the iron from deep within the earth, which indicated the long journey of the water, the copper residue from the pipes in the diner, the manure from piles stacked by farmers in the winter and swept away by the melting. But there had not been a melting! The tastes were from his mind and not from the water. He rushed to the men's room and had the dry heaves.

Cooty was waiting for him at the checkout counter. It was time to return to the shack, he said. Howard insisted on driving him home. The shack was on Spaulding Brook Road in the town of Donaldson. Howard knew the area: deer country, thick with the tips of young evergreens amidst ledges. Indeed, Donaldson Center was only two miles from Howard's town of Darby. But a century ago leaders from the two towns had feuded about the upkeep of the stagecoach road, which crossed the rugged hills that divided the towns. As a result the road was closed, never to be reopened, and it was a ten-mile drive from Donaldson to Darby by the valley road.

They left in the pickup, Cooty's bag in the back. Howard drove by Reason's house. It glowed in the sunshine. He looked for the woman's car and didn't see it. He wondered whether he really would have shot her, or whether he might yet shoot her, and why he had the idea in the first place. They left Keene on the bypass. The sky was blue and immense, warming, it seemed, although the air was still cold, and he could see low clouds in the hills beyond. He must stay close to Cooty. He was beginning to believe that the old man had been sent to save him.

"Howie, you don't look so good," Cooty said.

Cold ran through him. The old man's words seemed like a

prophecy. He could feel himself slipping into the same incoherent beastliness that had possessed him the night of the town meeting. He shook it off, telling—no, shouting, he realized—the things that had happened to him since the shop closed and how now he was close to murder.

He could see the old man's hands tremble in his mittens, then hug himself, as though the arms were his only companions, and the sight buoyed Howard's spirits, and his mind became clearer. It was as if the old man were doing his suffering for him. He touched the old man's hand. It quivered with the peculiar strength of a dying bird.

They were almost to the Donaldson turnoff when Cooty told Howard to stop the truck. Howard pulled the vehicle to the shoulder and backed up about two hundred feet. In a patch of grimy snow pushed up by the snowplow was a dead cat. "Road meat," said Cooty.

The cat was a tom with red hair and scarred ears. Howard deduced what had happened. A car had hit the cat and broken his back. For a minute or two the tom had had command of the front half of his body. With his front paws he had dragged himself toward some imaginary, unnecessary cover in the snow, snarled at the universe, and died. His teeth were still bared. The teeth were sharp and white and yet delicate, but the gums were black and meaty.

Cooty lifted the body, feeling it with his fingers. "Too stiff," he said. "I don't like 'em when they're stiff. I ain't going to take him; I got meat already." He was bragging.

They laid the cat's body beside the drainage ditch that paralleled the shoulder. Here the grasses would grow with the spring rains, providing wonderful cover for a cat on the prowl.

"There's all the meat a man needs along the highways, Howie," said Cooty, beginning a speech. "There's dogs and cats, which are very abundant; mice and other frightened little things if you're looking for 'em; and skunks when you're hard up; and foxes with mange; and you'll find birds of every description along the highway, and porcupines and now and then a deer that the dogs chase into the path of the cars; and I imagine that when summer comes there'll be turtles and snakes and lizards and rabbits—I forgot rabbits, which is strange, since I found my first just yesterday. Howie, there ain't a kind of animal or bug in these parts that ain't been hit by a car. The cars don't know the difference, see, and don't care. I turn down enough road meat in a week to feed a family of poor people in India or Europe, or someplace. I'm a rich man, Howie, just because I walk along the highway and put road meat in my bag. This time of year it stays fresh a long time, but sometimes the road salt gets to it and I won't eat it. Some of the road meat ain't got a mark on it; I swear it dies from fright. Sometimes it's all run over. Sometimes it's so run over you don't know what it is. One thing I learned is, and that's that you can't change guts. I mean you can run over a face until it ain't a face, but you can run over guts all day and it's still guts. Some of the road meat, if it's fresh, still has an expression on the face. Surprise, mostly. A car going sixty miles an hour hits and kills, but it don't hurt. After a while, maybe five hours, the expression goes away and the thing looks deader than before. I think the expression is the soul of the thing. The meat gets killed real quick, and the soul don't know what happened for a while, and then when it realizes that the body's dead, it leaves and that's when the expression goes away. I think there's souls everywhere, souls floating around that were once in people and in cows and in dinosaurs from long ago and from fleas and a million other crawling things and hooting things that hoot still, if you listen. I ain't saying this is all good or all bad, but some of both; I'm saying there's no place on the face of the earth where a man need feel lonely."

The Frenchman's cabin was just barely visible through the trees, although it was only about a hundred feet from the road. Like many shacks and trailers in the county, it had electric power, and a television antenna stuck out of a nearby tree, but there was no inside plumbing. Beside the cabin was a path, which once had been the old stagecoach road from Donaldson to Darby. From the narrow deck of the cabin, Howard could just make out the outline of the old road, flanked by stone walls green with moss, winding up the hill, disappearing. The snow was still deep here; it was hard, crusty, ugly, changing like the forest floor itself. The Frenchman had built the cabin in the woods, it seemed to Howard, so that one could only peek at it through trees as one approached. Even the sun had to peek. In a sweep of the eye he counted eight different kinds of trees: gray birches in clusters, doomed to die in the shade as greater trees rose above and took their light; white birches, which to the Indians must have looked like boats growing out of the ground; maples, whose species he could not immediately identify; a huge wolf pine that left its needles on the snow and on the cabin roof; poplars upslope, an indication of ground water, a spring perhaps; wild cherry trees about six inches in diameter, growing as they liked—in pairs; a single balsam fir forty feet high, straight as a flagpole; and hemlocks, whose bases enveloped rocks as though out of love. "Tough trees—hemlock," said Howard. Cooty wasn't interested; he was anxious to get inside, and his shaking hands fumbled with the padlock on the front door. The cabin was tiny, about twelve by sixteen feet, Howard guessed, sheathed with rough pine boards, the building set into the hill on wood piers, dark from creosote preservative. It would have looked like any number of shacks in the New Hampshire woods except for the windows, which were long and very narrow and arched at the top. Howard couldn't imagine where the Frenchman had got such windows and why he would want to put them in a shack. The effect the windows created was to make the cabin look like a chapel in the great cathedral of the forest.

Inside, a broth bubbled sweetly on the top of the Canadian box stove. The aroma mixed uneasily with the smell of the old man's sweat, which rose, it seemed, from yellowed sheets on a cot. At the foot of the bed was a television (twelve-inch), which rested on a crudely made dresser, which did not rest but balanced uneasily on collapsed casters, which cut into a floor of pine boards, softly aging to yellow. The furniture included a hot plate, an undersized refrigerator, a GI footlocker with smashed hardware, a folding card table, and one straight-back chair, which, from the severity of its lines, appeared to have been designed to make standing preferable to sitting. However, the cabin was dominated not by the large objects in the room but by a thousand tiny things—apparently things Cooty had found, things that had no relationship to one another, except that someone had thrown them away—which were nailed and tacked and Scotch-taped and glued to Sheetrock walls papered with (of all things) a repeating scene of two little girls chasing butterflies. Howard sat on the cot.

Cooty laid out the things from the sack on the table and stooped over them, touching them, pondering them, judging them, throwing most of them away, displaying the rest: A button was taped to an empty bottle of Canadian Club whiskey; a popsicle wrapper was affixed by a paper clip to a photograph of John Kennedy; a used safety was pulled over a wooden knob, part of a ridiculous Tinker Toy construction hanging by a hair ribbon from a cabin collar tie; and so on. When he had finished, the old man began to breathe differently, as though he were coming out of a trance; and then he sat beside Howard on the cot and put his feet up on the table (thus signaled, Howard did the same), leaned his back against the wall, and lit, with much difficulty, his corncob pipe. Rich curls of Half and Half tobacco smoke filled the room, and Cooty said, "I just took up smoking last month, and boy, I sure like it."

They talked for an hour, giggling and illogical as two small boys riding in the back of a pickup.

Howard remembered when Freddy and the Mooney kid— what was his name? Alvin or Elvis or Alkali, or some such thing—rode in the back of his truck while he drove them to Yardley Pond on sultry evenings for horn-pout fishing, and the fun they had—fumbling in the dark, swatting mosquitos, staying up too late, stalking fish of no redeeming value.

"Christ, I hate farmers," Howard said, unaccountably.

Cooty was anxious to tell Howard about the Frenchman, a man respected by his friends—and even by the inmates of the hospital in Concord—for his calmness, his good sense, his good honest Republican distrust of the weird, who nonetheless carried in his heart a secret, dirty dream for twenty years before he made it real and destroyed himself. The Frenchman lived in Keene in a tract house with a big lawn and no trees, with a wife who had babies every other year for ten years. He worked in a shop, behind a drill press, where amidst the repetitive sounds of steel on steel he nurtured his dirty little dream. He managed to save money without his wife's finding out, and eventually he bought the piece of land where the cabin now sat. Bit by bit, lie by lie, he built the cabin from the blueprint of the dream. The cabin was finished after two years of part-time labor. Here the Frenchman hesitated. He deferred; he compromised the dream. He would tell his wife he was going fishing or hunting or drinking at the Moose, and he would drive to Fitchburg and buy dirty books, and he would take the books to the cabin and read them. Then he would go home and ravage his old lady. She greatly approved of his fishing. But the Frenchman was not fulfilled. In Bellows Falls he found two whores who lived in a trailer park. He would bring the whores to the cabin and make them undress, and while they did dirty things to each other he would take their pictures with a Polaroid camera. The police found the pictures (Cooty pointed to the footlocker) and confiscated them. Still, he wasn't satisfied. The dream must be brought forth whole.

"I daresay, a man with ideas like that ought to keep 'em to himself," said Howard.

At this point in the story, they went outside to take a leak; there was no toilet in the house. Cooty used the forest for his bathroom, like any other creature of the woods. When the warm weather came and melted the snow, he would build an outhouse, he said. It was now late afternoon, and the cold had held. It would hold through the night and deep into the morning, Howard guessed. Then would come the melting.

He watched the old man pick his way cautiously among the trees until he found one he liked. What could it be about a tree that made a man want to piss on it? Ridiculous. Howard pissed on the naked snow and walked over to the old man, who had climbed the old stagecoach road a ways.

"Can you hear 'em, Howie?" said Cooty.

Howard strained to listen—and heard the baying of dogs running deer far up in the hills.

"Sometimes they run 'em from my side of the ridge," said Howard. "More dogs this year. Don't know why. Do they come down this side much?"

"They stay up there," said Cooty, pointing skyward. "They run them deer to a strange place."

"You've been up there," said Howard, and the old man nodded. Howard's mind was set in motion.

They went back inside and Cooty finished his story about the Frenchman. What the Frenchman really wanted to do with the cabin was to use it for a dollhouse for little girls to play in. He preferred a certain age, about eleven, when a girl is on the brink of changes. He got away with it for about a year. He found girls around school grounds. He would buy them things and be nice to them. Eventually he would take them to the cabin, which he furnished with everything a girl would want—dolls and other pretties—and he would pose them in grown-up women's underwear, bras and negligees and high-heeled shoes. They liked to pose, the Frenchman claimed. Indeed, some of them thrilled to it. Some he got to pose in the altogether. He never touched the girls; he took his lust out on his wife. Of course the authorities caught him. The odd thing about all this was that they could find nothing wrong with the man. He was neither crazy nor criminal but merely a man bringing a dream into the world of the real. They locked him up anyway.

"The story ain't true, is it?" Cooty asked, getting, it seemed, to his central question.

"I don't know," Howard said. "Could be. Anything anybody can make up probably can happen."

"Could be," said Cooty. They let the tale hang there, something about it still untold.

Howard asked Cooty to tell him what he had seen up in the hills. The yards where the deer congregated in the winter were about a mile up in rugged country, the old man said. He had seen the deer earlier, huddled together for warmth, but they were gone now. The dogs had scattered them. Almost round the clock a pack of dogs was chasing deer. The dogs ran the deer, as if by plan, into a steep, narrow valley and killed them. The place was an execution chamber for deer.

Cooty stirred his broth, and Howard could feel hunger, deep and pure, in his belly. Things were becoming clear to him now. The dream, the gun rack, his own rage, even Reason's foray into his mind—these were signs, which inevitably had led him here. He was a soldier recruited in the service of an unknown army. His stomach was calm; he could feel; the earth seemed a place of vast possibilities. There was work to be done.

He asked the old man to take him up on the ridge.

"It ain't that I care about the killing," the old man said mysteriously. "I mean, it wouldn't hurt me to kill. It would scare me. Course a lot of 'em, kids for example, like to get themselves scared so they can feel the difference when they're not scared. Not Cooty Patterson. Cooty Patterson is scared about being permanently scared, and is not interested in trucking in activities that start a person on the road to being scared. . . ."

The old man rambled on about subjects beyond Howard's understanding, and then he fell silent. Finally, he nodded.

They agreed to climb the hill at dawn.

It was now getting toward dark. Howard drove to the general store in Donaldson and called Charlene, telling her to put Heather up for the night. Charlene sounded frightened of him. It made him sad. He considered calling Elenore but changed his mind, not knowing exactly why. He bought two bucks' worth of gas for the truck, two six-packs of beer, and some cigarettes.

When he returned to the cabin, Cooty served the broth,

thickened to a stew now, and bread and butter. The stew was dark and strong. It contained the flesh of rabbit, deer, a strange bird, fat from a porcupine, and numerous vegetables. Cooty was proud of it. The food filled Howard's belly like dollar bills filling a wallet: He felt fat and rich.

"I found that bird in the woods, fresh dead. Some critter got him and killed him. I watch the birds in the trees, and I come to the conclusion that birds are more like people than the other animals. They don't like each other. They're always pecking at each other, chasing themselves for sport, screeching at their neighbor. They fight over a branch; and they fight just to pass the time of day. If you gave a bird a machine gun, he'd shoot up the countryside with it and probably plug his neighbor."

After the meal Cooty reclined on his place on the bed and watched television. Howard went outside on the deck. It was cold, starlight through the trees. He could just hear the dogs, high up on the ridge. The quality of the sound had changed from the afternoon. It was a different pack, he figured. Apparently the dogs worked the deer in shifts. Some might run the deer for four or five hours, tire and return home for a rest, take water and a light snack, and then go back to the hunt, called by some unknowable command as now Howard himself was called to hunt the dogs. It occurred to him that the earth itself was a living being and all its creatures its living fibers—as, in turn, each of the creatures was full of its own fibers and secrets and ways of their own, unknown by the host, and so on ad infinitum outward into the stars and inward into himself, the whole making up God. He would like to explain this concept to Elenore, he decided, but that was impossible. He would forget; she would not understand. At any rate, the idea, like most of his ideas, had passed through his mind without words, and any attempt to form it into words would fail, indeed might chase it from his mind.

He stayed outside until he got good and cold, and then he went inside and warmed himself by the fire. He watched television with Cooty. The two men drank silently, watching the glowing thing. Aspects of other lives, other places. About ten o'clock they went to bed, Howard lying on the floor by the stove. He ran his fingers through his hair and knew it was full of smells from the cabin. He lay there in the dark, listening to the old man breathing. He was asleep, in a moment it seemed. How was it, he asked himself, that someone as nervous as Cooty could fall asleep so quickly? Amazing. Amazing. So many amazing things.

16 : THE DOGS OF MARCH

Strangely, that night he dreamed about his daughters. They passed in review before him, as if he were dying—sweetly and full of medicine, in bed—and they had come so that he could photograph them for the album of his mind to take with him to the next world.

Charlene: He suspects she knows the dark secret he has tried to keep from her, that he had socked her pony between the eyes and permanently disabled the animal. (So it was in the dream; in fact, the horse had recovered.) She stands before him as she will be in ten years, a big-boned woman filled out with childbearing, her hair reddish blond, stiff as wires, under the dye getting gray, maybe, who knows? She wags a finger and scolds him, and there his mind photographs her.

Pegeen: A child neither lovely nor lovable nor strong nor wise nor lucky, she seemed to have existed only to make others grateful for their own modest gifts; a child he rarely spoke to, rarely felt much for, but merely watched grow, as one watches a stunted tree struggle upward from poor soil into poor light. He sees her now, still a child, having climbed a tree, scared to stay put, scared to come down. He goes up after her and encourages her to fall into his arms. She leaps, and there—frail as her mother, eyes hunted, throat choking with a scream, halfway between the limb she is out on and her father's mighty arms—she is frozen by the camera of the dream.

Sherry Ann: "Don't play favorites," Elenore says. But he loves Sherry Ann best, and he can't conceal it. You can't spread love equally, like fertilizer, the dream says. Love doesn't fall like rain. You can't aim love like a gun. Love comes from outside the warring earth like a comet, dangerous and beautiful, a headlong celestial object guided by its own plan. Hard to believe Sherry Ann had been a tomboy, fishing with him, cheering him on from the infield when he raced cars at the track on the county-fair grounds, refusing to wash, beating up boys, raging at no one in particular, like some wild creature in a cage, hungering for freedom. Almost overnight she grew up, striking as a movie queen, and then she ran off with a sailor or a Marine, or whatever the hell he was. Howard never heard from her again. He had made no mistakes with this one: She had come and gone, like the comet, beyond his influence. He sees her now, running across his field, dodging the derelict cars, moving up the hill, never turning, disappearing.

Heather: "You spoil her," Elenore says. And so he does. The girl is meant to sing; let her sing. There is only one thing wrong with her, the logic of the dream now reveals. Heather is buck-toothed. At this point Howard loses the helm of the dream. His body is in a casket, quite dead, his spirit floating above the moving—yea, gossiping—album of his daughters, Charlene, Pegeen, Sherry Ann, and Heather, when unaccountably he finds himself in a dentist's office. Songs hang on the walls and in magazine racks, as if songs could take that form. Sitting in the dentist's chair is Heather, but he cannot see her, because the broad, white-gowned back of the dentist blocks the view. The dentist moves to the side, and Howard can see Heather now. Her teeth are straight and perfect. She arises, plucks one of the songs from the magazine racks, and voices it: "Daddy weren't the man we thought he was / Daddy was an ignor, ignor, ignor-aaaaa-mus. . . ." The dentist stomps his heavy foot, accompanying the music. Wolf hairs cover his face, a smug, triumphant face, the face of his son, Freddy. . . .

Howard slept surprisingly well that night. When Cooty awakened him, about half an hour before dawn, his mind was clear, thoughts under direction. They breakfasted on stew, bread, and hot coffee served in white foam cups. They ate without speaking, because Cooty watched his favorite television program, early-morning educational TV.

A professor spoke gravely and importantly about ancient places. Cooty was soothed by the voice, if not enlightened, Howard guessed. It was as if the professor's words were things for the mind, to be displayed and enjoyed for their own sake rather than for any meaning they might hold. "Mesopotamia was not always the desert it is now," said the professor. "Once it was a lush and green land, a land in which to stop wandering and till the soil between two rivers. And yet beyond the fertile crescent were dry, craggy peaks. Surely the people of those early times must have looked to those peaks, swirling with fierce weather, mysterious rumblings with caves full of real and imagined ogres." A pause. "In the valleys man invents tools; in the mountains man invents religion. No wonder Mesopotamia is the cradle of civilization. My apologies to the Chinese. . . ."

The rest of the lecture was lost on Howard. He was thinking about the hunt. The topography of the ridge was wild and varied. There were old fields giving way to young trees, much favored by deer for their tender buds. There were dense forests of evergreens, where the sunlight scarcely touched the ground. Here the deer herds would be yarded up for the winter, unless by now the dogs had them moving and divided. Hunters made for good hunting, he knew. During the early part of deer season the deer were cautious and hard to find. Once the season progressed, they would be in an almost constant state of panic. They would be moving into the guns of hunters. The same situation must hold in March, the deer season for the dogs, he figured. Therefore, he could expect to find deer—and dogs running them—scattered throughout the ridge. There were great outcroppings of ledge and steep gorges hidden by the trees. And there were flat marshes that seemed—like the ledges and gorges—out of place, without origin. There was a little bit of everything New Hampshire had to offer on that ridge, thought Howard.

They left at dawn, Cooty stuffing the pockets of his overcoat with already crushed sandwiches in wax paper and a Thermos of coffee, Howard carrying only the rifle and ammunition. The hill was enveloped in a great cloud of morning fog that would burn off in a few hours. A light, unpredictable breeze flew among the trees, carrying the fog to and fro. There would be moments when the fog would fall upon them, as though by intent, and obscure their view of the path, and there would be times when the path would suddenly open, a wide corridor of inviting light, again as though by intent.

They followed the stagecoach road, plodding slowly in deep, crusty snow, until after about five hundred yards a snowmobile trail merged with the road. The trail was now hard, and walking was easy. Cooty had heard the dogs earlier, but it was not until he was halfway up the hill that Howard heard them. The sounds were scattered, and it was difficult to figure what they meant. It seemed to Howard that there was a main pack toward the center of the ridge, but there were other dogs, too, perhaps a score of them, running in all different directions, following no apparent route. It was impossible to tell whether their howls meant they were trying to join up with the main group or whether they were on trails of their own. At any rate, Howard guessed that the deer had long been chased from their winter yards and that herds would be divided, does separated from the bucks, from their recently dropped fawns. Chaos reigned on the ridge. He determined that the main pack was moving in a predictable direction and could therefore be intercepted. Eventually he and

Cooty would have to leave the road and bushwhack to meet up with the dogs. Probably the pack was driving the deer to the place where Cooty had been, a place he had not described well but that appeared to be a steep gorge hidden by trees, the execution chamber for deer.

There were other sounds in the forest besides those made by the dogs, sounds at moments heightened, then dimmed, by the wind and the fog—sounds of a stream plunging downward through worn rocks; birches clacking like gossiping women, evergreens brushing together in mighty argument, and ancient limbs creaking in criticism; a distant, threatening owl; a jet plane far ahead of its own roar. The old man was by turns awed, frightened, amused, and touched by the sounds. Howard heard the sounds only dimly, although his experience in the woods helped amplify them.

At a group of ledges, heavy and menacing in the fog, the road turned one way and the sounds of the dogs the other. They struck out across the crusty snow, which was spiked with thick brush. Beyond was a stand of spruce where Cooty said he remembered a trail that led to the strange place.

"We're in the puckerbrush now," said Cooty.

"Story of my life," said Howard.

The way cleared into a tiny, frozen marsh, which brought them to the wood, dark beneath the cloak of the evergreens. They walked for about half an hour. They did not find the trail Cooty thought he remembered. The sounds of the dogs were as far away as before, and seemed to move helter-skelter, a trick of the wind or the fog or both. Without discussing it, both Howard and Cooty knew they were lost. They stopped to rest by a fallen log, swept clean of snow, dry and mysteriously warm to the touch. Cooty reached into the depths of his overcoat and produced the Thermos of coffee and cups. He poured. The two men looked like a pair of the Marx brothers, Cooty resembling Harpo and Howard a husky Chico.

The old man pulled things from his face—thin gray hairs from his skin, strings of hard mucus from his nose, rusty wax from his ears, tiny scabs from wounds created by previous pickings—and he rolled the things in his fingers and considered them, as though they were codes of thought and memory.

Howard sipped the coffee. It was dark and bitter. He lit a cigarette and watched the smoke drift aimlessly, like the fog. His mind went blank for a time, and that look came across his face that made nice people think, Oh, what a stupid brute. Thanks be to God I'm not like him. Then he heard a bird call. *"Whooo-eeee, whooeeee,"* the bird said, but Howard thought he heard something else; he thought he heard the bird call his name, not the name he carried in his wallet but the name that was lost.

One day Uncle Jack had called him from the fields. (Haying was one of the few farm chores Howard liked: He liked the smell; he liked the need to have to work fast to beat the rains.) Even then there was something suicidal about Uncle Jack. He had a bent for teasing big men, not for pleasure but to get himself hurt, maimed, killed.

"What's that, Howie?" said Cooty, still picking at the things on his face.

"I say, the coffee's good, good and stiff."

Uncle Jack had sat Howard down at the kitchen table and put papers in front of him, paused a moment to watch his annoyance, because he knew Howard hated papers, and then said, "They lost your name, boy. They lost half the places you've been, and somewhere along the line they lost your name. They've been calling you by the name of whoever you was with at the time. Howie, do you recall your correct name? Did you ever have a name? Don't know, do you? Well, we got to come up with a name to put on all the dotted lines you're going to be seeing for the rest of your life. I'd give you my own, but I don't believe you'd take it. Would you? Nope, didn't think so. Let's try on a few for size. Jones. Howard W. Jones. HWJ, Esquire. Won't do, eh? How about Gates? Howard W. Gates. . . ."

And on and on he went, half serious, half mocking, fully mad.

And as Uncle Jack spoke, Howard had been thinking, seeing in his mind's eye a huge tree from somewhere in his childhood in an unremembered town on an unremembered lawn, gripping the earth, springing forth from the earth, rising into the sky. "Call me Elm," he had said, and Uncle Jack had written on the paper "Howard W. Elman." So he had a name—if only a made-up name. Eventually he dropped the *W* because the initial had been Uncle Jack's idea. It was Howard's way of saying "Up yours" to Uncle Jack's ghost.

The elms were dying. He learned this fact, oh, about 1955. They had been dying right along, but he hadn't noticed. The trees died in the open, but there was nothing public about their dying, unlike men crashing in airplanes or slipping silently from hospital beds into the public obituary columns of newspapers. One year a dying elm had fewer leaves, and the next year fewer still, until it stood bare in the summer as it was in the winter, the actual death having come in utmost privacy. In the years following, the bark peeled, the tree's bones turned gray, its sap drained into the earth, the wood drying and twisting, until the tree was a monument to the treeness of trees; and about that time the tree was recognized as such by men, and the men wrote it down, "Big tree at Calhoun's Corner"; and then the wind knocked it over, at night, with no one looking. Something from the earth was killing the elm trees, but—what the hell!—something from the earth was always killing something else from the earth. "The rule is killing, set from on high," Ollie Jordan would say.

But what did Ollie Jordan know? He was just another ignorant shitkicker, wise about a few general things, stupid about the particulars of his life. So it was with all men: wise here, stupid there. Dumb luck whether what you were good at fit the world or fit your doom.

Cooty had stopped picking at his face. He was shivering slightly, and he looked confused.

"Howie, I'm lost," he said. "They keep changing the furniture out here with every wind and storm. I couldn't tell you how to find that place now if both our lives depended on it."

Howard listened for the call of the bird. He heard it no more. Indeed, for the moment the forest had fallen into relative silence. He heard only the dogs in the distance and the fog closer, slipping with the wind through the trees.

"Did you hear that bird?" Howard asked.

"Agh?" said Cooty, puzzled.

"I heard a bird a minute ago. Made a funny sound," said Howie.

"Oh, yes, I remember now. It went '*Whoo-eeee.*' "

"Howie Hooey—that don't sound like too good a name to me," said Howard. "How's it sound to you?"

"Why, I don't know what you mean, Howie," said Cooty.

"Don't mean nothing. Nothing at all. If you want to go back, I ain't going to blame you. As for me, I ain't got nothing better to do today but to shoot dogs running deer."

Howard headed up the slope, and the old man followed. They blundered about in the deepening snow for a while, their footfalls crunching loudly as they broke through the crust. They kept going higher and higher, and they had some luck. The fog cleared temporarily, and they found themselves within seeing distance of the path Cooty had been looking for, an old logging road. With the discovery, the sounds of the dogs seemed to draw closer.

"We're not too far from the place now, maybe a twenty-minute walk," said Cooty, rallying. "I can find it now. I know I can."

The trail came to the spine of the ridge, following it upward. The wind was stronger here, the trees shorter—stunted—and they were draped in hoarfrost. When the fog settled in, it was heavier, almost tangible, like an icy rain. It was here, right on the trail, that they found the first dead body. Oddly enough, the body was not that of a deer but of a dog, a black mongrel, gray around the mouth, and fat, as old pets get. His haunches and genitals were eaten away.

Howard read the tale of the old dog in the snow. About fifty yards away, perhaps ten dogs had downed a deer, a young buck, Howard judged from the tracks. The dogs had torn away great chunks of flesh from the flanks and belly of the deer, which somehow got to its feet and went on. The old mongrel had got his jaws into a piece of meat, and he had dragged it to a defensive position, where other dogs threatened him for it. The old dog hurried to eat his prize. He'd have all of it, and those other dogs could go bark at the mailman. Howard opened the dog's jaws. The deer meat—still fresh—was clogged in his throat. The old dog had strangled on his meal. The other dogs had sniffed him, cautiously at first, until their noses told them he was dead. And then they fed on his haunches, and went home and barked at the mailman.

"Kinda got what he asked for, didn't he?" said Howard. The old man nodded, but he didn't understand. The story in the snow was not revealed to him.

On they went, Howard loping like a busy bear, Cooty struggling to keep up.

The main pack was still a ways off when they saw two stray dogs sitting on the trail ahead. Their tongues hung out and their chests heaved. They were resting. Howard shot them both. He crippled the first, a purebred collie, with a shot to the shoulder and finished her with a shot to the brain. He killed the other dog, a musty gray mongrel terrier, with a single shot to the brain. The animal was dead before its last crying bark screamed through the woods.

The .308 was a good gun. It was holding up, and he was shooting well.

"Practice makes perfect," he said.

The old man shuddered.

The old man felt the world around him, absorbed it, reflected it, consumed it and was consumed by it, was so much a part of it that he could not possibly understand it. Howard envied him. Howard felt apart from what he was a part of. His drives came from inside and not from outside. He could shoot a dog or a deer and feel nothing except a curious mellowing—or deepening—of his inner rage, of which he had as little understanding as the old man had of the things that he collected and of the collection he was part of. Howard understood everything about catching fish and nothing about water. The two of them put together made something like a whole man, Howard thought.

The sound of the dogs was coming toward them now, was coming toward them until it had enveloped them, and for a minute they saw no animal, no evidence of a chase, just heard the sound. The pack was spread over a much wider area than Howard had thought. It was like a great boom of sound sweeping the ridge for deer. And then they saw the buck running right at them, tongue hanging out, rack held high, until the old man moved and the buck cut to his right at the movement, and they saw, hanging tenaciously from his haunches, a toy poodle, shaking like a tiny bell, then falling, Howard whipping a shot at the dog, missing, the tiny dog now attacking them, Howard shooting it dead at his feet, the event occurring within a matter of seconds, although Howard had got a clear picture in his mind of the deer. It was doomed. Its entrails were hanging out, flanks ripped, sex organs torn from its underbelly. The buck had been down and up, and once they had it down again, it would be the last time. He examined the tracks. The sharp hoofs plunged through the crusty snow in clusters of four. Blood was sprayed on the snow.

The sound of the pack still engulfed them. They saw no more dogs. But the dogs were there on all sides in the woods. Howard started tracking the deer, but the old man stopped him.

"We ain't far now," he said. "They'll drive him to the place for sure."

The dogs ran the deer in shifts, Howard thought. They ran the deer to the same place, almost as if they had conspired to do so. The dogs were experts in chasing. The deer knew nothing but fear. The dogs had taken something they had learned from the mind of men and married it to the mind of dog—the dogs were a society, the deer a herd—and the result was chaos on the ridge.

They continued, and it was as if they were still and the hemlocks were walking toward them, passing like ships on the sea. They crossed ledges and began to descend. Hemlocks getting bigger, branches broader, like baggy green sails. Sounds of the birds growing dim. The wind dying. The fog creeping. Dogs—where were the dogs? He imagined them excited and frothy from the smell of the deer's blood on the snow.

"What did you say, Howie?"

"Didn't say nothing. Thinking out loud. Wondering where the dogs went."

"It don't matter," said Cooty. "They take 'em around the long way. We'll be there before they are."

They came to a stone wall, just a pile of rocks, really, a winding, snowcovered hump in the woods, four to ten feet wide and three feet high at the peak of the hump. Years ago a farmer had cleared a field here, Howard figured, tossing the stones in this crude course, swearing his damn head off all the while, "Fuck thou, rock; up thy nooky, stone," or however they swore in those days. Today the farmer was dead, the cows that grazed in the fields forgotten, the field itself returned to the forest. Only the wall remained: "Fuck thou, farmer."

They followed the stone wall downward for a short while until they came to worn cups in the snow, the old man's footprints from weeks ago. The prints turned into the trees for about fifty feet and then vanished, as if the old man himself those weeks ago had reached a point where he became weightless.

They plowed through the heaviest cover of hemlocks yet, and then quite suddenly they reached a clearing of ledges and a steep, narrow valley, partly obscured by fog.

"The dogs run 'em in from the far side—I don't know exactly where—and then the deer he can't get up the sides, and he's done for," Cooty said.

The fog was heavy in the valley, with only a few drifting

patches of light below. The place was littered with jagged boulders, formed as though by explosions. Howard remembered stories about mining operations in these hills years ago. Perhaps the place was an old quarry, where they had mined granite for gravestones or mica for windows. He wasn't sure. At any rate, the place was different from the other parts of the ridge: Here, it seemed, nature had failed, lost a battle with some greater, more cunning force. Stunted shrubs and hemlocks struggled to grow out of a few mugfuls of soil.

Below the fog might be standing water, he guessed. It was impossible to tell from where the dogs drove the deer, but there must be an entrance. He would find it, and then when the dogs came in, they would be trapped, as they expected to trap the deer.

Howard and Cooty began to descend.

The air was heavier, colder, than on the ridge. The fog was dense but moving in an unfelt wind. It was, thought Howard, as if there were no real fog at all, no valley, no anything, as if he were living the tail end of a life that was merely an apparition.

"Even the snow has a hard time keeping a grip here," Howard said.

"Make no mistake—the place has a plan," said Cooty. He was extremely nervous, Howard could see, sweating profusely, touching his face, clacking his tongue, the gestures of a man reassuring himself that he was real in an unreal place.

A hole in the fog opened below them—for a moment, it was as if the hole of light were moving and the fog were still, permanent, and then the fog was moving again—and they saw on the jagged rocks the body of a dead deer, a young doe, her face perfect, untouched, eyes frozen open, front hoofs gripping the rocks as if to climb. The rest of her was carnage. Her haunches had been eaten to the bone, the inside of her belly caved in, eaten from the inside. Not ten feet away lay her unborn fawn, frozen in its translucent net, but untouched by the dogs.

It was unclean, Howard thought. Not the carnage itself, but

that he had seen it, that it had not been disposed of. Where was nature to clean up this mess? Where were the skunks, the raccoons, the porcupines, the meat birds, and other small, curious scavengers for which Howard had no names? (He imagined dark, slouching men—dwarfs carrying black sacks—patrolling the wood paths and highways for carnage to pick up.) Where were the butchers with their bloody aprons, their glinting knives, their white paper on rolls? Where was the melting to bring the final custodians, the insects?

They came to another cadaver, a spike-horned buck. The same story. The dogs chased the deer for miles, attacking the hindquarters until the deer was weak from loss of blood and from exhaustion, and then the dogs drove the deer into this valley, and the deer could not climb the steep, jagged boulders, and the dogs brought down the deer, feeding on the insides, which steamed in the cold, working from the sex organs forward into the chest cavity and backward to the haunches, the deer conscious, if powerless, during much of the process.

"I think I got to go to the bathroom," said Cooty. He was shaking. He dropped his trousers and squatted. The next time, the old man would shit his pants, Howard thought. Cooty must be calmed. Using his foreman's voice, Howard ordered him to gather some dead branches and build a fire so they might warm themselves. The old man busied himself, and Howard went on alone. Without thinking, he flipped on the safety of the .308, which he always did when the country was so rough he might slip.

The place was dead still. The steep walls of the valley and the dense tree cover blanketed the sounds of the dogs, the sounds of the highway in the distance, the very sounds of the forest. There was no bird show, no wind in the trees, no red-squirrel complaints, but only the meticulous sounds of his descent—the grinding of snow under his boots, the swish of a branch as he brushed it, the halting, tenuous drownings of his breathing.

The ground was flat now, and when the fog cleared temporarily, he could see he had reached the floor of the valley. Close by was a small pond, the frozen surface dirty with deer carnage. The pond was imprisoned on three sides by ledges. The dogs had pinned the deer against the ledges and destroyed them—bucks, does, thrown fawns, and fawns still in the bellies of the does. A narrow, rising trail led away from the pond and wound out of the valley, an old road perhaps. The snow on the trail was full of confused tracks. Here was the entrance to the valley where the dogs would drive the deer he had seen earlier into the entrance. He stationed himself at the juncture of two boulders, out of which grew a hemlock. He cut some green boughs, sat upon them, and leaned his back against the tree. He had an excellent field of fire. He was at once relaxed and coiled to strike. His life had come to this: Save a few deer from the jaws of dogs. He was a small man sent to perform a small task, or so it seemed to him.

Images spilled from his mind: Cooty under the looms working (hiding?), lint fuzz sticking to his face like white leeches; Filbin inspecting web, as much with his fingers and nose as with his eyes; the ass of Fralla Pratt chugging down the aisle like some marvelous engine; Elenore tumbling down the stairs (but they said she hadn't fallen); a big bird, an eagle or hawk—he didn't know—socking a duck with his closed foot in mid-flight, the duck tumbling (picture of Elenore interrupting) and the big bird catching the duck (Elenore) ... the thing repeated in his mind, duck (Elenore), duck.

Dogs.

Closer than he expected, their sounds came out of the trees above. The unfelt wind moved the mist and the sounds, so that he was not sure whether the dogs were yet on the trail. And then he saw the buck, stark for a moment in a patch of light. Howard's eyes fixed on the tongue hanging out. It was deep red, almost blue, enormous with arterial blood, the color as out of place in the forest as a woman's scarf. Two dogs were nipping at the deer's hindquarters. The other dogs were in the mist, and he couldn't see them. He took quick aim at one of the dogs he could see, a beautiful black Labrador mixture. He fired—and the gun did not go off. "Jesus H. Jammed," he said. "Sweet Christ of death." And as he swore, despite his rage, somehow he knew it would be like this, that the gun could not operate in this valley, that he would have to face the dogs on their own terms. He shouted, trying to distract the dogs from the deer, which had vanished into the mist. "Go on home and chase cars," he yelled. He ran, stumbling along in the fog-shrouded, boulder-strewn valley floor.

The valley, heretofore silent to the point of oppressiveness, now reverberated with the sounds of barking dogs and a screaming man.

Howard reared up like a bear, waving his arms, one of which carried the .308. He shouted, "Constipation for life to the lot of you!" and then he growled, insensate and wordless. A few of the dogs were frightened by his voice and slunk off. Some ignored him, intent on the deer. A few turned to him, as though he were some new game or enemy. One of these was the Labrador, which faced him with bared fangs and bristling neck. Howard swung the rifle at him like a baseball bat and missed. The dog leaped for him, and Howard caught him in the chest with the rifle butt. The dog's scream was high pitched, like that of a woman in fear. Howard drove the butt into the dog's head, which was wedged against a rock, and the dog was silent. A smaller, mixed-shepherd bitch made the mistake of getting too close, and he picked her up, grabbed her tail, and battered her against the rocks.

The sounds of the other dogs faded and then came together. They were on the pond, he thought. They had trapped the deer on the ice. He moved toward the sounds in the mist. He felt strong, full of war spirit. He moved, bearlike and growling, until he could see the forms of the dogs on the pond and the deer carnage on the ice and the dark form of the ledges in the background. He startled a small poodle, which looked at him curiously for a moment and then foolishly bit him on the boot. Howard flipped the animal in the air, caught it in his hands and brought it down against his knee, breaking the dog's back. It wriggled away, snakelike, legs useless. The deer was down, backed against the ledges, surrounded by dogs. Howard shrieked a challenge and plunged into the mass with his rifle swinging. It seemed to him at the time that he was beating, biting, kicking, dogs, killing them all. In fact, as he would realize later, he had merely driven them off, inflicting little damage.

After his initial charge, only one dog remained at the body of the deer; the dog stood there holding its ground. The sky opened, and Howard could see the colors of the animals clearly now, the deer's tongue, still enormous and deep red, and the dog, saliva and blood dripping from its mouth. And for a moment he had a hallucination, himself in the place of the deer and the woman ascendent over him, and then the reality of the scene came into focus. He was looking into the defiant eyes of Mrs. Cutter's Afghan, Kinky. The hound leaped for his loins. Howard dropped the rifle and caught the dog's face with both hands. He eased his hands back to the neck and lifted the dog off its feet, and then slowly, with great care, he strangled the animal to death, a procedure that took several minutes and was accompanied by great thrashing on the part of the doomed dog. When the dog's body was still, he tossed it away and dropped to his knees. The deer lay panting, mooing blissfully.

"Howie, are you all right?"

Cooty was standing at his side. It was not until then that Howard realized he was so out of breath he couldn't speak. Light was falling on him. The fog had lifted, burned off by the sun. It was going to be a warm day. The melting had begun.

He rested for a few minutes until his breath came back, and then he began to quake and feel cold, and he was sick to his stomach. He was in shock, he could tell. He searched for the gun, and then the old man was handing it to him. The gun had not jammed. He had failed to release the safety. Stupid. He was going to finish the buck, but the deer was so far beyond pain that Howard decided to let him enjoy the last few images of life slipping away. He found two of the dogs he had crippled earlier and shot them both through the head.

He did not remember the walk back to the cabin. He remembered lying on the old man's bunk, sipping whiskey from a bent tin cup held by Cooty's shaking hands. The old man's smell surrounded him like a blanket. "You sleep now, Howie," he heard the old man say, and he shut his eyes and felt the tiredness of his limbs. And then it was as if, between sleep and waking, his full intelligence, like a great fish, surfaced into his experience for one brief look: He was an ignorant and stubborn man who only now was reaching adulthood. Further, it was clear to him what he must do to hold what he deserved in the world.

Outside, the snow was melting. Even with his eyes shut, he could feel the sun coming through a path in the trees and through the tiny churchlike windows of the cabin and warming his face. He was free and sad with knowledge.

It was the second day of the melting when Harold Flagg, charged with spring fever, decided to ask Mrs. Zoe Cutter (for sure this time) to be his wife. He drove to Keene and got a haircut and, for the first time ever, a shave, after which his face was sprinkled liberally with after-shave lotion by Shorty the barber. He didn't even mind Shorty's meaningless small talk. ("How you, Mr. Flagg? Still running the store there in Alstead? Oh, yah, Darby. These small towns is all the same to me. I see the price of bread is up again. No wonder they call it Wonder Bread. It's a wonder you can pay for it. Heh-heh....")

Harold had heard it all before and heard it now, yet did not hear it. He was thinking about Zoe, his mind traveling from her vast holdings to her slim, aristocratic body, down, down, down, to the tips of her red, red toes. He saw himself in Swett's old bedroom (he never liked Swett; a petty, vicious man), looking at *his* trees, *his* fields, *his* walls. With the acquisition of the Elman land (that had to come any day now), he and the woman together would own more of the town than even his forefathers had. Surely he would have to run for the legislature. Maybe he'd do a little gentleman farming. Never mind raising a few pigs and cows for the meat counter. But get a good-size dairy herd and some decent hired-on help. What the hell, he'd give the store to Arlene. Get her a couple of boys to take care of the shelves. He'd still do the accounts. He liked that kind of work, and he could keep a hand in the business.

He practically bowled Shorty over by tipping him a dollar and exclaiming "I'm getting married, you can bet on it, Shorty" as he left the shop with a grin. (Shorty said to his next customer, Sergeant Abrams of the Keene police force, who always got a crew cut, "I don't know what Flagg thinks he's going to do with a wife. I believe that gut of his has prevented him from seeing it for years. Heh-heh.")

On impulse Harold stopped at the florist to buy some flowers.

"What kind of flowers do you want?" asked Mrs. Kasmire, whose hair was tinted blue-gray, like no flower that had ever existed, so that she looked strangely alien in the shop she and her husband had run for forty years.

"Want courting flowers," said Harold, catching the woman's somewhat awed look.

"Roses?" she asked.

"Red roses," he said, knowing just at that moment what he wanted. "I'll take ten of the reddest long-stemmed roses you've got." One for each toe, he thought, and he could hardly keep from laughing at his little private joke.

Oh, he was in a good mood, all right. For one thing, he had taken care of the Ollie Jordan matter. He had sent the Jordans' landlord in Rhode Island a vaguely threatening letter saying that the town might no longer allow him to rent land that did not meet state requirements for septic systems. Then he had sweetened this bitter medicine with a friendly phone call in which he indicated that the Darby Planning Board, which had turned down the man's subdivision request some years ago, now might reconsider a revised plan. The man got the message. The Jordans had been evicted; they had until May the first to get out. Harold had also sicced the social-service agencies on the Jordans. It seemed he saw caseworkers every day in his store—nice young, guilt-ridden men and women whose favorite word was "supportive." He was certain they would take Ollie from the helm of the Jordan family, for the mutual good of all concerned.

Harold stopped at Dunkin' Donuts and bought half a dozen, three over his limit. What the heck—it was time to celebrate. On the drive back to Darby, he drove ten miles over the speed limit; he gobbled doughnuts; his heart pounded with anticipation; he played with himself with the élan of an adolescent. His senses seemed to cry for stimuli. He turned on the radio very loud. He finished the doughnuts before he reached the Darby turnoff, and now he could smell the roses. He put the flowers on his rampant lap, opened the paper, and breathed in their scent, an aphrodisiac to him. He imagined himself with Mrs. Cutter, both of them bare, in a roomful of roses. The realization that the roses had whiplike, thorny stems further excited him.

Indeed, Harold was so preoccupied with passion that under normal circumstances he would not have noticed Howard Elman approaching in his pickup. What made him notice was that Elman—like himself—was driving much faster than usual, dangerously so. The drivers startled each other, appearing to be on a deadline for a crackup on the narrow road, before each pulled away at the last second. It crossed Harold's mind, if just for a second, that Elman's speeding was very strange.

God, it was a beautiful day. It was as if summer had come in a day. The road was wet with rivulets caused by the melting. The sun lay on the woods like a sweet kiss. The stream crossing under the road was heavy with runoff, cold, blue, rushing to the ocean. Oh, it was romantic. Beautiful. The melting, the melting. . . . "Someone should make a song about the melting," he said to the radio. It was at that point that he saw the smoke, curls of it, rising near Elman's place. Somebody burning brush. Had to be. He was annoyed now. Somebody burning brush—

somebody doing anything in the town—without his knowing it caused him annoyance. The smoke was thickening. He turned the corner and saw that the smoke was coming out of Elman's house.

All his good feelings turned to rage. A fire. A goddamn fire was going to ruin his day, this day of days. He pulled into Elman's driveway and opened the kitchen door. Smoke poured out, and the room was hot. "Anybody in there?" He tried to think. Elman gone—speeding. Wife in the hospital. Boy in college. Young girl in school. There would be nobody in the house. He dared not go in to use the telephone. He ran back to the car and headed into town, to the firehouse. He was puffing. Elman speeding? Then it dawned on him: Elman had set fire to his own house for the insurance! For sure. And in broad daylight! The gall of the man, the unmitigated gall. Harold raced the car back to town. He was sweating. The exertion was greater than he had thought. He was having trouble breathing. He could taste the doughnuts. His chest was filling with something. Oh, my dear sweet Jesus, he thought, I'm having a heart attack. The road was wet, and his next sensation was of spinning. The car went up on the bank, rolled over once, settled on its wheels, and spun completely around. It was now broadside in the middle of the road. Harold dimly realized that the car would have to be moved before the fire engine could get by; then he realized that this matter was extremely unimportant, that nearly everything but life itself was extremely unimportant. He discovered that he was half lying, half sitting on the seat and that the chest pains were gone. He felt curiously detached, analytical. He could smell the roses. They were lovely.

Zoe Cutter also saw the smoke pouring from the Elman house. She called the fire department, jumped into the Mercedes, and drove down to the fire. She shouted, "Yoo-hoo, anyone inside?" When she was convinced no one was there, she decided to drive to the store. She might be able to arouse the local volunteer firefighters before they could be reached by the county dispatcher in Keene. She saw Harold's car blocking the road. She parked and ran to it. Something was terribly wrong. She opened the door and was greeted with a marvelous smell—roses. Harold lay open-mouthed on the seat. He seemed dead but uninjured. His fly was unzipped. He was covered with roses. The enigma presented by the situation sent a rush of pleasure through her.

17 : THE TRAILER

Summer that year was deep green. Mornings were heavy with dew; afternoons, hazy. Evenings were drenched with showers that made the Big Boy tomatoes in the Elman garden as fat as melons. Elenore canned enough spaghetti sauce to last the winter. She could struggle along now on leg braces and crutches, but she preferred the wheelchair. There was no uncertainty about it, no pain. After supper she would roll out on the ramp to the garden and sit while Howard weeded and picked vegetables. From here she could contemplate her new mobile home. It had wall-to-wall carpeting, built-ins, and a cathedral ceiling—and there was no pain in it.

She only dimly remembered what the house looked like. But she remembered how it felt—cold and immense. It had been his house; this was her house. The loss by fire had been his, and he suffered with it. Good. He was earning credits for heaven. He crawled about the garden on his hands and knees. The position pleased her because it was close to the position of kneeling for prayer. He was a better man these days. The hearing aid caused him to lower his voice; he seemed more gentle, humbled. She liked what his classes were doing for him. Instead of reaching for curse words when he was frustrated, he found big words they taught him at night school. Sometimes she couldn't understand him at all, and this thrilled her. She fancied he was becoming cultivated. He came to her now, filling the apron on her lap with tomatoes. "There you are, Mother," he said. Then he wheeled her up the ramp and into the kitchen. She sat thinking, the tomatoes red and beautiful and soft as babies in her lap, while he went to the living room to work on his lesson. Her prayers had, for the most part, been answered. Life had changed and settled. So be it. But already she was conceiving another prayer project. The next step in their lives, she decided, was that they should both be formally brought into the Roman Catholic fold. Then on Sundays he could take her to church. The idea staggered her. She was touched by a sentimental feeling that she translated as God stroking her. She ran her hands over the tomatoes—they were so like flesh—and prayed.

Howard read aloud: " 'Ta-Ta the cat cleaned her claws with her red tongue.' Absurd, indubitably absurd," he said. "Absurd" was the word for today. "Indubitably" was yesterday's word. Mr. Phelps said that if you used a new word three times, it was yours.

Why should a grown man have to read a book written for children? It was absurd. He would bring the subject up with Mr. Phelps at the next class. "It is indubitably absurd that an adult must be expected to peruse"—Friday's word—"material such as this," he would say.

He put the lesson down and picked up a copy of *Time* magazine. Any man capable of reading *Time* ought not to have to put up with Ta-Ta the cat, he thought. "Up yours, Ta-Ta," he said.

"What did you say?" Elenore spoke from the kitchen.

"Nothing. Didn't say nothing. Just perusing my lesson," Howard answered.

He believed everything he read in *Time* magazine, not so much because he trusted *Time* reporting but because *he* had read it, as though reading could create truth on the page.

He read for a while, fidgeting with his reading glasses because he didn't like the way they felt around his ears. "People."

"Sports." "Health." "The Nation." He had to admit he still didn't grasp it all. There were words he didn't understand, certain arrangements of words that threw a knot into the lead of his thought, references to events and people that were only shadows to him. No matter. He'd learn. He was confident that one day he would know enough to pass his GED test, and then he would say to the world, "Up yours."

"I'm ready!" A command from Elenore. He hurried to her. He wheeled her into the living room, turned on the television, and fetched her rosary beads. Indifferent to him, she began to whisper her prayers. A voice on the television said, "I'm going to bust you wide open."

During the day she got along just fine by herself, but as bedtime drew near, she insisted on being treated like an invalid. She scolded him, sent him on senseless errands, complained of invented pains, talked his ears off—manipulated him, stunned him, halved his thinking. It took him a while to catch on to what all this was about: She feared him in the night. Keeping him busy was a tactic to keep his drinking down. He approached the subject with her once but failed to get anywhere. "How'd you like me to stop bringing home beer?" he had asked. "I'd know you was drinking on the sly," she had replied. And so he continued to drink at home—but less. All right. His drinking gave her something to suffer over, offer up to her God, and when she saw he had cut down, she could take credit for his moderation. Then, too, he needed punishment to purge a nagging guilt. He was still at odds with himself over what had happened that night when he came home drunk after being with Fralla Pratt. Had he knocked Elenore down the stairs? Had she fallen of her own mistake? Had she faked the accident? He didn't know and probably never would, because she would never tell him. The knowledge was something to hold over him, a power. So be it.

When she was settled, he went into the kitchen and opened a big accounts book. At his feet lay a pot full of peeled tomatoes. They were still whole, and their flesh had all the tenderness and agony of living animal flesh with the skin stripped from it. He was reminded that deer season would be here in a few months. The .308 was oiled and ready; he had plans for hunting, although not necessarily for deer. He smiled maliciously to himself. Elenore had her ways; he had his.

Heather came home past her hour, as had been her habit recently. "Where you been?" he asked.

"Down the road," she replied. She reeked of the smell of Mrs. Cutter's house. "Aunt Zoe wants to take me for a ride to New York City," she said.

"Ah-umm," he said.

"Can I go?" The summer had touched her, changed her. She was at the age when she was beginning to discover that you could lie and God would not strike you down.

"Why, sure, you can go," he said. She came toward him, as if to kiss him, but did not. Her mouth fell open and she stepped back, shy. The braces on her teeth made him think of little steely traps.

Mrs. Cutter had won victories over him but none so costly as the taking of Heather.

After the insurance man had investigated the fire (he gave Howard no trouble; why should a man burn down a twenty-five-thousand-dollar house for five thousand dollars in insurance?), Howard rented a bulldozer and, with the help of Cooty Patterson, cleaned up the mess. The old man had pointed to the paint-charred two-and-a-half-ton truck and said offhandedly, "Howie, why don't you take up dumping?" At that moment "Burning Barn Trucking" was born. They did a neat job of cleaning up, pushing the debris into a big pile and taking it to the dump, altering the landscape so you couldn't tell where the cellar hole had been. He worked deliberately, with a plan. He could imagine the woman on the hill taking all this in. She would see this smoothed, perfect spot surrounded by his derelict cars. She would be thinking, scheming. He would not call her; he would wait until she called him. The first one to speak would be the loser. One week passed. He settled Heather in at Charlene's and moved into the cabin with Cooty. Two weeks passed. He started to collect welfare and enrolled in the night school as part of a tradeoff with the government. Three weeks. He launched his trucking company, and he and Cooty were busy each morning collecting trash. Four weeks. Elenore was released from the hospital, and he moved in with her at Charlene's. Five weeks. The tension in him mounted, and he was on the brink of visiting Mrs. Cutter when she finally contacted him, in a way he had not expected. Freddy called him—from her house, he guessed—and asked him to come over. She had a proposal.

When he arrived, Freddy had gone. Good. He didn't need a third force to deal with.

It was a cool night, and he made a display of warming himself by the fireplace.

"Where's the doggie?" he asked innocently.

"He's been missing for weeks," Zoe said. "I think someone stole him. He's a very valuable animal, you know."

"I imagine he was," Howard said.

They beat around the bush awhile longer, until finally she made him an offer.

"You want the whole piece," he said.

"Howard," she said, and he was offended that she called him by his first name, "we've had our differences, you and I, and I don't expect we'll ever love each other. I suppose we're two of a kind—insistent people. Howard, I am sincerely fond of your family, of Elenore, of Frederick, of Heather. They're fine, lovely people, and I know how much you love them. . . ." She paused, waiting for a word, a gesture, from him, but he continued to stare at her blankly. "Heather is such a beautiful girl," Zoe continued. "She has a future, you know. She has a beautiful singing voice; she has presence; she has the will to perform. It would please me to pay to fix her teeth."

He understood Mrs. Cutter's offer for what it was, not a gift but a condition of the sale.

"I expect you could do the girl some good," he said.

"I believe so," she said. He could see that she thought she had him on all fours.

He let the proposal sit in silence for a full minute, until he changed his expression to one of exaggerated concern and said, "Course you know I'm mighty fond of that piece of land, and all my children call this town home. And just the other day Elenore says to me, 'I can hardly wait to plant the garden. I can taste that sweet corn now.' Suppose, Mrs. Cutter, that you let me keep half an acre."

She was suspicious.

He pressed on, his mouth dry and false from the taste of his words, but his voice steady and persuasive. "I don't believe I could bring myself to part with that land unless I could keep a garden spot. There's just too much sentiment attached to it. I expect I could find some realtor in town who maybe wouldn't offer me what the land is worth but at least would let me sell it my way."

"What plans would you have for this half acre?" she asked coldly.

"Oh, just a vegetable garden," he said. "Course I wouldn't rule out a little retirement cottage for Elenore and me by and by, but that's a long ways off. Elenore, she wants to be in Keene near our eldest daughter, and that's where my business takes me these days."

Zoe rose and walked soundlessly to the window. Howard watched her. She wore a white skirt, and her brown legs were slim and faultless, not a vein or a bulge showing, and the muscles in her calves were displayed like the streamlines of a new car. She was a good-looking woman—no doubt about it. He figured she was searching with her eyes down the valley, calculating what his garden might do to her view.

"No junk cars," she finally said, bluntly, eyes still toward the window.

"Ain't much room for a garden and cars on half an acre," he said.

"And practically none on a quarter of an acre," she said, and with that he knew that though she had won the major battles, he had won the war.

"Agreed," he said.

They signed the papers the next morning, and that afternoon her men came and hauled away the derelict cars that littered the field. One week later he moved the twelve-by-seventy-foot trailer in on the quarter acre and set it on concrete blocks. Elenore picked out the trailer. She loved it. He hated it, but it satisfied his purpose, which was to wound Mrs. Cutter. He would have given anything to see the look on her face when she pulled the drapes to gaze at her hard-won view and there, conspicuous as a pig, was a trailer.

He knew Mrs. Cutter's time-payment plan. She would educate Heather, dress her, change her ways of speaking, alter her completely, turn her in subtle ways against him, until he would not recognize her. He had his land, such as it was, and he had his revenge, such as it was, and he had some wisdom about the world, such as it was, and he had paid the price.

He laid the bills out on the kitchen table along with the big accounts book. The television in the living room spoke: "You scum, you weasely scum, I'm going to bend you over double." And Elenore whispered loudly into her rosary beads. In her room, Heather strummed her new guitar: *dee-dang, sppporang.* Howard turned off his hearing aid, and the world was suddenly smaller, more compact, like a stone. He hadn't quite mastered accounting, but he knew he was making money at his business. There were still things beyond him—for example, reckoning with taxes, figuring Social Security for Cooty—but that would come.

It had been Mr. O'Brian at the unemployment office who launched him. He had told Mr. O'Brian about the fire and about his thoughts on starting a business with the dump truck, and Mr. O'Brian had taken him (at one point, literally by the hand) across the street to another government office and helped him fill out half a dozen forms he had no understanding of, and he had signed papers. For all he knew, he was being drafted. He trusted Mr. O'Brian, as one trusts a doctor. Somehow he made a deal with the United States government. They were going to give him money to start his business, and in return he was going to let them school him. They gave him tests and sent him to Manchester for a physical. The next thing he knew, he had a hearing aid, and the world was large and full of company, crazy and beyond his comprehension, but he went along with it, because the encounter on the hill and the fire had charred his soul, pained him beyond the will to resist what was next, left him somehow rich for new growth, like a burned-over woodland. He didn't care anymore how old he was. Fifty, forty-eight, fifty-two—it made no difference. A good man was by turns old and young.

He finished the books, turned up the hearing aid, and opened a can of beer. There was silence from Elenore's chair in the living room. She was asleep; if she had been awake, she would have called for him when he opened the beer and busied him with some senseless errand. The strumming in Heather's room had stopped. Only the television went on: *Music. Gunfire. More music. Death gurgles.*

He gave himself over to reverie. In the spring he would buy a new truck with a compactor body. Maybe he could get Freddy to go into business with him. "No, put that from your mind," he said to himself. The boy was lost to him forever. The boy had his ways, or at any rate was developing ways, and they were not his father's ways. He wondered where the boy was today. Gone some damn place. The last time he had seen him was in Mrs. Cutter's boat-teak, or whatever the hell the name of the place was, and the boy had looked at him with love and guilt. No doubt the boy had put Mrs. Cutter up to fixing Heather's teeth. It popped into his head that the boy had done it to Mrs. Cutter. "Goddamn," he thought, "he done it to her and he done it to me and I done it to her and I done it to him and she done it to me and she done it to him. One big circle jerk of love. Strange, lonely."

"What?" Elenore from the living room, coming awake.

"Nothing," he said.

"You were saying something."

"Nothing," he said. "Indubitably nothing."

"What?"

"Nothing."

"You said something."

"Nothing."

"I heard you."

"Nothing."

"I heard you say Freddy's name."

He was on his feet, and he was walking into the living room, and he was struggling to control his temper, and he stood over her and spoke. "I didn't say nothing. Okay?"

"Ah—"

"Nothing."

"It's time to go to bed," she said, and that ended it. The bear in him moved off. He wheeled her into the bathroom, pulled down her pants, and set her on the toilet. After she had cleaned herself, he put her back in the chair and watched while she washed her face by the sink and combed her hair in front of the mirror, seeing and not seeing, like a man taking aim at an animal. He wheeled her to the bedroom, undressed her, and placed her in their bed. She was asleep in a moment.

He returned to the kitchen and drank another beer, and then he prepared for bed. He stopped by Heather's room, but he dared not go in. "What do you want?" he thought he heard her say from inside, but of course she had not spoken.

"Nothing," he said. "Indubitably nothing."

He returned to the kitchen and drank another beer, his mind as dull as a church service. He drank another, one over his limit, and went to bed.

Teeth, straight teeth. The thought surfaced in his mind, and he pushed it back into the depths. *Come to fix the lights?* Ollie, where was Ollie? Off somewhere, hiding his idiot son in a cage. They paraded in Howard's mind. The state had taken Turtle from Ollie and put him in a school. Ollie had fled with Willow. Who knew the fate of the Jordans? Howard wondered. What did it matter? What did it matter that Mr. Lodge was kissing babies somewhere? Even Howard knew that Jimmy Cleveland would whip Lodge's ass in the primaries. What did it matter that Sherry Ann could not bear him, or that Freddy had gone to California to learn book writing, as Elenore explained? "Well, I'll give him something to write about." He found himself voicing the thought, awakening Elenore briefly.

"What—?" she said, and was asleep.

"Nothing," Howard answered, although he knew she had gone to sleep again. "Indubitably nothing."

ERNEST HEBERT

BACK IN THE 1970s when I was reading contemporary New England writers, it seemed to me some things were missing. The people I grew up with in Keene, New Hampshire, appeared in the fiction of the literary masters only as stereotypes or to reflect the light of the main characters (who almost always seemed to be from out of town). Also what I reckoned to be the great New England drama—the displacement of local people by wealthier, more educated classes from down country—was being passed over. As I saw it, native versus newcomer was "the" New England story, "the" American story, right from the moment Columbus landed. My father lost his job after forty-five years in a textile mill. My wife Medora— like myself a New Hampshire native—encouraged and inspired me to write about these matters that meant so much to me. In the story that would become *The Dogs of March,* I set out to tell a native versus newcomer story from the point of view of the invaded and to present local people as fully fleshed out, true-to-life characters.